ANGEL
DOWN

ANGEL DOWN

DANIEL KRAUS

ATRIA BOOKS

New York Amsterdam/Antwerp London
Toronto Sydney/Melbourne New Delhi

ATRIA
BOOKS

An Imprint of Simon & Schuster, LLC
1230 Avenue of the Americas
New York, NY 10020

This book is a work of fiction. Any references to historical events, real people, or real places are used fictitiously. Other names, characters, places, and events are products of the author's imagination, and any resemblance to actual events or places or persons, living or dead, is entirely coincidental.

First Atria Books hardcover edition July 2025

ATRIA BOOKS and colophon are trademarks of Simon & Schuster, LLC

Simon & Schuster strongly believes in freedom of expression and stands against censorship in all its forms. For more information, visit BooksBelong.com.

For information about special discounts for bulk purchases, please contact Simon & Schuster Special Sales at 1-866-506-1949 or business@simonandschuster.com.

The Simon & Schuster Speakers Bureau can bring authors to your live event. For more information or to book an event, contact the Simon & Schuster Speakers Bureau at 1-866-248-3049 or visit our website at www.simonspeakers.com.

Interior design by Esther Paradelo

Manufactured in the United States of America

1 3 5 7 9 10 8 6 4 2

Library of Congress Control Number: 2024059947

ISBN 978-1-6680-6845-8
ISBN 978-1-6680-6852-6 (ebook)

Dedicated to
MICHAEL RYZY,
BROTHER-IN-ARMS.

But they are hideous creatures—degraded beasts of a lower order. How could you speak the language of beasts?

EDGAR RICE BURROUGHS, *The Son of Tarzan*

Élan

and Cyril Bagger considers himself lucky, he ought to be topped off, gone west, bumped, clicked it, pushing daisies, a new landowner, napooed, just plain dead, not only dead but scattered around in globs, for the last thing he saw was a shell dropping on top of him with the noise of colliding freight trains, a jim-dandy of a shot from Fritzy the Hun, and kind of ironic, seeing how the whole reason Bagger prefers burial duty is artillery shells can't reach this far behind the frontline trench, but this shell sure did, the way he always pictures it in dreams, a red skull of fire screaming down, giving him one second to think, *That old Bagger luck has finally run out,*

and the afterlife, for the brief time he knew it, had been delectable, he was gentled back into the arms, and the long, long legs, of Marie-Louise, the prostituée on whom he'd lavished all his francs when the Butcher Birds of the 43rd had been stationed in Vosges, pretty, dry, warm, quiet, bloodless Vosges, where every inhale was Marie-Louise's La Rose Jacqueminot parfum, her rosewater hair and periwinkle powders, every exhale the flutter of her dyed red hair and the lace whatchamacallits of her lingerie,

and so the last thing he wants is someone fucking with him and demanding, "You alive?," to which Bagger responds, "Fuck no," to which the man laughs mirthlessly and pulls him up by the armpits like a breech birth, so Bagger the newborn unseals his eyelids, a crust of mud, oil, and embarrassing tears, and discovers he's being lifted from the burial pit he'd been digging when the mortar hit, now blown to triple its size and is stacked with triple the dead, all being sprayed with quicklime and hastily carpeted in soil,

and Bagger would have been buried alive if not for this sharp-eyed private, he really ought to reward him with a cigarette, but Bagger's distracted by the corpses packed slick hot on all sides of him, one dead doughboy nearly beheaded by a pelvic bone, another who bit it collecting his intestines in one of his boots, a third stomped so flat by a shell that his spinal column protrudes from his gaping mouth,

and yet Bagger, by his own baffled accounting, is intact all the way down to his little piggies, so how the fuck is he alive when every-one who'd been near him, by the look of it, was exploded, shredded, and scattered, he tries to credit the corpse he'd been carrying, it must have absorbed the shrapnel, but a nagging voice insists it's a miracle, which only pisses him off, he'll be goddamned if he's going to start believing in miracles here in hell,

and once his ass is on solid ground, more or less, he realizes this marshy patch of land between the Argonne Forest and River Meuse has fallen quiet, and there's nothing more suspicious, a Western Front quiet is tetchy, one side always gets itchy and opts to bleed a few hundred more men over a few inches of land so ruined only a maniac would want it,

and so Bagger sits up with vision aswirl and shoos away the filthy pelt of air, the pigeon-gray smoke and eyeball-white fog, and beyond the hills of diarrheal mud and the pappy craters from whence those hills were upchucked, Bagger sees trucks and carts and wheeled guns crunching east, looks like the whole fucking U.S. First Army, III Corps, 43rd Division has vacated the scene with the likely exception of Bagger's lowly Company P, forever dangled like a gonorrheal dick from the brigade's leftmost flank,

and Bagger feels for his haversack, still there, and extracts his Bible, and opens it, and stuffs his nose into the gutter, and inhales, doesn't give a fuck about kings and shepherds and carpenters and prophets, but the damp protean smell of the book's red leather and the woody scratch of its onionskin pages, each one half-mooned by his father's finger-stains, has a smelling-salt effect on Bagger, has since he was a kid, it brings him back to the cramped study over the church where Bishop Bernard Bagger labored on sermons, back when Cyril's heart, now filled with smoke, was filled with what must have been hope,

and it's only through the motions of inhaling that Bagger feels a brittle tightness, his face is glazed in dried blood, clearly not his own, and he orders himself not to imagine whose, it's best when blood has no deeper meaning than rain, especially in the Argonne where so few trees remain to block the October wind that flash-dries blood so rapidly to your skin,

and while there's no telling which boy bled this blood, what *kind* of blood is a different matter, fourteen days into this cyclone of carti-lage and lead, Bagger has developed a sommelier palate for the tart fizz of brachial blood, the fudgy sorghum of femoral, the meaty sludge of heart wounds, the rancid reek of any gut juice at all, and the warm salt lick of arterial blood he now licks from his lips, and it's good the Bible is here to push him through it, Bagger takes a loud, greedy sniff, sinuses bathed in the aromatic nostalgia of comfort and solace, then reluctantly pockets the book and sticks fingers into his ear holes to clear out the creamy plugs of mud and blood, in this trenchworld hearing is so much more vital than seeing,

and the world's noises whoosh back, and Bagger catches his breath at a rubbery wail that overrides everything, another minenwerfer dropping, the same kind of shell that ripped his fellow buriers to cutlets, oh no, oh shit, but hold on, wait, no, this is different, less a wail than a *shriek*, no rival to a minnie on a decibel level but with an edge that chisels through the end-times grumble at a pitch he's never heard,

and though there's plenty of attack machines in extremis out in No Man's Land, their death moans are as predictable as hinges, while this shriek is organic, as alive as Marie-Louise's pleased moans or Bishop Bagger's stentorian damnations, it could be male or female, human or animal, but whatever it is, it's dying, dying slow, dying loud, ripple after glissading ripple of agonized lament,

and Bagger, already weighed down in mud and blood, further heavies in the dreary certainty that the shriek won't ever end, just like the war won't ever end, like the carnage won't ever end, it's a sentence in a book careening without periods, gasping with too many commas, a sentence that, once begun, can't ever be stopped, a sentence doomed to loop back on itself to form a terrible black wheel that, sooner or later, will drag each and every person to their grave,

II

and Bagger wipes his face with his forearm and five pounds of matter plop off his head, his brains, he supposes, all that blood on his face was his after all, and because he's become educated in what brains look like, he stares into his lap for confirmation but all he sees is yellow clay, there's nothing more ordinary than yellow clay in the Argonne,

and while he's staring at the claybrains, he notices a voice,

and the voice feels like part of the shriek, an undertone,

and Bagger knows undertones, he grew up enveloped in the polyphony of the church's old pipe organ, the Swell, the Choir, and the Great woven like flutes, strings, and reeds, but this undertone is from a yet uninvented keyboard called *voice*,

and the voice says, *Bagger,*

and it's stimulating how the word seems to buzz from within his own flesh, that's how it felt when standing beneath the sanctuary pipes, though Bishop Bagger would have told little Cyril that's only guilt murmuring from inside you, a sentiment the adult Cyril Bagger refuses to buy, he's worked too long to bury such weepy notions along with the hundreds of dead bodies,

and so he ignores the voice, it's just his skeleton vibrating from the mortar strike, and takes a big, fetid inhale, all right, Bagger, your division's on the march, not good, but otherwise things are as you left them, which is to say absolute shit, Jerry's shells have slashed a half-mile cleft through the trench system's doglegs so that front, support, and reserve trenches all reside under a fourth designation called smithereens,

and within those smithereens Bagger verifies that Company P indeed lingers, there's Lieutenant Aquila's gorilla limp, there's Sergeant Rasch's crow caw, but instead of slumped like mutts in post-battle stupor, Company P is on its feet, bumping like windup toys between fat tongues of displaced mud, and Bagger wonders if the shriek is driving them mad, too, damn sure something strange is afoot, and Bagger's got to goose himself to life if he's going to outfox it same as he's outfoxed everything else,

and so he imagines General John. J. Pershing lording over him, demanding, *Where are you, Private?*, and he saying, *France, sir!*, and Pershing saying, *More specifically, Private!*, and he saying, *Bois de Fays, sir, and bois is frog for woods, sir!*, and Pershing saying, *Very good, Private, and do these look like woods to you?*, and he saying, *No sir, but they might have been woods a few years ago, sir, before the giant trolls came through*, and Pershing saying, *And what were those trolls' names, Private?*, and he getting the gruff old army commander to crack a smile by saying, *Marne, sir, Verdun, sir, Somme, sir, stomped the shit out of everything, sir,* and Bagger laughs, and it helps more than the Bible, hallelujah, hoist the flag and let her fly, Yankee Doodle, do or die, Private First Class Cyril Bagger feels more like lucky old Bagger again, the Hawkeye Hustler, the Sioux City Sharpie, the Council Bluffs Crossroader, the Dean of Dubuque, nicknames he earned from being banned from half the riverboats on the Mississippi, not that he doesn't own a tackle box of disguises capable of getting him back on those boats the second he gets home,

and once he's back in Iowa, he'll rerun the same schemes, the flop, the ring reward, the pigeon drop, mine salting, pig-in-a-poke, the fake-counterfeiter, he'll even do a classic melon drop just to prove he still can, hell, before the Army nabbed him, he even toyed with psychic boobery, finagled a metal rod to jut from a hidden leather cuff to make the table seem to rise beneath his hands, a total bust, though he knows the spiritualism con is a growth area, grievers make the best marks and postwar America's going to be lousy with grievers,

and it's this same sleight of hand that has kept him safe out here, that and a bacon can packed with dominos, bottle caps for shell games, loaded dice, a pen for drawing pips on sugar cubes in case he loses those dice, and marked cards, and when it's too dark to read those marks, he razes the card edges with a fingernail he keeps sharp, or puts literal cards up his literal sleeves, there's always a cornpone private unable to identify him as a shark who has more teeth than Iowa has corn, and those boys bet everything, lives included, when their manhoods are impinged, and here in frogland, challenges to one's manhood crop up every few seconds,

and the result is soldiers who end up so far in arrears they have to pay back Bagger in derring-do, infantry charges mostly, they go over the top in his place and get on a first-name basis with bullets while Bagger steps back, way back, keeping to latrine and burial duties, where flying lead doesn't whistle past one's ears but rather whines like late-summer mosquitoes,

and when he's not working a shovel, he's insubordinating in front of every captain, major, lieutenant, and sergeant in the 43rd so they'll "punish" him with more backline duty, and by accident, he's gotten good at those duties, he's practically become the 2nd Battalion's burier-in-chief, planting fellow doughboys in the dirt makes him feel like a proper goddamn artiste,

and the idea of other men doing Bagger's work job while he was briefly unconscious offends him, what does the HQ staff, those signal men, cooks, clerks, quartermasters, bugle boys, and stretcher-bearers, know about burying bodies, nothing, that's what, the savages probably laid them head-to-head instead of head-to-feet and neglected to cover their faces, and when they came across disarticulated parts, a foot or a head or a perfectly preserved bottom jaw, they probably chucked them in like olives into cocktails, and furthermore, probably failed to note the coordinates of the burial pit, not that it's worth a crap, no recovery detail is ever coming back to exhume doughboy bodies and everyone knows it,

and, what the hell, there it is again, that voice, *Bagger*,

and then it's replaced by something louder, realer, "Bagger! Bagger! There you are, Bagger!" and Bagger's vertebrae crackle as he swivels his neck to see Lewis Arno dancing around upended oak roots and furry-looking clumps Bagger identifies as moss, only to feel stupidly naive, there was a minnie, there was a burial pit, and that's not moss, Cyril Bagger, you dumb fuck,

and Bagger's guts thicken like they do anytime he sees Arno, the
kid's fourteen, lied about his age to some Nebraska National Guards-
fuck trying to make quota, and ever since has been a tick sucked
to the 172nd's underbelly, devoid of skills but too damn small for
the Germans to hit, and Bagger resents the kid, really goddamn
resents him, the kid complicates Bagger's otherwise flawless loathing for everyone out here, there's not even any point in swindling
Arno, the kid doesn't have a penny to his name,

and Bagger also loves seeing Lewis Arno, and there's nothing he
hates more than love, so he snaps, "What do you want? Little trench
rat," and Arno sets aside a Chauchat rifle bigger than him, stares
big goose eggs, and whispers, "Are you dead?," the second time
Bagger's heard this, he must look really goddamn bad, so he snaps,
"Yes. I'm a ghost. And I'm going to haunt the fuck out of you,"

and this seems to satisfy Arno, who presses sooty palms over sooty
ears and asks, "What's that noise?," which gives Bagger some re-
lief, if Arno hears the shriek, it means Bagger's not loony, he's not
gone 4-F, not yet,

and so he gins up the wildman grin he knows the kid wants to see,
and replies, "Sounds like someone's letting the air out," and Arno
asks, "Of what?," and Bagger says, "The whole big balloon" with
a mad chuckle, though what he imagines is quite sad, the earth,
punctured by a 105mm heavy, leaking air, cratering inward, with
all of them along for the crash,

and Arno says, "It hurts," juvenile but accurate, the shriek *does*
hurt, though not the ears, feels more like a small, feminine hand
sliding into Bagger's chest through a shrapnel wound and squeez-

ing his heart arrhythmically, and if he wasn't already kneeled, he'd have to take the posture, so damn the kid all over again for making the hard parts of him go soft, "You're bellyaching to the wrong soldier," Bagger gripes,

and what impresses him about Lewis Arno, from a con man's perspective, is that the kid's not easily bluffed, Arno points at him and says, "You got face on your face," a statement that, at any other time and place would be gibberish, but there's only one interpretation here, a real unfortunate one, and Bagger gingerly touches his own face, cracking the blood glaze into fragile plates, and Arno grimaces, and Bagger traces the grimace to his own right jaw, where something dangles, slight and flexible like a human ear,

and Bagger peels it off his face and holds it before him, and that's exactly what it is, a human ear, clotted with clay and matted with a tuft of blond hair,

and he wipes his face of the face, and the only way not to throw up is to make a joke, so he takes the ear by its helix, holds it out to Arno, and says, "Ear you go,"

and the joke lands flat, the kid is appalled, so Bagger tosses the ear over his shoulder, devil-may-care, but he does care, he *does*, so much he wants to spin around and find the ear and pin it to his lapel, a medal more useful than the Croix de Guerre, one that might lend him super hearing to better understand the unending, undulating shriek,

and it's within this phantasmagoria that Arno asserts an even harsher reality by stating, "The major general wants you," and because that's preposterous, Bagger pshaws, "You gotta learn your stripes, kid," but Arno shakes his head and insists, "I know my stripes," and Bagger peaks an eyebrow and says, "You mean the first lieutenant," but Arno shakes his head harder, "No, the major general," and Bagger levels a look, "Major Chester?," and Arno shakes his head hard enough to untwist the fool thing off, and Bagger asks, now with a cramp of concern, "Brigadier Motta?," and Arno moans in exasperation, "The major general! The man with the tiny little arm!,"

and descriptions don't get clearer than that, Bagger's face goes slack, which causes more mud to slough off, unless it's really brains this time, and it might be, that's how hard Bagger's thinking, he's done an ace job fleecing privates, corporals, lieutenants, majors, brigadiers, and captains, but no way does a lowly PFC like Cyril Bagger get the chance to interface with the commander of the U.S. 43rd,

and that might mean tales of Bagger's bamboozles have gone all the way to the top, which could lead to a court-martial, to prison, and to cover his dread, Bagger tries to play it off like nothing, asking, "Yeah? He say why?," to which Arno shakes his head earnestly, so Bagger just blinks and breathes, blinks and breathes, and sits at the edge of the mass grave, just him, the boy, the fear, and the shriek,

and it brings him close to voicing a fantasy he's nurtured like a houseplant, in which the two of them, Bagger and Arno, simply stroll the fuck out of this cunting nightmare, Arno sitting atop Bagger's shoulders like a kid brother, livening Bagger's path through shell craters and around dead horses, until the terrain goes dreamy, twitching clover patches, handcrafted stone fences, until they find a wee farm more charming than its Iowa equivalents, and acquire it, and live there, the two of them, accruing personal trivia, the only swindle being the years they wasted anywhere else,

and fuck it, it'll never happen, a fruitcake fantasy to be kept close to his chest, same spot he wanted to pin the ear,

and so Bagger struggles skyward, and Arno holds out a hand to help, and Bagger clubs it aside same as he does trench vermin, because he's *not* the kid's big brother, he's just a guy who's going to get through this war by living how he's always lived, not giving one shit about anyone, regardless of age or innocence, but he rises too fast, he's dizzy, he buckles and pitches and weaves and flounders, a necessary struggle, or else he'll fall into the soupy mass grave he never finished digging but the kill-happy world dug for him, for every last one of them,

III

and as Bagger's strides are man-sized, Arno has to rabbit his pace to keep at Bagger's heels, and the kid asks, ignorant as ever of being a pest, "You think Korak's going to kill Baynes?," and Bagger replies, "Nah. Baynes is going to chop up Korak and make stew out of him," which sets off loon laughter from the kid, who goes about listing all the reasons Korak the Killer is too powerful and crafty to be taken down by the silver-spoon likes of Morison Baynes,

and Arno prattles on, "You think Korak is going to rescue Meriem again?," to which Bagger snipes, "If I hadn't lost my sewing kit, I'd sew your lips shut," but the kid's happy chatter proceeds un-bothered, characteristic of their daily palaver, in which the kid asks a thousand dunderhead questions about whatever they're reading and Bagger doles out the most upsetting answers possible,

and their current book is *The Son of Tarzan*, published in 1915 by Something Something Burroughs, little boy stuff, but Arno is, in fact, a little boy with a little boy's passions, and as far back as Camp Winn at Fort Sinclair, the kid was badgering recruits about their dime novels until they started tossing their finished books at the kid, never realizing that just because Lewis Arno liked adventure stories didn't mean he knew how to read, and you get one guess which soldier Arno chose to confess his shame of illiteracy, fuck the luck, and before long the kid was begging Bagger to read him *The Prisoner of Zenda*, and though Bagger initially told the kid to scram, war is a slog even when you're not warring, and at last came the day Bagger was too pooped to resist the kid's begging and ripped the book from Arno's hand and began reading aloud with plans to insert passages of sickening violence and shocking pornography, only to find himself engaged by the plot,

and it's bar none the biggest mistake Bagger's made in the Army, and worse still, he keeps making it, *King Solomon's Mines*, *The Count of Monte Cristo*, *Treasure Island*, and now *The Son of Tarzan*, a tale in which, so far anyway, Tarzan barely appears, the stage ceded to the ape-man's civilized son, who follows his daddy's footsteps to become Korak the Killer, an idiotic coincidence, but diverting enough as Bagger, of course, inserts explicit content, Tarzan revised to be a randy sodomite and Lady Greystoke a nudist cannibal, to which Arno only nods along, suggesting there's no atrocity Bagger can concoct the Great War hasn't reduced to believability,

and with Arno still at it, "Big Bwana is really Tarzan, right, Bagger? Bagger, you can tell me!," they pass a side of human ribs still flexing, powered by the heart, always the last organ to let go, and because there's no time to direct Arno away from it, Bagger stomps the heart before the kid can notice it, and the heart feels like his own,

and here come several aching somnambulists through the fog, HQ staff dragging wagons so heavy with carnage they need to be yoked through the mud like sleds, arms and legs and scalps and entrails swinging from the sides, so Bagger distracts the kid, yanking him close, shouting, "Mind that hole!," to which Arno cries, "Whoa!

Close one!," except there is no hole, and Bagger wonders if Arno knows it and they're both just playing the role the other needs,

and Bagger drops into the shallowest stretch of trench he can find, knees like hamburger, and when Arno crouches like he wants help, Bagger pretends not to notice, he's not the kid's daddy, and he walks off and hears Arno splat down in the mud, so what, they're all muddy, though he wishes it was the kid's landing that made the trench quiver instead of the war machines over the next slope, either that or a hundred thousand of Ludendorff's Huns exiting the fortified pillboxes of the Hindenburg Line, a choppy sea of pointed helmets heaving south,

and it could also be the shriek, palpitating everything,

and whatever it is, it's bothering the Butcher Birds of the 43rd, they low like Iowa cows needing milking, mud slurping at their hooves, and Arno scurries ahead to lead Bagger through a U-shaped elbow, a turn that reveals the remains of Company P, there's Lieutenant Jules Aquila blurting inspirational falderal and slapping the chests of men dead on their feet, there's Sergeant Moss DiStefano passing a salt vial beneath the noses of those who need it,

and it's all because P Company, too, is finally on the move, forming a column to march, which means Bagger needs to fall in, but before he can, Arno swerves left, away from the line of forty-some drooping men and past Father Muensterman, who pukes into his own carefully cupped hands as if he intends to pass off the vomitus as both body and blood,

and they bank into the lopsided amphitheater of a shell crater, a striated bowl of clay scalloped as if from a giant's closing fist, painted by vertical stripes of blood that rise up the sides of the bowl, a pattern accentuated by a mash of tissue right where a clock should hang, something yuletide about it, the color of fruitcake, the shape a wreath, and only the ornaments of a dozen teeth tell Bagger it used to be a human head,

and the next thing he notices are three men, not dead in the mud but standing in formation with Springfield rifles at their sides and spines at high attention, and though Bagger has but seconds to look, he identifies them as the three most disposable men of Company P, a label that makes him curl his lip with detestation and superiority before he gets to the demoralizing punch line, that it isn't the *three* most disposable gathered here but the *five*,

IV

and with a flare of coat hem, a man in the center of the crater turns, a soupçon of operatic grace in the graceless affront of the gutted countryside, and Bagger jerks back, he didn't see him there, though the high-laced field boots are unmistakable, and surprising, for one might expect a sideways lean from the man, given the lesser weight of his withered right arm, but no, his martial stance is ramrod, all crookedness resolved by the golden walking stick clawed by the leather-gloved hand,

and it's Major General Lyon Reis's costume that's most often mocked by the Butcher Birds, the shin-length wool trench coat, once ivory, now smoke-stained and unbuckled to affect a cavalier's flair, three coin-sized medals dangling over his left breast from pentagonal ribbons, typical for his rank but arranged with a space reserved for a medal not yet earned, which, according to rumor, is the Medal of Honor, that's how certain Reis is that the war will win it for him, how sincerely he believes it's his due,

and it's highly irregular for Reis to be speaking to privates without his staff, who must be busy pushing carts through mud, or without the leaders whose ranks fall between Major General Reis and Private Bagger, in this case, in ascending order, Lieutenant Aquila,

First Lieutenant Hollis, Major Chester, and Captain Greisz, none of whom like Bagger, and the feeling's mutual, though now Bagger feels a pipsqueak yearning for those authority figures to protect him from big, bad Major General Reis, whose light brown eyes have gone arachnid with the points of several lanterns,

and Reis asks, "Did little bunny get lost in the warren?," and Arno, Tarzan fantasies forgotten, replies, "No, sir," and looks like he's going to blabber a more detailed excuse, so Bagger knuckles the kid in the back and takes over, saying, "Sorry, sir, we took a pretty direct hit back on burial detail,"

and Reis lifts his lips to his nostrils, a disgusted inhale that siphons the lower half of his face into his sinuses, which broadens the Van Dyke beard the major general inexplicably finds time to manicure, the vanity of youth, some of the boys say, for Reis is the youngest division commander in the Army, though reports of his age hitch higher with every strategic blunder, Reis was thirty-three in Alsace, thirty-five in Vosges, forty on September 26 when the 43rd jumped off at Bois de Malancourt, and now, two weeks into the lathe of the Meuse-Argonne, Lyon Reis is nearabout sixty, seventy-five on a bad day, and this is a very bad day,

and Reis leans his head back, back, back, the way the upper crust always look at cretins who dare intersect their path, which tilts his gold-braided cap so the two stars pinned to the front catch fire in the lantern light, eyes more fiery than Reis's own,

and he echoes, "Direct hit. You think you know about direct hits?," a question to which Bagger would say yes, if not for the three men slashing him with their eyes to say, *Why won't you shut up, Bagger, why must you always make it worse?*, a complaint true enough to make the fly trapped inside Bagger's rib cage fling itself against prison bars of bone,

and the fly's been with Bagger since Camp Winn, where there was a poster tacked to the barracks door, I WANT YOU FOR U.S. ARMY, unsound grammar Bagger would have disparaged if he hadn't been so struck by the man painted on the poster, a top-hatted, red-bow-tied, billy-bearded Uncle Sam who looked uncannily like his father, Bishop Bagger, drowned to death two years prior when the RMS Lusitania was sunk by a U-boat torpedo,

and once Bagger swatted away the Tennessee flies, he found this Uncle Sam, too, to be more cadaver than man, skin tight to his skull, pearled with putrescence, the ripe pouches of flesh beneath his eyes ready to burst with maggots, and Bagger thought it boded poorly that the man who most wanted him in the army was already dead, it made Bagger reach for the poster to trash it, comeuppance be damned, and that's when one of the goddamn Tennessee flies zipped right into his open mouth and down his throat,

and now the fly, also named Uncle Sam, lives in Bagger's chest, all that's left of Bagger's father, and though Bagger's tried to drown the fly with moonshine, incinerate him with cigarettes, even dope him with opium, Uncle Sam's a tough little bastard, but at least Bagger has him trapped, and one day the shamefly, as Bagger thinks of him, will die, and with it will go that pestering nip of shame, that filmy wing flutter of guilt, and Bagger's life will be launched anew,

and Reis's challenges excite Uncle Sam, which Bagger takes as his own challenge, he'll show the shamefly that he doesn't kowtow to imbecilic militance, so he says, "Yes, sir, Major General, sir, direct hits are my area of expertise. If the major general would care to visit, I'd be happy to show him all the pieces. It's hardly III Corps anymore, sir. More like III Corpse, I'd say,"

and Reis's face drops like claybrains and his eyeball arachnoidism spreads until suddenly he's got too many lower appendages, some legs and a cane, and he's racing at Bagger like an out-of-control carousel horse, up and down, the leather case of his field glasses pendulating, the Medal of Honor gap gawping like a eyeless socket, and he's in Bagger's face, same height yet shouting downward because Bagger is shrinking,

and Reis barks, "*I see you find American sacrifice funny, Private Bagger!*"

and it can't be good the major general knows his name, Bagger's stunned, and it must read on his face as easily as a Tarzan book, for Reis smirks and says, "That's right, I know you. Shirker. Archschemer. I call you Private Gravedigger," and he cuts a look at the others, "I have names for all of you. I make it a priority to receive reports on the division's disreputables,"

and all Bagger can think to do is double down, he shapes himself into a caricature of soldierdom and says, "Major General, sir, I was merely making a lexical observation!,"

and Reis flattens his mustache with an equine blast of hot air and says, with great odium, "You are a mosquito, Private Gravedigger. Imminently squashable. And you will be squashed before this war is over. I won't do the squashing myself. I wouldn't give you the honor. Nor do I believe your end will come from one of your 'direct hits.' Your demise will be typical to vermin. Your long, greasy tail caught in some trifling mousetrap. And when your tail is thusly pinched, who will come to your aid, Private Gravedigger? These men?," and Reis jabs his walking stick at the glowering soldiers, before swinging the stick toward Company P's column and asking again, "Those men?," and Bagger knows he's right, none of these boys give a shit if Bagger lives or dies,

and Reis swears, "You will be solitary in your suffering, Private Gravedigger. No man will risk anything to assist you, as you have risked nothing to assist your fellow man. They might return the favor you gave to their fallen brothers and toss what is left of you down a hole. I should think you deserve your own hole, one of your signature latrines, perhaps, the sort that collapse upon the first stream of piss. Of this resting place, no record will be made, though I do fancy a sign to warn farmers to keep their flocks away. What lies beneath is a man made of poison,"

and with that, Reis sneers, "Wipe the blood of the valiant off your face, Soldier. On you, it is profane," while Uncle Sam goes amok in Bagger's chest, the same wingbeat of shame he felt seeing off his father on that final doomed voyage, Bagger wants to punch back now like he did back then, maybe this time literally,

and he could, Reis is no physical specimen, adenoid eyes, noodle neck, a matronly pelvic misalignment that sets his feet to a 10:10 configuration, shortcomings Bagger presumes originated from whatever defect blighted Reis's right arm, which all the boys snicker about, one claiming to have seen the little arm employed to brush Reis's mustache, another swearing Reis keeps a tiny box of tiny cigars to be held by the tiny fingers, but it's bullshit, no one's ever seen the arm, it hides inside its specially tailored uniforms and coats, and even if Bagger saw it, he wouldn't stoop to ridicule it, the arm's not the major general's fault, it's how he's twisted his life in reaction to it that has turned his men against him, his refusal to adhere to the frontline rotation the Great War has made standard, his threat to outright shoot deserters, and his belief that flank attacks are unworthy of the 43rd, which forces hundreds of men to directly assault machine-gun nests until they are no longer men at all,

and before Bagger can force Uncle Sam the shamefly down and make a cutting jibe, *Very creative, Major General, sir!*, Reis's left arm, the good one, whip-cracks Bagger's shoulder with the walking stick, and son of a bitch, it fucking hurts, though not as much as a bullet, a fact of which Reis will happily remind him if he produces even a squeak,

and "Formation!" is Reis's order, so Bagger stumbles left, blind beneath black plumes of pain, the only sign he's in position coming from the bump of the next man's shoulder, and then the crater goes silent, except, of course for the shriek that continues to unfurl in an infinite ribbon, and since Bagger can't see so good right now, a tableau forms in his mind, the shrieker as a grief-stricken villager watching these five men standing on the gallows, a hooded executioner gripping the lever that, when pulled, will send them swinging till they are dead, dead, dead,

V

and Reis paces the slime in smart spiderleg, indifferent to the day's necrosis, while just past the vomiting chaplain, the poor devils of Company P force themselves to stay upright on their blisters, awaiting Reis's order, knees singing, brainpans percussive, eyelids blue flame, radiating loathing for the five flunkies, all of it rancid gravy down Bagger's throat,

and Reis looks like he could pace like this all day, the far-off booms of enemies and allies as pleasant as garden-party chatter, while magenta clay oozes down the crater like liquified skin, until he says, "It is unlikely any of you have ever been nominated for anything. This, indeed, is how you came to stand before me," and Reis points his walking stick rather casually at the sky and asks, "What do you see up there? Private Goodspeed,"

and despite Reis and his cane, despite the fresh welt on Bagger's shoulder, Bagger creeps his eyes left to glance at Private Vincent Goodspeed, a man he knows only by reputation, but who exudes a squirmy, squirrelish air, as thin as birch bark stripped from a tree and topped with a tight bowl of blond hair and the steel-rimmed pince-nez of Woodrow Wilson, so tightly applied the spectacles dig grooves into the sides of his nose, and what's most suspicious about Goodspeed is his cleanliness, nobody's clean out here, even your insides are filthy, you drool mustard gas, sneeze soiled gauze, cry soot, shit mud, but since the start of the Meuse-Argonne Offensive, rumors have circulated of a private who goes over the top willingly enough only to stop ten yards out to *clean his boots* while fellow Butcher Birds meet Jerry's iron hail, and it has to be Vincent Goodspeed, his olive drabs still olive, the brass buttons of his ammo patch bright as pennies,

and Goodspeed follows Reis's walking stick to the continent of smoke shifting tectonically over No Man's Land, darkening the frontline to the crisped paste of an uncleaned oven, and with a sniveling grin, Goodspeed replies, "Sir, that's artillery smoke, sir, they say we've got over four hundred thousand artillerists now, the French 75s, the Schneider 155s, the long-range GPFs, they fire higher and farther than anything ever built, sir, and I'm proud to fight alongside them, sir, I'll say that much,"

and it's the breathy tumble of a schoolboy eager to cozy up to the king of the playground, and Bagger, a former king, aches to dole out the smacks such bootlickers deserve, he'd love to sock Goodspeed right in the kisser, for although Bagger prides himself on knowing as little about the U.S. Army as possible, he knows Goodspeed is spewing agitprop, American and French arty are Tinkertoys compared to Tommy's guns, and even those pale alongside the Heine heavies, just look at the size of these shell craters, you dunderhead,

and Reis withholds a head-pat, in fact glares at the ass-kisser, then shares that glare with the others, saying, "And here is the problem with the lot of you. Devoid of vision, melancholic of spirit. Why have I been cursed with the First Army's most sullen and fatalistic men? The injustice rankles. There is a limit to what a man can accomplish with such donkeys," and he shakes his stick at the sky and demands, "What else do you espy? Private Popkin,"

and Bagger has to suffer the horsey lip-smack of Hugh Popkin drowsing to life, he's always privately called Popkin *the lummox*, and oh, how he wishes it were the lummox's blood splashed across his face, he's hoped to find Popkin's head in every new pile of doughboys to be buried, and only his head, as Bagger doesn't think he could lift Popkin's full corpse, he's like one of the ape kings Korak duels in *The Son of Tarzan*, a tank physique that suggests greatness but only mirrors the impotent French landships Company P found junked along the south bank of Le Wassieu,

and, all right, okay, to be frank, they have history, Bagger and Popkin, the lummox having found a genuine diamond ring glinting up from between his planted feet at the latrine, the latrine Bagger himself had built, which meant, Bagger figured, that the ring was rightfully his, and so, casual as hell, he bet Popkin's ring against everything Bagger owned that he could win five of five blackjack hands, the only game Popkin could follow, and of course Bagger won, the lummox was too slow to catch Bagger's palmed aces,

and naturally Popkin had raged and tried to hit him, but he moved too slow, everything about Hugh Popkin is slow, he talks slow, he moves slow, look how long it takes him to follow Reis's gesture, his huge mouth drawbridging down to reveal the worst case of trench mouth Bagger's ever seen, gums hotdog red and swollen around gray teeth so guttered by ulcers they look as long as fingers,

and though Popkin is two men to Bagger's left, the mouth's gamy odor conquers all other stinks, and to top it off, the lummox forgets himself and lifts a hand from where it's supposed to remain at his side, and scratches the scabs of a scalp nearly bald from chemical gas burn, the result of an ill wind that blew the battalion's mustard gas back into their trench, Popkin's got nothing left but sprigs of red hair, and he replies, "Sky? Sir? Blue sky? Sir?,"

and Bagger's surprised, he's hasn't noticed any blue sky, but when he scours the battlefield canopy, he'll be a monkey's uncle, a blue spot soaks through the brown haze like the fishing holes Bagger once drilled through Lake Zabriskie, the only indication that it's not, in fact, the middle of the night, it's the middle of the goddamned afternoon,

and Reis drives his stick into the clay and cries, "Our ogre, the seer! He's correct, boys. See for yourself. The inevitable clearing of smoke, the cyclic passage of black skies into clear. If a man of Private Popkin's bovine intellect can see this truth, how, I ask you, can the muckety mucks nibbling their biscuits in Souilly be so ignorant? Of the give and take of battle. Of how the strategic retreat of a cunning leader can swiftly turn the tide,"

and these might not be hypotheticals, but the only man left to address them can't be expected to do it, for a man like Lyon Reis doesn't speak to a man like Ben Veck, Bagger identified Veck as the anvil of their life raft the moment he entered the crater, the surest sign their fivesome was doomed, for Negroes don't fight alongside whites, yet here Veck is, and has been, for an astonishing seven days, a mystery that the men of the 172nd have chosen not to solve in favor of spitting both saliva and invectives at him,

and the only reason Bagger knows about Veck at all is that his arrival marked Lewis Arno's sole success as a runner, and the kid, big for his britches, jabbered Bagger's ear off about Veck's history, how the all-Negro 368th Infantry Regiment failed to plug a hole at the west end of the line and had been exiled to Marbache, of little consequence until P Company's last flamethrower operator was burned alive, and because Major General Reis was partial to flame-throwers, he requested, nay, demanded a prompt replacement, who arrived, led by Arno, in the form of Ben Veck,

and Veck arrived damaged, he'd seen battle to a degree the Butcher Birds haven't, it's clear from the way his eyes ping side to side, the wormy vein in his forehead, the contorted way he creeps, as if every step is certain to trigger a mine, and the truth is, Bagger doesn't feel safe around a man that jittery strapped to combustible tanks,

and the tanks are part of the French P3, the latest iteration of the Schilt "liquid fire projector," Bagger's seen the two-tanker spit a ten-second arc of flaming oil and petrol a hundred yards, and here's the kicker, P3s are supposed to have two-man crews, but Ben Veck wields the lance and turns the propellent valve both, impres-sive, Bagger supposes, but sooner or later something's going to go wrong,

and though Bagger always understood Veck's arrival as the writing on the wall for the 43rd, only now can he read the whole sentence, the division is being marched not only out of Bois de Fays but off the line entirely, and because General Pershing can't afford to lose a whole division, that means the 43rd is being organized under a new leader,

and Bagger is caught in an eddy of giddy delight, Reis is being re-placed, the Butcher Bird's butcher is actually being replaced, and that explains Reis's fixation on gray skies turning blue, the un-fairness of being retired before he can enact the counterstrike that will change everything, and Bagger suffocates a grin, Reis's Medal of Honor gap will never be filled, hell, it's an outrage the major general wasn't yanked within a half-day of H-hour,

and while Reis peers through field glasses at the splotch of blue, Bagger looks around to share the victory with the others, but Arno's attention is on a scampering lizard, and Goodspeed's lips rustle through private calculations, and Popkin only stares back with lax hostility, no indication he's caught on, leaving only Veck in rigid formation, or as rigid as a man can get when afflicted with perpetual tremble,

and they all adopt Veck's posture when Reis slips his field glasses into their case and drops his dreamy gaze back to the singed planet and, following a stare as sharp as a billhook, says, "We have ten working eyes here. But do we have a single working ear?," and he cocks his head to reference to the shriek, always the shriek, forever the shriek,

and Bagger's ribs shiver and marrow stirs, the shrieker has not quit shrieking, not paused for air, not cried for water, which re-minds Bagger of something his father said, that God built parents to feel stricken when babies cried so they didn't simply eat their children, sensitivity to shrieks is what keeps the human race roll-ing, apocrypha Bagger now fully believes,

and Reis says, "I imagine hearing such a cry is quite the incon-venience. I imagine it disrupts the pleasant music in your heads. While you happy wretches have tended to your own concerns, other men, better men, have cleared Bois de Fays of the injured. Some of whom might even live. Do you have any inkling, I wonder, what it is to live? I think not. Your kind of survival, bought on the backs of the brave, is a walking death,"

and defiance pushes from Bagger's belly, his only sin is duping rubes who ought to know better, it's Reis who shoves men into a delicatessen slicer with no plan other than to slice them up thinner, but Reis muses onward, "No longer will I risk such men. We must," and here Reis locks his jaw for strength, "we must be on the march. But the United States Army does not leave a man behind,"

and Bagger only appreciates the blood crusted over his face as a protective mask after it starts sliding apart with sweat, as Reis distills his order to its briefest essence, good military practice, it could even be mistaken for conviction if Bagger didn't know better,

and Reis says, "Stay behind. Find the man. Help him,"

and Reis's pained smile is as unexpected as the daub of blue in the brown-bruised sky, he looks transported, to where Bagger has no idea, but he longs to be there, too, where soft clouds roll over a clean, contented populace whose workaday niceties convey quiet affection, a vision that nearly moves Bagger to tears, except, no, that can't be what waters his eyes, it must be one or another toxic fume,

and Reis extracts a handkerchief, tidies his gloves, and delivers his final words without the favor of eye contact, "Élan, boys. Élan,"

and because it's famously the major general's favorite word, Bagger despises it, it's French for *sprint*, but Reis uses it to mean soldiering with unsnuffable zeal, an impossible ask amid the wet clay, the mashed rats, the human innards, but Reis snaps his handkerchief clean of mud and with the poise of a man choosing to stand erect before a firing squad, strides across the crater, grand-marshaling his walking stick, his missing Medal of Honor no longer a dragging weight,

and so Major General Reis exits the crater a better man than he entered, a fact Bagger knows will gnaw at him, and the second he's gone, Bagger looks and finds panic slithering like chemical gas between Goodspeed, Popkin, Veck, and Arno, they know as well as Bagger the euphemisms endemic to the Army, and "help him" is one they don't need translated, for in the eyes of the First Army, it's always better for a dying doughboy to be finished off by a fellow American,

VI

and the men unlock postures, puddled and dangled, and cover their ears, the shriek a screwdriver to the earholes, and Goodspeed rips a stick of chewing gum from his pocket and stuffs it in his mouth, seems the wait nearly killed him, his chewing sounds like a child being spanked, and Popkin flattens one nostril with a thumb and ejects snot from the other, and Arno blinks at Bagger in confusion, while Veck remains the obelisk, eyes closed and quaking,

and Arno aside, they can't look at one another, a sensation Bagger recalls from Camp Winn, where recruits were divided into teams every day for internecine bullshit like obstacle course or rope-pull, and because Bagger was emptying everyone's wallets at craps, no one wanted him on their team, a revenge Bagger mocked until team selection was down to him and one other guy, at which point Bagger's smirks cooled to wax replicas, for being hated together is so much worse than being hated alone,

and, you know what, to hell with it, Bagger slaps on his helmet, takes up his Springfield, and goes into the trench, can't see Reis but hears the marching orders, which kick off an orchestra of weary groans, jangled buckles, slorping boots, and clunking rifle butts, all of it contributing to a terrible *crunch*, an entire society gnashed between titan jaws, and beyond the murk, the Germans crunch that way, too, like an Iowa county fair contest, who can eat the most hamburgers, the most pie, the most world,

and huzzah, the parade of troglodytes begins, Father Muensterman the sole loiterer, the old chaplain's pressed from the same mold as Bishop Bagger, he holds his Bible aloft and points a Grim Reaper finger at Bagger, as his chin, crudded with vomit, joggles in supercilious glee, they call Bagger a hustler, but Muensterman plays a harsher three-card monte, the Father, Son, and Holy Ghost,

and Muensterman cries, "You'll find the devil out there, Private Bagger!," and Bagger grins, a long zipper of teeth unzipped, he enjoys this, the chaplain's so much easier a target than Lyon Reis, not to mention the Reichstag army,

and Bagger says, "It's devils you're after, padre? Well, that'd be us. Private Mephistopheles reporting for duty. Over there you'll find Private Beelzebub, Private Baphomet, Private Lucifer, and Private Antichrist. I know there's only supposed to be four horsemen, but it's the War to End All Wars, so we went all out,"

and Bagger detects a ratlike scurry, and checks over his shoulder, and it's Arno, naturally Arno, and over the kid's head he glimpses the last marchers vanishing centipedially around a trench corner, the gunmetal sky glowing off the canteens clipped to every pack so it looks like there's a big, silver hole punched through each soldier, the air thick with the molar grind of men overburdened with matériel, the drowsy clops of horse-pulled supply wagons, the asthmatic hack of covered trucks dragging fifty-ton howitzers over cratered rubble, and it's misting, but mist is a gift in the vulgar deluge that has been every day of the offensive, where only rain stops the bullets, and the men would prefer the bullets, so with Arno back at Bagger's heels, he leaves Father Muensterman with his sanctimonious face drained of blood, a not-bad Pierrot act, and snakes through fifty feet of trench before the underfoot mud slopes ten inches beneath black water, each stomp sending toads hopping and rats paddling,

and because the trenches are French-built and only recently wrested from the Boche, all intersections are marked by darling little replicas of village road signs, which means, of course, that all of them are in fucking French, not that it matters, the international language of *BANG* pulls Bagger toward the battlefront, still going strong to the west in Bois de Romagne and to the east across the Meuse, feistier fronts with soldiers more saturated in élan,

and as Bagger blinks away the ash that snowfalls heavier with each northward step, he imagines it as the whispery tickle of falling ticker tape, New York City mistaking him for the kind of guy who, back when the war was raging, gave a flying fuck,

and he finds the frontline trench looking like a mouthful of busted teeth, the tops rounded by the fretting of bayonets or the clawing of soldiers on their way out or back in, while inky water covers Bagger's boots and runs in rivulets down the walls like blood down a riddled body, but Bagger leans into the front wall anyway, a puppy into his mama, and the wall leans back into him, as if seeking the same comfort,

and he scans for a periscope but it looks like the Butcher Birds took them, though a wooden ladder waits like the cross of an absconded Jesus, each rung whittled by thousands of metal-studded trench boots pushing men over the top, so Bagger lodges his foot onto a rung and feels it vibrate like a bicycle wheel, and he imagines a bike chain routed around his scapulas, pelvis, femurs, and patellas, by taking this rung, he's threaded himself into some sort of machine,

and Uncle Sam's finally quiet as Bagger extends his calves to peek over the trench's muddy crenellations at the black world hulking beneath the slow cyclones of smoke, he can only see ten or twelve yards into a landscape reminiscent of soldiers he's seen pulled from fires, their outermost layers of charred skin peeled to reveal a soft, pale hypodermis,

and beyond that are foundations of obliterated buildings like the vertebrae of buried gods, lying beside slag heaps of bricks of no obvious origin, as if German Fokkers have taken to dropping brick in lieu of bombs, though some of these bricks must have once been homes, for there's an upright piano out there, gap-toothed, down two legs, but still technically a piano, its exposed wires droning in the scraping wind,

and Bagger ducks down, it's like surfacing from water, breaking back into breathable air, where Arno waits with big red eyes, asking "Bad?," to which Bagger gives him a flat look and replies, "Not at all. They're selling popcorn. Go get some,"

and a leathery hiss of drabs heralds the galumphing elephant train of the others, Veck first despite his shakes and the weight of the P3, followed by Goodspeed and the shrewd assessments of his blue ice-pick eyes, then Popkin, lollygagging a good twenty yards back, his beefy bulk making it hard for him to reach the back of his neck, he reaches, and reaches, could be a rat there, usually it's a rat, and this time it's a tongue, a human tongue that had been hiding in the trench like an asp viper, and wow, tongues are long when detached from their heads, Bagger wonders if the lummox might keep it, it's got to be superior to the one infected with trench mouth, but Popkin flings it and takes a moment to collect himself, looking like he's going to puke, or cry, or shoot himself in the face, all of which Bagger has seen before and none of which would surprise him,

and the weight of No Man's Land strains against the men's shoulders, no longer twenty thousand pairs of shoulders, only five, five versus what could be ten thousand Huns who still think there's a 43rd Division there to absorb their next barrage, and Bagger considers this as the shriek shrieks, and tree bark sizzles, and mortars explode close enough to filigree brimstone onto the drifting whales of smoke, which cause Bagger and the others to do the trench dance, it's easy to do, you hold your helmet down, you do a little dip, and you believe in the fiction that being six inches lower will save you from the wrath of God,

and Popkin says to no one, "Yeah, well, I ain't going. Reis wants this screamer so bad? He can go. Go get his guts unwound,"

and Goodspeed brushes soil from his uniform as quickly as the soil appears and says, "Who said we have to go out there? We don't have to go out there. You have to look at what the man actually said. He said, 'find the guy.' He's found, isn't he? It's not like we don't know where he is, he's straight thataway, shouting like mad. Reis wants him to shut up is all," and Goodspeed titters, "I say we just wait till he shuts up," and a third voice, a new one to Bagger, says, "Waiting won't work," so whispery Bagger wonders if a sandbag is draining sand until everyone turns to Ben Veck, one more of the day's surprises, Bagger's never heard the flamethrowing Negro say a word and doubts anyone in the 43rd has, but the whites of Veck's eyes wolflight like trench lanterns, he has indubitably spoken,

and Popkin's forehead doughs over his eyes and he says, "That guy out there? The racket he's making? He don't make it to sundown. No way, no how," and Bagger actually thinks the lummox would take a swing at Veck if not for the tank of combustible oil strapped to Veck's back, so Popkin's belligerent fists hang like dual scrotums, and he grunts, "I think the darkie's gonna tattle,"

and though Bagger has no reason to defend Veck, boy, does he hate Popkin, so he says, "Well, tattling's what you do to bad little boys, Popkin,"

and it's a risky thing to say, given Popkin's size and mood, but Bagger's got no interest in hors d'oeuvres of violence before a main dish of violence, and maybe Popkin feels the same, for all he does is spit tobacco at Bagger's feet and say, "I'll make boots of you," a threat that Veck, anyway, weighs with his deadlights before he nods his head at No Man's Land and says, "No telling how long that boy will go on yelling. Reis might send a runner back to check up on us,"

and Popkin scoffs, "That bastard's got bigger problems," and Veck, in a frankly shocking display, locks his jaw and rasps, "The major general is a good man," and Bagger can't help it, he laughs, and asks, "How do you figure?," to which Veck stretches his knotted body into a prouder stance, and says, quietly and firmly, "He chose me,"

and Bagger could dispute that, Reis wanted a flamethrower operator, not specifically a battle-rattled one, but the world makes his
point for him, a blast from the west, trouble in V Corps, a peach au-
rora like dawn's youth soaking into the age-old dark, and Veck hits
the deck, slams himself into muddy water, the habit of the shell-
shocked, and though Popkin laughs, Bagger is envious, must be
cool under the water, and quiet, and what he wouldn't give for both,

VII

and it's too much for Arno, who sits down, something Bagger hates to see, mud's going to soak through the kid's drawers like he's loading a diaper, and under his dented helmet, Arno does look pretty shitty as he mumbles, "He's not stopping. He's been yelling for longer than anyone's ever yelled," and he screws the heel of a palm into his eye, "It hurts my head,"

and Bagger wonders if the kid's onto something, what if the shrieker is some new kind of Hun weapon, a sonic cudgel intended to drive doughboys batty, turn them against one another to release the pressure in their skulls, and if so, it's one more reason not to dally, either they do this task or they don't,

and so Bagger says, "The kid's right. So's Veck. We don't mop up this mess, Reis is going to find out. If he gets replaced, that only makes it worse. He's not going to drift peacefully out to sea, you know? He'll drag us down with him. He'll make his last act sticking us with court-martials," a threat that descends until Popkin hurls it away like the tongue,

and Popkin grunts, "No one's gotta know what we do or don't do. Nobody's gotta tell nobody nothing about nothing. You hear me, darkie?," and Bagger smiles big, lets the ash turn his teeth as gray as Popkin's, and says, "Your belief in us is downright touching, Private Popkin. You're right. There's no way any of us would ever turn against our bosom pals. Or talk about how one private wanted us to just hunker down till the guy out there stops screaming. Nah. We wouldn't dream of it. We're all-American heroes, all five of us, fresh off the assembly line,"

and Arno concurs with a single-word moan, "Nantillois," mispronounced but with enough dread for Veck to agree, "Uh-huh. Those blinded Germans at Nantillois. Reis told Company K to question them. Instead they killed them. Reis found out and there was hell," but Popkin butts back in, insisting, "Company K did right. They did what ought to be done," and he makes a finger gun, aims it at Veck, and goes, "Bang,"

and Goodspeed, high-pitched as rifle fire, says, "Hold on, everyone just hold on. Maybe you're right, Bagger, maybe we gotta do what Reis said, but it's cockamamie for all five of us to go over the top like we're a whole brigade when we're not even a platoon, not even a squad, just a piss-poor five-man detail, couple of pop-guns and a flamethrower. You have to be honestly joking,"

and Popkin aims his finger gun at Goodspeed and goes, "Bang,"

and this is rich coming from Vincent Goodspeed, Bagger closes his cold hands over the cocking piece of his Springfield, one quick twist and he could crack Goodspeed's jaw in half, but instead, Bagger strokes his chin and says, "Only one of us should go, is that right? I wonder why that would be so important to Private Goodspeed?

Why he'd want to be alone with our dead bodies," to which Goodspeed's squinty face unclenches into gasping offense,

and it's an act, they all know it's an act, Goodspeed combs over battlefields like a prospector, harvesting every tradable object so the men
who do the actual fighting have to visit the Goodspeed General Store
for war souvenirs, he's got German slouch hats and pickelhaube
covers, ideal playthings for stateside sons, and horse gas masks that
look like the heads of nightmare stallions, and epaulettes your girl
can sew into a quilt, and weapons, they say Goodspeed lugs around
an arsenal of saw-toothed bayonets, Mauser cartridges, brass-topped
gas shells, even German officer pistols,

and because carrion birds aren't choosy, Vincent Goodspeed, also
known as Vincent the Vulture, also robs the American dead, or
so they say, as well as the American *dying*, there's a corporal who
swears he saw Goodspeed cut the thumb off a dying doughboy to
get his wedding ring, not that Goodspeed could ever trade such
contraband to fellow Americans,

and that might explain why Goodspeed has gone AWOL during
battles only to return from the direction of a village, pockets larded
with francs, which isn't even the ugliest hearsay, that'd be the
rumor that Goodspeed makes his best deals during night visits to
the German trench, he's been seen humping across No Man's Land
at dawn, fingers shiny with the military-issue butter he trades to
Huns reduced to eating their horses, and it's fitting he licks those
fingers clean, Vincent the Vulture has no morals, only appetite,

and though Bagger knows his own morals aren't much better, he
regrips his Springfield, aware that if he swings it hard enough,

Goodspeed's whole head, including that exaggerated look of insult, will pop right off, but Hugh Popkin is the faster draw, pointing his finger-gun at Bagger, lips peeled back to reveal the overripe fruit of his gums and the long roots of teeth as gray as chicken bones,

and he says, "Bang, Bagger. Right in the balls,"

VIII

and Bagger's patience tears away like a pair of old britches, there's no question which of these men he'd condemn to crawl out there if he had the power, and that's the thing, he *does* have the power, part of what makes him the Hawkeye Hustler is his ability to spin a yarn, it's how he lures a fellow into horse betting, how he convinces widows their dead husbands had nearly finished paying for a surprise jewelry gift, how he coaxes men into believing he's a stockbroker, please read my brochure, *How A Modest Fortune May Be Made From A Small Investment In Wheat And Corn,*

and it's a skill he picked up from his father, Bishop Bagger's sermons made the obscurest Bible tales as suspenseful as photoplay serials, and Bagger has learned it's easiest to swindle the rich or sophisticated, who despise admitting that they have been rooked, which means getting through to Hugh Popkin won't be easy as there's no intellect to manipulate,

and the laughing lug appears to read the shift in Bagger's demeanor, Popkin takes hold of his own Springfield with a defensiveness Bagger thinks he can capitalize on, the lummox is childlike, after all, and children love stories, and so Bagger begins, carefully, "All that bang-bang. You're good at it," and Popkin warns, "I told you, I'll make boots of you," and Bagger says, "I know. But hear me out first," and Popkin says, "You ain't good enough for boots. Rags to wipe my dick," to which Goodspeed giggles and interrupts, "Show him, Popkin, show him your pork and beans, wait till you see, Bagger, the worst case of clap you ever saw!," and Popkin's lip curls up as he gamely holds open the front of his pants,

and Goodspeed says, "Get yourself a gander, Arno, here's a lesson in social hygiene," and the kid looks terrified, he saw the same VD posters, they all did at Camp Winn, HE PICKED UP MORE THAN A GIRL! and BOOBY TRAP!, neither of which worked as the Army intended, for the poster artists couldn't help but draw the tainted girls as absolute knockouts worth any VD risk, though now Bagger hopes the posters' small-print curses come true for Popkin, insanity, blindness, heart disease, sterility,

and after Popkin's pants snap back to his gut, Bagger says in his father's doxological tone, "I want you to listen, Popkin. I want you to imagine. You're out there. Zero hour. Over the top," to which the lummox snorts, "Is this storytime?," and acts like it is, closing his eyes and leaning into the clay, so Bagger says, "Storytime, sure. Now, in this story, you're belly-crawling over No Man's Land. Jerry's bullets zipping through your hair,"

and Popkin snorts, "Oh, good, I got my hair back," and Bagger goes with it, "You and your big head of hair crawl till you find the shrieker," and Popkin singsongs, "I told you, I ain't going," but Bagger soothes, "It's just storytime. All right. So you find the shrieker. He's caught in barbed wire like a steer. It's bad. It's bad like we all know it's going to be. But you do your duty. You do what you're so good at," and sure enough, Popkin hits his cue, forming his finger gun and going, "Bang,"

and Bagger says, "Correct. You *help* him. Like Reis said," and Popkin laughs, "Yeah. With élan," and Bagger dares a glance at the others, even amid the death rumbles and offal stink, perhaps because of it, they have the translucent look of Bishop Bagger's rapt congregation, because stories are hope, stories have all sorts of fantastical twists, underdog victories, and heavenly interventions, all things soldiers yearn for,

and Bagger continues, "Then you crawl back here. The rest of us greet you like a hero. Because you *are* a hero. Finally, the hero you always knew you could be. You did what the rest of us couldn't. And we vow to give you all the credit you're due," and Popkin says, dreamily, "Lift me on your shoulders," to which Goodspeed protests, "You might get your block shot off," but Popkin warns, "I'm the star of this story,"

and, sure, whatever, "We lift you on our shoulders. We carry you all back to the division. Hollis sees us first. Can't believe his eyes. Sends for Motta. Motta's beside himself. Greisz shows up. Greisz gets the whole story. Greisz calls you 'son.' Now word reaches Reis. The Generalissimo's never looked so shocked. Forget a court-martial. Reis shows you off to Bullard. Bullard shows you off to Pershing. You're the best thing to ever come out of the 43rd, and the honors? They're only beginning," and Popkin murmurs, "Medal of Honor. I get one before Reis,"

and Bagger's on a roll, "Here's the best part, Popkin. Tonight, as early as tonight, a few hours from now, you're cozied up in the driest spot of the camp because heroes don't sleep in mud, and you ask for pencil and paper, and I know writing's not your strong suit, but you get your point across, I bet," and Popkin says, "Figure I do. Who'm I writing?," and Bagger pauses long enough for artillery blasts to tenderize the lummox's heart before he forks it, "Effie,"

and here we go, Effie Inez Barbeau, Darling Inez, Effie Weffie, Effie My Hart's Desire, *Hart* pronounced with a seal's *arf* to mock the misspelling the recruits saw on letters Popkin let slip to the floor, where men were pissing into brand-new boots to soften them overnight, and had it been only one soldier teasing him, Popkin probably would have murdered the guy, but the whole damn barracks razzed him,

and though Popkin tried to hide his future letters, as well as the girl's replies, he's always failed, and thus his tragicomic relationship with Effie Inez Barbeau became Company P legend, how Popkin had enlisted at Effie Weffie's request, or at least that was Popkin's understanding, as Effie Weffie, in her imitable, playful way, wrote repeatedly that she hadn't asked Popkin to join the army *specifically*, rather that she could only love "a fighting man," a distinction that, at this point in the war, feels really fucking important,

and Popkin's letters sop with obsessive accounts of the times Effie Weffie let him hold her hand and how his loins burned, a different burn than the clap, Bagger assumes, and of the times Effie Weffie spurned his kisses, which always lead to the same list of questions, why did she refuse to kiss him after he signed up, why does she still refuse to say she loves him, does she know he fantasizes about her every night, P Company sure knows, the lummox can't keep Effie Weffie's name from his masturbatory sighs, and it's probably fair to mention all the boys are obsessed with Effie Weffie, the girl is trouble, a real minx, and yet, like the VD vixens, she inspires lust through her painstaking descriptions of the boys she dates back home, boys who aren't "fighting men" at all, each detail a bullet into Popkin's chest, a feminine barrage from four thousand miles away, she's driving the lummox insane, a different shell shock than Veck's,

and Popkin's eyes twitch behind his lids as he asks, "Why'm I writing Effie?," a justified suspicion particularly when it comes to Bagger, as it was Bagger's rigged blackjack game that unloaded Popkin of the diamond ring he'd intended to present to Effie upon returning home,

and so Bagger replies quickly, "All your letters have been complaints. That's no way to win a lady. This time, you'll have something to brag about," and Popkin asks, "Yeah?," and Bagger says, "Tell her about the letter of commendation you're getting. About the medal you'll show her when you get back. The medal you'll show *all* the girls when you get back. That ought to do it, don't you think?," and Popkin licks his lips of tobacco and blood, and growls hungrily, "Yeah,"

and Popkin's eyes open slowly thanks to the weight of mud and the intoxicating notion that he, at long last, might be the driver of his own sexual future, and there's a dull bison glow to his eyes that unsettles Bagger, makes him worry that, if Popkin does get out of the war alive, Effie Inez Barbeau will need better protection than a well-manicured slapping hand,

and Popkin's eyes roll toward the trench top, and Bagger holds his breath, and Popkin leans away, the clay slurping as it lets him go, he's picturing No Man's Land, how he can keep his big body low, how he might bludgeon the shrieker to death so as not to tip off Jerry sharpshooters, deep thoughts for a lummox, but this is how good cons work, your mark's imagination finishes the con for you,

and Popkin takes a single step, the first station of the cross en route to the trench ladder, the first stage of keeping the rest of them safe and sound, when the whole effort is ruined by the kid, the goddamn kid, bouncing up, hands bolted to ears, screaming,

IX

and it's enough like the shriek for Bagger to believe the shriek is a new social disease, the kid's infected, the rest of them soon to be infected, too, and when Reis sends a detail back to get them, they'll find five men with mouths agape like baby birds, unable to eat or drink or talk, only shriek, and they will be taken to Paris, still shrieking, installed in a sanitarium, still shrieking, last rites performed by a priest, still shrieking, until Saint Peter welcomes them to heaven with one last joke, opening his mouth and shrieking,

and Arno claws red gems of blood from his temples and shouts, "It's killing me! It's killing me!," and the men stare, and Arno whimpers, "Isn't it killing you?," so Bagger holds up a hand, "Kid. Hey, kid. It's okay. Things are going to be," but the kid interrupts, "Nothing's going to be okay! We're just sitting here! We have to do something!,"

and, Jesus, this is bad, Bagger looks for something to help and sees the stiff yellow clay of the trench's substrata, and digs out two plugs, and holds them so Arno can see before he pushes the blobs into either of the kid's ears, which recalls the sensation of the dismembered ear stuck to Bagger's face, no good deed goes unchased by bad memories, and Arno goes quiet to gauge whether the plugs help as a black wind teases the overgrown hair fringing his helmet, and there's motion, and Bagger looks, and Veck's screwing a finger into his own ear, and Goodspeed's rubbing his ears, too, it's happening, the shriek's worming its way into their systems like typhoid, diarrhea, pneumonia, trench fever,

and Popkin stares at all of them, appalled, before he investigates his own ears, and Bagger's ribs roast in fury, all the gains of his Effie Weffie gambit lost,

and Veck says, "Only one of us should go. But we gotta choose fair," and Goodspeed snaps, "How do you do this fair? This is like the story of the sailors on the lifeboat, they're starving to death so they randomly choose who's gonna get their leg cut off so the others can eat it, and right after they cut it off, a rescue ship shows up, and now they gotta live with it, what they did, all of them have to live with it,"

and Bagger's had enough, "Give me a break. The shit you do? You seem okay living with *that*," and Goodspeed goes goggle-eyed, "The shit *I* do? That *I* do? You're the only one of us without a scratch, not a ding-donged scratch!," and Arno gasps, he knows Bagger's going to do it, going to break Goodspeed's skull, but Veck asks, "How'd they choose? On the lifeboat?" and though Goodspeed gestures wildly at the missed point, he replies, "I don't know! Straws?,"

and Popkin, fully roused from Bagger's spell, points a finger at him and says, "No straws. Not with him. He cheats," and Bagger laughs, "How do you cheat at straws?," even though he knows exactly how to cheat at straws, but Veck interjects, "Something you can't fake.

Flip a coin," and Bagger's gut tightens, rigging coin flips takes god-damn time, so he bluffs, "No one's got any coins," and it's Arno who fucks him over again, gesturing at Goodspeed and saying, "He does,"

and it's true the main thing stopping Goodspeed from being an effective No Man's Land operator is the weight of money in his cartridge pockets, and Goodspeed folds more gum into his mouth, a defensive gesture, "You expect me to hand over cash? I give you a single franc and you'll lose it, and then you'll ask for another and another. Maybe you don't like how I earned this money, but I'm not going to let you toss it in the mud, I won't do it,"

and suddenly everyone has an opinion, Popkin says they should arm wrestle, Veck says they should guess numbers, Goodspeed says they should bid valuables, Arno says they should go in birth-day order like they do in school, and Uncle Sam the shamefly goes wild, incensed by the festival of cowardice, every soldier living down to Reis's opinion of them,

and that's when Veck, over the woodpecker dill of distant machine guns and the porcelain clack of his jaws, says, "Rochambeau. You know it?" and Bagger's breath catches the way honest folks' breaths do at the sight of a glorious sunset,

and so much hot opportunity creeps from the collar of Bagger's scratchy wool coat that he has to choke it back down, you can't pull off a fleece if you betray excitement, but Ben Veck has handed Bagger a different kind of trench ladder, one he can climb right up out of this mess, so he holds his tongue and lets the others think they're the ones choosing the game, and Goodspeed shrugs to say of course he knows Rochambeau, he's no lunkhead, and Popkin grins like his knowledge of the child's game is a palpable point of pride, and Arno asks, "Is that the rock, paper, scissors game?,"

and Bagger nods, yes it is, and he cycles through masks of skepticism, reluctance, and capitulation, before shrugging his willingness to go along with the idea, and he observes the straighter postures, replanted boots, and exchanged glances of men confident they have attained the upper hand, the poor, confident fools, the word *confidence* is right there in the phrase *confidence man*,

X

and what they can't know, can't begin to imagine, is that Rochambeau was Bagger's first grift, he took it up around the time pa-
rishioners began breaking from his father's church, an overdue
exodus, as Bishop Bagger had gone hardshell following the death
of Bagger's mother, who'd always been the one to focus on fellow-
ship, he said, and without her, the Bishop got lost inside the cave
system of his intellect, learned Hebrew even, and passed his un-
easy revelations onto his flock, forgetting that flocks don't want
truth, truth is too much to take on a Sunday morn,

and the only invulnerables were the church's children, too bored
by preachments to care, and like millennia of brats before them,
they turned to games, Rochambeau reigning supreme in pew play,
pocket money changing hands in silent tournaments with no child
achieving supremacy, and because Cyril Bagger, the Bishop's son,
had no pennies to wager, he spent months studying matches that
seemed based on predicting what your foe would predict that you
predict, a chain of prognostication no one could sustain for long,

and Bagger's eureka was how a player's *reactions* to success or failure
gave away the store, and so one day, after mapping current trends
inside a hymnal, Bagger entered a Rochambeau round-robin on a

five-cent loan, which he paid back at triple interest, and proudly, for if Bishop Bagger was going to set fire to their lives for things as stupid as belief and ideals, young Cyril Bagger would need to start looking out for himself,

and that's why Bagger, beneath the carbonation of gunfire and digestive upset of falling shells, humbly suggests to his fellow doughboys how to arrange their little contest, imagine if you will the pentagon shape of the Medal of Honor ribbon Reis has all but forfeited, and draw a line between each point, a five-pointed star, which is to say each player plays every other player once, zero points for a loss, one point for a win, math even the lummox can handle,

and Bagger sighs woefully, "At least this will be fast," and the men, these chumps, these stools, these patsies, think they smell blood and draw close, there's nothing like war to habituate you to physical proximity, forever are you jostled by wet, cold, filthy male bodies, the group lurches within inches of Bagger, hands out, fingers flexing to work out the bone chill,

and it begins without ceremony, Bagger and Veck, the former feigning nerves, the latter swallowing the bait, his lantern eyes irising to pinpricks, an intimidation tactic that is Bagger's best clue, for while it's true naive players lead with rock forty percent of the time, it was Veck who suggested Rochambeau, so he's not naive, or doesn't consider himself to be, but Bagger also knows paper is the classic first choice of players who fancy themselves clever,

and Veck raises his fist, the call to arms, and Bagger mirrors it, and together they drum the beat, *one*, eyes locked, *two*, breath held, *three*, Bagger lets insight flood through the seams of his skull, Veck's too smart for paper, but no way does he go for scissors, on no planet does a man who's been through what Veck has been through choose the fussy, fallible gadget of scissors when it's been rocks thrown at him all his life,

and so it goes, Veck with rock, Bagger with paper, and weight leaps from Bagger's back like a gargoyle, the hardest round now behind him, he can forget about Ben Veck forever, good riddance, quickly he logs Popkin's result, paper, and Goodspeed's result, scissors, and the absurdity wallops him, they are five soldiers, lost in forsaken craterlands, wedged into a collapsing crevasse, playing a child's game beneath falling ash while earth convulses around them,

and it's no more absurd than the opposite, world leaders in play costumes of braids, buckles, aiguillettes, pompons, tufts, cords, plates, and sashes, in playpens of castles and state rooms, pushing wooden blocks around a game map, a magic trick that shoves millions of men across actual battlefields, it's really the same game, rock crushes kaiser, paper covers tsar, the scissors of the Entente snips Europe into new configurations,

and Popkin comes at Bagger like a hellbeast, purple-ringed eyes, nostrils pink and crusted, face a flaky agglomeration of red clay, brown blood, black mud, and orange tobacco, everything shellacked with sweat, the lummox gasping like a fish, a furor that makes it easy for Bagger to see the future, *one*, human nature is to replace a losing weapon, *two*, but Popkin will overthink it to the extent he can think at all, *three*,

and Popkin's scissor is dispatched by Bagger's rock, the lummox goes down fuming while Bagger eyes the other matches, Arno faring poorly, Goodspeed cruising until Veck beats him, prompting the Vulture to check over his shoulder in hopes he might accuse the

Negro of cheating, but Bagger won't have it, he reaches through the
pyre of men's arms, grabs Goodspeed, and pulls him over, Goodspeed wily enough to know he's being cornswoggled, *one*, crying,
"You can get into their heads, Bagger, but not mine, not mine!,"
two, but it's not Bagger getting into the Vulture's head, it's the
shriek, *three*,

and it's Goodspeed, paper, and Bagger, scissors, and while Goodspeed spits gum, Bagger watches Veck dispatch both Popkin, who
bellows like a bear, and Arno, who looks betrayed by the flamethrower operator he once escorted from the 368th to the 43rd, with
whom he shared his cup of corn meal mush and kidney beans
when Veck's shaking hands dropped his own cup, for whom he
pilfered a piece of chalk so Veck could write his wife's name on the
P3 fuel tank, dozens of small testaments of affection,

and amid the clerical brouhaha of proclaimed wins and unjust
losses, the kid pouts at his winless fist, as futile as his Chauchat,
before looking up at Bagger with naked vulnerability, for that's the
only duel left, Bagger versus Arno, and if Bagger wins, that's it, it'll
be the kid, not Popkin, going over the top alone, and Bagger, like
those apocryphal cannibalistic lifeboaters, will have no choice but
to live with it, same as he lives with everything else,

XI

and here's the scammer's tightrope, to really scam someone you need to get to know them, but the worst thing you can do is get to know someone *too* well, you want to flirt, not fall in love, Bagger watches Butcher Birds make the mistake every day, an offered cigarette, a smile of acceptance after some expulsion of fear or bodily fluid, the trading of photographs, this sweetheart for that, friendship is what Army leaders count on, that a buddy's struggle becomes your struggle, and for them you'll gladly die,

and it's propaganda, the same pablum peddled by every cop who's ever dragged Bagger off a riverboat by his collar, don't you care about your fellow man, Mr. Bagger, not really, sir, what has this so-called fellow man ever done for me, but the problem with Lewis Arno is that the kid never shuts up, and so Bagger knows things about him he wishes he didn't,

and that includes how Arno's an orphan, a sad little pauper straight out of Dickens, and though the kid's never explicitly said he fibbed his way into the Army to procure a family, it doesn't take a genius to see it, orphanages are staffed with, at best, backward nuns and, at worst, opprobrious careerists, and are either way devoid of adventure, leading the little dope to seek adventure above all else, safe enough when listening to Bagger read dime novels, but lethal when plunged into the murder machine of the War to End All Wars,

and now their shared sagas of jungle avengers, false kings, desert plunderers, and viperous pirates twist between them like taut rope, Arno watching Bagger so ardently he worries the kid might salute, this feels less like a game now and more like he's re-delivering Reis's assignment, and as much as he hates to do it, he knows it's best to deliver it with axe brutality,

and the kid says with a pained smile, "Didn't win a single one. Just unlucky, I guess," which requires no reply from Bagger, yet he feels himself shrug and say, "Wild was the way to play it. You did right. Just wasn't your day," and Arno winces upward, Reis's blue sky still permeating the battlefield smoke with the luminescence of hungry bluegill beneath frozen Lake Zabriskie, the cracks of distant guns nothing but expanding ice,

and Arno asks, "What happens to Korak?," and Bagger replies, "You want to know how it ends?," and Arno nods, "In case I don't make it," and Bagger is reminded of dressing deer as a boy, he's got a hunch Arno has hunted before, how else to explain how the kid knows how to cut a heart out while leaving other organs undisturbed,

and so Bagger says, testily, "You haven't lost yet, kid. Like I said, play it wild," but the smile Arno returns is that of a kid who knows Santa Claus isn't real but appreciates an adult's attempt to preserve the ruse, and Goodspeed cries, "What's all this chitchat? It's cold and getting colder, get on with it!," while Popkin glares with spooky red eyes and Veck holds his clackity jaw shut with both hands, and all three scratch their ears, the shriek a scythe through skin, muscle, and bone,

and Arno raises his fist like he's holding his neck out, and Bagger's briefly furious at the world, what sadistic author plotted their dime novel to this disconcerting climax, but as the shriek dives about their heads like a conventicle of magpies, Bagger just does the fucking thing, lifts his fist in the air like felled men do to signal stretcher bearers,

and quickly he whispers, "Korak and Tarzan end up having to fight to the death," and Arno gasps, "To the death? Does Tarzan win?," to which Bagger nods sagely, saying, "There can be only one Lord of the Jungle," an ending he's just made up, but Arno ponders it, before smiling and declaring, "Good ending,"

and at that, the kid drops his fist and Bagger, too well trained, matches it, *one*, and now he's scrambling to recall the kid's symbol history thus far, *two*, before realizing the kid's doing what Bagger suggested, truly playing wild with no idea what symbol he's about to throw, the kid's Korak and Bagger's Tarzan, and the only way for the son to defeat the father is to become the Killer, *three*,

and Arno drops his hand a beat too soon, an error that gives Bagger the split second he needs to choose whatever symbol is required to win, which makes him wonder, in that flash, if he has it in him to deliberately lose, but the symbol Arno chooses isn't rock, or paper, or scissors, his hand is curled into a C-shape like he's back home, a home he never had, hand wrapped around a mug of hot chocolate made by someone who loves him, and it's the biggest choke Bagger's ever seen, he could fucking murder the kid, and Popkin howls, "He lost! Arno lost! You all saw it!" and while Arno examines his hand like it's a reptile he's got by the tail, Bagger's own fist, symbol still unchosen, melts away, and he really feels the melt, skin and muscle sliding off his bones, seems fitting, his inability to choose a weapon only his latest failure to fight,

XII

and if forced to choose, Cyril Bagger would say the ugliest minutes of his life are the five it takes Lewis Arno to prepare for his solo mission to dispatch the shrieker, doughboy packs weigh seventy pounds and the kid weighs probably ninety, so he disencumbers himself of everything he won't need, canteen, magazine belt, SBR gas mask, shelter canvas, entrenching tool, soap dish, mess kit, sewing kit, shaving kit, which looks brand-new because the fucking kid's too fucking young to fucking shave, and, of course, *The Son of Tarzan*, a sight that hurts Bagger more than any bullet,

and yet he doesn't do fuck-all about it, he feels filleted as the others shoot the shit like Arno's already gone, and Bagger joins in only to cover the flapping wings of an incensed Uncle Sam, "Who do you think's out there?" Goodspeed fakes, "Gotta be some cornholer, he screams like a lady," Popkin fakes, "Strong voice. 2nd Battalion have any good singers?" Veck fakes, and "Duck Casey could sing. Kept half the division awake before he bit it," Bagger fakes,

and Arno places his first aid kit into one pocket of his coat and his wire cutters into the other, eyes half-lidded, his mind's somewhere far off, tucked into bed, while his physical form takes the sides of the trench ladder and climbs it, artichoke-colored mud seeping where the ladder presses into the trench, and Arno peers over the top, his M1917 wobbling like a cereal bowl, the Army never did make a kid-sized helmet,

and because life is cruel, and because Bagger deserves it, the kid looks back at him one last time, and there's so much Bagger could say, words of encouragement, words of regret, but Uncle Sam is livid and Bagger can think of nothing but the shriek, so he flaps an impatient hand and snaps, "What? Get going already,"

and Arno obeys, and Bois de Fays rumbles as it digests him,

and Bagger stares at the empty ladder, the cowlick of grassy mud where Arno's boot pushed off looks like a scalp, and Bagger has the urge to slip it into his pack, a memento truer than anything Goodspeed sells, while behind him, the others stir,

and it goes, "Don't look at me like that. What did I do?," and "Shut your face. Or I'll shut it," and "I've been the one. Plenty of times I've been the one," and "The one what, darkie? To get their face rearranged?," and "To jump off like that. No one cares if I live or die," and "So he's a kid! So what! We're all kids! We all have to take our turns!," and "Bury me. Just bury me here," and "Darkie. I'm warning you,"

and a new voice, saying, *Save me,*

and the words are so clear, Bagger assumes they come from a fellow Butcher Bird, a loiterer who played dead in No Man's Land until it was safe to drag himself back to the line, but it's not, the voice, *Save me,* comes from inside Bagger, the same way it did back when it first called to him, *Bagger*, which Bagger had thought had been Arno, but clearly he'd been wrong,

and Bagger searches himself, *Save me*, it's nowhere he can pinpoint, *Save me*, if it was only in his head he'd ascribe it to the mortar blast, *Save me*, if it was only in his heart he'd reject it as maudlin bunk, *Save me*, but it comes from the center of who he is, like his every molecule has been halved with a shrieking mouth, *Save me*,

and Bagger's going to fall, suddenly fall, so he hooks an elbow through a ladder rung, which swings him so he's facing the duckboard shelf of Arno's belongings, and there's *The Son of Tarzan*, abandoned, unfinished, once a book, now a headstone, leaving Bagger to make the graveside conclusion that the voice is a ghost, or not-quite a ghost, a pre-ghost, Arno begging Bagger to be the man Uncle Sam wants him to be,

and though Bagger never reached *The Son of Tarzan*'s end, come on, there's no doubting that Tarzan, Prince Greystoke, Lord of the Apes, will show up in time to save his son, Jack Clayton, aka Korak the Killer, the novel isn't a novel at all, it's a chapter-and-verse psalmbook that has been training Bagger better than any Camp Winn drill sergeant, to be Tarzan, finally Tarzan,

and so he does it, just goddamn does it, starts stripping himself of the same impedimenta Arno did, but with none of the bedtime fastidiousness, off comes the shovel, the mess kit, all of it except the gas mask, each piece hurled like a punch, the lighter items lodging into sticky clay, the heavier items splooshing into the ratty moat, and Bagger pauses only once to open the red leather Bible and inhale its strength before cramming it back into his pack and putting that pack on his back, he'll bring the Bible and the Bible alone, and Popkin sputters, "The fuck. Where you going? Where's that fucker going?" and Goodspeed cries, "Stay down, you stupid asshole!" and Veck, in a multioctave splinter, begs, "Bagger, don't," but none of them give a shit, they only know that, if Bagger goes over the top, the cowardice they have hidden away will break through the dam and engulf them,

and there's no battle cry this time, no Reis, no Greisz, no Motta, Chester, no Hollis, no Aquila, no *P Company over!*, no *Butcher Birds advance!*, no *Bash the Boche!*, no *Spite the kaiser!*, no lies of elation, of glory, of grandeur, of nobility, of triumph, of pageantry, of exaltation, of magnificence, of sublimity, of dignity, of honor, of prestige, of extolment, of idolization, of worship, of rapture, of radiance, of ascendence, of immortality, which leaves only the lie Bishop Bagger might have offered his son if the old man could have broken free of his mind's prison, the lie of forgiveness,

and the lie goes like this, Bagger tells himself, you deal this one card honestly, my boy, this one single card cleanly off the top of the deck, and maybe all the bad deals of the past will be pardoned,

XIII

and if you imagine it from Arno's perspective, it's quite the fright, first the kid's elbow crawling, a misnomer, you'd have to be an idiot to use your elbows, that'd put your noggin into prime exploding range, more like he's dragging himself shriekward with his hands, one of which has to carry along his no-good rifle, he's in and out of rain-swamped craters, holding his breath for the underwater slither, chin and neck rawed by the detritus of shells or casings or belt buckles from annihilated men, he's alone, so alone, a bug on a leaf, his death will be insignificant, but that don't mean it won't hurt, and so when he feels a bear-trap grip his ankle, he's gobsmacked to find not gristled flesh back there but Bagger's hand,

and that's pretty much how it goes except with a lot more screaming and kicking, Bagger has to hiss for the little fucker to shut up, and even after Arno does, he looks uncertain whether Bagger is real, and as much as Bagger hates to further degrade his noninvolvement, he can't help but splash a swaggery Tarzan grin onto his face, he's not going to make a habit of this hero business, but it does feel pretty fine,

and he points at what looks like a long pale string of lower intestine but is really the white tape the engineer regiment laid out this morning to mark the charge boundaries, as if war followed tennis-court etiquette, and though most of the tape has been tramped beneath mud, enough remains to indicate the kid has crawled off course, while the shriek sounds to Bagger like it's resounding straight down the engineered lane,

and so they go that direction, mud-slicked torsos reading a belly Braille that details four years of voracious futility, wagon wheel spokes, snapped trench knives, spent magazines, detonator plungers, incinerated flare pistols, scabbards bent to right angles, an airplane altimeter if you can believe that shit, soggy piles of puttees that might have unraveled from severed legs, and all Bagger and Arno can do is keep crawling, keep reading, and hope the story ends up like the other books they finished, the good guys easily definable and victorious,

and the shriek, good lord, the shriek pervades everything, so shrill it rings harmonies from the dead, altos of discarded guns, sopranos of spent stick grenades, booming basses of riddled canteens, so blistering a dissonance that Bagger's relieved when he has to crocodile through a marshy crater, it's quieter in water, even with Arno gagging beside him,

and the sky is slashed with yellow howitzer shot revealing body parts in the stew through which they squirm, two severed arms holding hands, boots still potted with feet, a set of shoulders that dangles a curtain of hairy chest, nothing alive here but opportunistic animals, a stoat dragging away a complete digestive system, a blackbird perched atop an opened head to peck at the brains,

and Arno freezes, and Bagger's almost glad, and if the kid wasn't here to rouse, Bagger's not sure he'd ever move again, so he takes

Arno by the sodden wool and hefts him up the crater incline, never mind that half a horse, that field telephone box filled with blood, that pair of lips still pursed over a cigarette, "Élan," Bagger says, Reis's word but he's stealing it, "Élan" on the inhale, "Élan" on the exhale, and the kid, a sign of life, echoes feebly, "Élan,"

and at the top, Bagger rests his face in the crook of his arm, but Arno slaps him and gasps, "Light, Bagger, look at the light," and Bagger thinks, well, shit, Jerry fired a Big Bertha, the monster gun capable of lobbing two thousand pounds from six miles away, shells that only explode after embedding fifteen yards into the earth, a fairy tale to Bagger until he saw it happen a week ago, the forest floor leaping a hundred feet into the air, whole groves of trees airborne, if you gotta die out here, at least the Big Bertha does it fast,

and Bagger pulls a Lot's wife and looks up to behold his slayer, but instead finds a different kind of light fifty yards away, not the vaporous fireball of a plunging shell but a tower as newfangled as the Woolworth Building, except made of nothing but blinding white light, six feet in diameter, endless in height, an elevator between No Man's Land's world of slime and the fuliginous clouds,

and the kid cries, "Is it a plane?," and Bagger understands, it could be a spotlight from above, an ace trying to light their way, but no Curtiss can hold so tight a pattern, certainly no Nieuport, and although the RAF is capable of anything, the Brits are nowhere near Bois de Fays, which leaves the possibility of a German zeppelin, except zeppelins are fucking balloons, and no balloon could have survived the day's firefight,

and the light scintillates like fire behind a waterfall, a depth Bagger feels more than sees, like when he was on the ship to Europe and feeling the Atlantic's depth by the flex of its topmost wave, and all around the lucid beam is an ash-and-soot darkness that reminds Bagger of pubic hair around a cock, a vulgar but adroit comparison, the way the light imbues the earth feels downright lustful,

and Bagger wants to cover the kid's virgin eyes from so intimate a scene, but Arno doesn't look abashed, he looks like he's being reunited with the parent he never had, there's a grin cutting through the kid's grimace, and though he's got both hands over his ears to buffer the metal-on-metal shriek, he's hollering over it, too, "Bagger, Bagger, it's her!,"

and of all the things the kid could have said, *Look, Bagger, it's a giraffe!* or *Hey, Bagger, is that Fatty Arbuckle?*, this single word, *her*, is the most jarring, the Western Front is Earth's malest place, an effluvium of burps and piss, jeers and jokes, strength and sacrifice, where any woman, from Red Cross nurses polka-dotted in blood, to the so-called war godmothers and their care packages, all the way to Marie-Louise and her sulky pout, exists so far to the fringes they feel like fading dreams,

and the kid's gotta be crazy, except he isn't, right there at the foot of the light shaft, snarled in concertina wire in a pose both pained and graceful, is a woman, there's no mistaking the copper sheet of hair, the delicate fingers splayed as if in want of a handhold, the gather of red dress over her hips, the swathe of blue cape off her slender shoulders, the cream skin, a living American flag in tortured repose,

and Bagger believed himself devoid of chivalry until this injection of gasoline into his heart, and when Arno says, "We gotta save her," Bagger nods, it's true, they do, maybe this is what gallantry feels like, and Bagger follows the kid's order with an obedience he's given no one else in the army, he grapples through mud, hurls aside forsaken gear, shuts down the lobes of his brain that short each time his hands touch cold, slippery body parts, while rainbows of death arc overhead and the *put-put-put* of machine guns throbs Bagger's chest like he's sprouted several new hearts,

and all of them seize in the unexplainable fear that this woman might perish, Bagger's never felt the need to save anyone, with the exception of his father the night before the old man left for the Lusitania,

and just as Bagger thinks it, barbed wire stabs inside his nostril, he sputters and draws back so fast the barb exits through the cartilage, a sting, a run of blood, Bagger slitted like the nostrils of the First Army's suffocating pack mules, that's how he feels, animalistic, here only to serve, to burro this woman out of here no matter how finely he gets minced,

XIV

and she's right there, Bagger could touch her if not for the wire sickles between them, the forest shakes so wildly from mortar-shell punches that the whole nest of spikes bounces like bedsprings, the pain must be indescribable, that's why she shrieks, it's this woman who's been the shrieker all along, and Bagger's guts flop, she lay here in agony while he and the boys sat around playing Rochambeau,

and then the shrieker writhes, a sinuous ripple from upturned face to pointed toe, and the beam of light over her ripples, too, and Bagger's struck stupid, the beam isn't pouring down *onto* the woman, it's coming *from* the woman, specifically her exposed skin, the dewy face, the extended arms, the bared ankles and naked feet, every inch cascading like Veck's flamethrower unleashed,

and she ought to be a latticework of charred bone, but only soft perspiration beads her closed and quivering eyelids, an expression that mixes pain and purpose, the look Bagger imagines on women giving birth,

and Arno arrives next to him with wire clippers in hand, a tool that comes with implications, you don't euthanize someone with wire clippers, which means Arno agrees this woman isn't to be *taken care of* in the way Reis suggested but rather *taken care of*, rescued at all costs, and the begrudging warmth Bagger feels for the kid leaps to a furnace burn,

and Arno rises to a kneel, a height that puts him in view of German sharpshooters, and though Bagger wants to yank the kid back down, he, too, takes to his kneecaps and pretends he's protected by this thicket of wooden posts and fist-sized knots of barbed wire so tortured Bagger sees faces in them the way he does clouds, except all these faces do is shriek, shriek, shriek,

and Bagger gets out his M1910 cutters, too, and he and Arno get working, finicky snip-snip-snips, like trimming a dragon's hair with tweezers, it's taking too long, killing her would have been easier, and so when a sugar maple a hundred yards to the left explodes into tangerine fire, a sure sign Jerry sees them, Bagger drops his wire cutters and uses his rifle bayonet to fight down the wire's rusty hedge no matter how many punctures he takes,

and he threshes loops of wire low, then stomps them lower and thicker, which allows Arno to start cutting two, three, four layers at a time, and suddenly Bagger's got fingers closed over the woman's wrist, though he can barely feel it, it's like dipping his hand into a pitcher of warm milk,

and he thinks how the blue cape must be snared by hundreds of barbs, which brings to mind the 43rd's nickname, the Butcher Birds, an embarrassment compared to the Red Arrows, the Buckeyes, the Cyclones, divisions that came to their nicknames honestly, instead of having a peacock like Major General Reis force it upon them because he liked the sound of it, butcher bird being a colloquialism for shrike, a bird that impales insects, vole, lizards, mice, and other birds on twigs, thorns, and yes, barbed wire, a means of keeping its kill fresh till the shrike wishes to eat it, a sadistic thing to call your division, if you asked Bagger,

and, oh, how things change, at last he feels like a Butcher Bird, this helpless woman impaled before him, his prerogative to nibble her, or eat her whole, or leave her for later, all options he discards, for he only wants to help her, so he pulls her arm upward in hopes he can rip her dress free of the barbs,

and the arm comes right up, not in fact snagged to anything, which seems impossible, but it's a gift Bagger won't question, he bends the arm around his neck, light as a scarf, and as he leans to get her left arm, accepting the fanged attack of wire into his crotch, he gets his first clear look at her face,

and hold on, what the fucking hell, he *knows* this woman, Bagger's mind starts spinning, could it be Marie-Louise, lovesick and pursuing him all the way to the trenches, no, he's known this face longer than that, perhaps a devout woman from his father's church who followed her preacher's footsteps across the Atlantic, or maybe a celebrity on the level of Mary Pickford, shipped abroad to inspire her fighting boys, only to get lost in the chaos,

and then her eyelids part, soft as a daub of honey,

and her shriek severs, abrupt as a rubber sole,

and gone with the shriek, Bagger realizes, is the undertone that had been buried in it since he awoke from the minenwerfer blast, *Bagger*, it had said, *Save me*, it had said, the words had come from this feminine effulgence, she had cried out to him, specifically Private Cyril Bagger, long before he could have possibly heard her, it's so outlandish an act he wonders if he died in the mortar blast after all, and this blazing oracle is a creature dispatched to drag his stubborn corpse to the hereafter,

and her eyes are brown, no surprise, because he *knows* her, and while he's transfixed, the whole pile of wire rollicks, it's Arno blundering into the thorny mesh, wire cutters abandoned, and the kid grabs the woman's ankles, the light from her skin so intense it functions like Röntgen's X-ray machine, Arno's hand flesh bright pink, each finger bone defined,

and the kid's weeping, which makes Bagger realize his eyes are leaking, too, and it's not like getting gassed or getting soot in his eyes, it's like the tears of the devout he used to see at his father's church, moved by some vision incomprehensible yet gorgeous,

and with Arno in the wire, Bagger gets moving, placing the woman's other arm around his neck, turning her over, the red dress as impervious to being snagged as the blue cape, and he rolls the woman into his arms, and in accordance with that roll, the tower of light falls hard as an axed tree and Bagger's abruptly eye to eye with the coruscating dazzle,

and it ought to blind him but doesn't, it's like being suffused in the sunlight of some arcadian glen, pollens and danders and seeds and fluff newly visible, an invisible world of wee floating things revealed, the October chill stoked to a cozy snug, the slaughterhouse reek sugared into a bakery bouquet, the gravel crunch of war muffled by a calming rustle of leaves, and then the woman's chin notches over Bagger's shoulder and her lighthouse beacon blazes toward the Allied trench, and the screech and talon and stink of the Great War resumes, nothing in front of Bagger but Bois de Fays smeared into the gray-purple of a flayed trout, and Bagger's chest pangs with the loss of beauty, like the last time he saw Marie-Louise, applying woeful wartime cosmetics, mascara of vaseline and charcoal, rouge of dampened red crepe, lipstick of red cake coloring, when Bagger was dragged from her bed by a corporal under orders of a bugle call, no basking one last time in the sarcastic curl of her lips, or kiss her nipple, or admire the arrowhead of hair pointing between her thighs,

and now that beauty's back, watch what you wish for, asshole, the sedentary murk of the northern forest blossoms into spectacular magnolias of Maxim fire, the Germans having seen the steeple of light topple and decided they'd had enough of the mystery, time to shoot, and it's the closest Bagger's ever been to machine gun fire, bullets coming in shiny ropes like spittle, like semen, everything in war is the residue of men,

and Arno tackles Bagger, that's a new one, all three of them splatted to the mud as the uppermost yard of concertina wire is sawed off by a chugging chain of bullets, individual barbs flung from the wire and embedding into Bagger's right hand, which protects the back of the woman's head, and Bagger pushes away from the wire with his boots but hardly moves, heels going nowhere in the loose mud,

and Bagger thinks, this is it and it serves me right, Reis was spot-on that the shrieker should be killed, you learn pretty quick out here, especially on burial duty, that there are ideas humans shouldn't have and tools they shouldn't build, and to allow a being of such purity to live within such sloppy Armageddon is wrong, even if she survives this assault, it'll ruin her, war isn't merciful, no matter if he and the kid were handed a mission of mercy,

and so Bagger, under darting sparrows of bullets, shifts his hands to the woman's throat, tender and slim as one of those pretty French poppies, so easy to admire, so simple to pluck,

XV

and Bagger will never know if Arno guesses the thought in his head or if the kid's simply a finer soldier, but the featherweight takes handfuls of Bagger's drabs and muscles him to his hands and knees, the woman safe beneath him, and the kid's screaming words Bagger can't hear over the clack and cough and zing of lead sparking off barbed wire in gold doubloons that expose the terrain, mud knobbed with the chins, noses, and cheekbones of embedded corpses,

and when the woman's head lolls, her citadel of light hinges west, carving across pitted landscapes, through skeletal barricades as well as actual skeletons, and into the bosks of the battle's perimeter, and, as far as Bagger knows, straight down the longitudinal line, a new kind of engineer's tape stretched through Bois de Romagne and Bois de Bas, erupting from the woods at Brest, spooking submarines in the Celtic Sea, a bridge of light all the way to Boston, a new border for a new world,

and just as Bagger accepts there's no way to evade Jerry's fire while carrying a human torch, Arno becomes a dressmaker's assistant, he pulls the sleeves of the long blue cape over the woman's arms, and tucks the hood over her head, dousing her phosphorescence, and Arno, crazy kid, he's got Bagger's Springfield 1903 lodged into his shoulder, his piece-of-shit Chauchat forgotten, and waves for Bagger to make a run for it, but fuck that, Bagger's not getting up, the kid's going to get decapitated up there, but Arno starts firing at the German trench, one kid versus the entire Hun army, so what the fuck else is Bagger supposed to do, he braces the woman tight to his chest, right over his gas mask, and tries to stand, only to spring right up, the woman weighs no more than her dress and cape,

and Bagger runs, oh shit, and with his arms over the woman, his legs have to do all the work, oh shit, tendon-stretching strides, heels planted into muddy marsh, warped metal, mushy organs, crackling bones, oh shit, and he sees at his periphery the red starbursts of Jerry's grenades and feels the hawkwind of the resulting shock waves, shit shit, feels fallen men claw at his shins, desperate for water, desperate for a bullet, hands that are really only rogue weeds, oh shit,

and he scrambles arcs around craters he can see and splashes through craters he can't, shit shit, while Arno's noises grow increasingly distant as the kid keeps stopping to shoot, oh shit, and all Bagger thinks is how he's never checked his ammo, why would he, he never shoots any, but cartridges bloat in wet weather, his Springfield might blow up in Arno's hands, shit shit shit,

and there, fifty yards off, is the long, toothless grin of the Allied trench, a shade darker than the sackcloth day, only first here's a dead soldier propped against an oak stump, facing the Hun trench like a spectator, a bullet caught between his front teeth, the guts in his lap still wispy with steam, and Bagger thinks this is why they call U.S. soldiers doughboys, you slit them open and their guts roll out like dough,

and Bagger looks at the dough too long, his right boot clips the corpse's knee, and that's it, his adrenalized dexterity is disrupted, he's spun, the battlefield a carousel of yellow gun blasts, his legs cycling too fast, can't extend his arms for balance, he's a runaway wheel, not falling, not yet falling, not quite falling,

and then a factory-made product of destruction lands, well, somewhere, and the earth digests it with an earthquake, and Bagger finally falls, twisting so as not to crush the woman, a dive into cold, hard mud, the trench but a few arms' lengths away, all Goodspeed or Popkin or Veck has to do is reach out and pull him in, if they haven't murdered one another or skedaddled,

and Bagger's heard men describe the whoosh of howitzers shot over their heads as they go over the top, both shit-your-pants scary and the apex of exhilaration, and here it is, oven-hot air singeing his neck, a shell with a German accent, yes, there's the minnie scream, nothing like the woman's shriek now that he hears it isolated, a barbarian noise, lionlike in solipsistic bloodthirst, its shadow a swelling, widening, black pool,

and, boy, it stings to have gotten so close to saving his own butt one last time, stings even more that he failed to protect this woman's breathtaking light, but at least Uncle Sam's gone quiet, happy and satisfied, at long, long last,

and then, so then, but then, it happens, a thing happens, a thing, it happens, how else to put it, Bagger knows he'll never grasp it, the thing, which happens, the thing that's like a pinch, like a thumb and forefinger pinch, taking him by the back of his olive drabs, same as a mama cat takes her kitten by the scruff, and he's lifted, that's the thing that happens, lifted right off the ground till he's watching mud dribble ten feet down from his dangled limbs, and though one of his hands holds the woman's hand, she's above him, it's like she's pulling him into the air, they're floating, and not only them, three rats and whole colonies of bugs, and who knows, maybe Arno, too, and then they are tossed, the lot of them, fifteen feet into the trench, and a second after this thing happens, the mortar lands, embeds, and detonates, the trench wall obliterated, but that's not where Bagger is anymore, he's way over here, inside a clay avalanche but alive, alive, what did Bagger tell you, he's always been a lucky son of a bitch,

The Gaff

XVI

and Bagger saw a moving picture once, nine chairs crowded into a wagon, *My Fearful Visage* was the title, a grayscale play in the form of rapidly cycled photographs, a tawdry melodrama acted out by thespians shrunk to pygmy size on a wall, followed by a sales pitch from a chap hawking a scald cream called Mr. Stick's Suffradine, all of which intrigued Bagger, he was always on the lookout for novel magics with which to bewitch his marks, and it's sad, really, that he never got to see another photoplay until right now,

and this one's projected on the inside of his skull, *Private Bagger Goes to War*, set in Davenport, Iowa, May 1915, our hero is twenty-two and reading a *Des Moines Register* piece titled MANY WOMEN AND CHILDREN AMONG LUSITANIA DEAD, and there, under the subhead *1,000 gone*, is "Bishop Bernard Bagger," drowned in the Celtic Sea when a U-boat, enforcing a Reichstag blockade, torpedoed the British liner, which the Bishop had booked in the desperate hope that ministering to Entente soldiers might restore his belief in a righteous God,

and it's hard to fathom it was only ten days earlier that Bagger had come, dragging the heels of his fringe-tongued, patent-leather brogues, nicely paired with shin-length checkerboard socks, back to the old church, now closed, and to the drafty apartment above, soon to be closed as well, where he'd grown up with his spartan father and his father's memories of Bagger's mom, who the old man described as having blond hair, chubby cheeks, and a lamblike soul,

and Bagger had been summoned to see his father off on the 20th Century Limited, which would spirit him to Manhattan's Cunard pier, with grandstands in sight of the White Star pier that was meant to have received the Titanic one year earlier, how about them apples, and finally onto a cruiser called Lusitania that would deposit him in Liverpool,

and how flippant Bagger had been, chewing ice, calling the ship "Lucy" to be a brat and asking, "Why not stay at the Biltmore, Pop?," though under no circumstances would Bishop Bagger stay anywhere but New York's most fleabagged of flophouses, just as he'd accept no Lusitania berth but the C-deck bunkhouse, and the old man's disappointed look withered Bagger as it always had, his father considered him a useless dandy, no matter how fine his finery,

and that's probably why Bagger lost his cool and spit his ice in the hearth and ranted how the old fool ought to get off his high horse, the only concern the U.S. had in Europe's war was cold hard cash, if the Entente vanished, so did the money they paid us for our goods, that's what Bagger read in the paper, and he concluded by accusing his dad of running from failure, the failure of his church, the failure of his faith, "You're looking for a purpose to save you!" he shouted, to which the Bishop, rather mournfully, replied, "Aren't you?,"

and it was a low blow, and Bagger got up to leave, but the Bishop raised a hand, fingers osseus, skin crepe, he'd aged a thousand years in ten, and he asked, with a tenderness Bagger had forgotten was possible, if Bagger wouldn't consider coming with him, C-deck still had tickets, and Lucy was, after all, the world's fastest, most luxurious ocean liner, a detail tailored to tantalize his son's poltroon interests,

and Bagger hesitated, what if he said yes, simply said yes, and got on that train, on that ship, and left behind the guilt of being the baby that killed his kindhearted mother in childbirth, left behind the shame of cheating others for a living, not to mention that the gambling on a boat like Lusitania would be gangbusters, though what if he didn't gamble at all, what if he stood by his father's side on the deck and found purpose in the sun, the water, the gold braids where the two forces met,

and what if Bagger died trying to save him,

and what if they went down with arms intertwined,

and when the *Register* confirmed that only one Bagger male had drowned, Bagger thought, well, old man, does that answer your question, it was either that or start sobbing, and he had a casino to get to, for while he knew plenty of boys who'd take their father's murder as a sign to volunteer against the Huns, he'd already lost half his life to dear old dad's suicide mission, and he'd be damned if he was going to lose the second half, too,

and what he'd never admit to anyone was that, before he polished his brogues and headed out to work that day, he picked up the red leather Bible, the single item his father had pushed into Bagger's hands before he left the apartment, and he inhaled deep from its pages in hopes of smelling the forgotten parts of childhood, the good things, paper, glue, charcoal, milk, chocolate, skin, fur, grass, and it was the Bible the Bishop had revelated from every Sunday of Bagger's youth, the leather adumbral with old sweat, gilt edges rubbed free of gold, silk bookmark frayed to a serpent's tongue, the only object that ever felt holy to Bagger, for nothing else had the power to drive the Bishop to his knees,

and how many times, while the flaking paint of the apartment flapped like shamefly wings from the vibrations of the organist downstairs, had Cyril tried to pull his father from his whirlpool of ponderings, pull him literally by the sleeve, only for the Bishop to gently, crushingly, extricate his son's fingers and hand him the Bible to read, the way Red Cross nurses give a man about to be amputated a rag to bite on, like all the answers were in this book, you only had to be willing to let them drive you insane,

and because the Bible had too many words, little Cyril instead studied the pictures bunched at the book's center, reproductions of famous paintings of the whole cast, Abraham, Moses, Jacob, Esther, Jesus, Judas, the two Marys, how he came to adore those portraits, the big, eccentric household Bagger never had,

and it's a household he didn't need anymore, after the Lusitania came the best part of *Private Bagger Goes to War*, all obligations to his father released, allowing him to barnstorm the Mississippi with impunity, imbibing wine, check, women, check, and song, check, and once President Wilson, reelected on the slogan of *He Kept Us Out of the War*, declared war, Bagger made paper airplanes of the loyalty leaflets that littered the streets, and enjoyed many a hearty guffaw at the suckers who rushed to enlist, and he began to see his draft dodging as a kind of vaudeville dance, look at Cyril Bagger go, maybe his purpose was to resist having a purpose, be the hedonist against which valorous sorts measure themselves, that's its own kind of service, for without villains there can't be heroes,

and so he hid behind the skirts of the women's peace movement, which included, to his delight, a bevy of shapely charmers in full swoon to his principles, until Wilson blew that up, too, with the Espionage Act, though Bagger would have survived that as well, if not for an enlistment officer who spotted him in a Des Moines red-light brothel, good and tipsy, and in possession of a card cutter,

and that was curtains for ol' Bagger, he was dunked in a horse trough to sober him up, and escorted to an Army office to fill out his Selective Service form under threat of jail, where he gold-bricked a final time by misspelling everything in hopes they would deem him daft, even writing *WAR IS RONG* at the top of the form, but they didn't bite, and thus *Private Bagger Goes to War* comes to its bittersweet end, our hero drafted into the American Expeditionary Force on August 10, 1917,

and four hundred and twenty-nine days later the AEF's still got him, and for a second time in as many hours he stirs from oblivion, the backs of his eyelids a-flicker with the photoplay's final words, *THE END?*, and the first thing he sees is Lewis Arno's face, will you look at that, his face is still on his head, his head still on his shoulders, his shoulders still on his torso, the kid's not only alive but whole, Bagger's luck must have rubbed off,

and before Bagger can see what Arno is up to, he notices three more faces far above, Vincent Goodspeed, Hugh Popkin, and Ben

Veck, each holding a lantern, a sure sign they'd been fixing to ab-squatulate when Bagger and Arno were delivered, but now the trio stares down in shock, not at Bagger but at Arno,

and so Bagger looks again, and this time sees that the kid is snuggled like a toddler into the side of the woman, her eyes closed, Arno's eyes closed, too, he's smiling beatifically, cauled with clay the others must have dug him from, and because the woman's lying face up, brilliant ivory light spears upward into the gloom,

and what felt so fantastical in No Man's Land, dancing along the razor of a dozen different demises, feels realer in this mudworld setting, the woman has all the upsetting tangibility of the two-headed lizard Sergeant Neil paraded around at Montfaucon, a worrisome aberration, for who can say if such a lizard, or such a woman, carries a novel disease, it could be seeping into Arno's pores right now, yet none of the soldiers do shit, maybe because the kid has never looked so happy,

and Bagger stands, legs bowing like rubber, and joins the others at a safer distance, and regards the bizarre tableau, his dizzied mind wilding, he goddamn *knows* this woman, and what's more, he's seen her in this exact pose, holding a child, it's a clue, but Bagger's cranium throbs too hard to seize upon it,

and that's how he remembers the minnie blast, oh shit, that's right, the facts sink in like tiger claws, the blast, the floating through air, the impossible everything,

and he wipes Earth's mucus from his eyes and really looks at the woman lit by lanterns, face a placid moon, features fine as china, cheeks the same pink as the petals of her lips, brows only a suggestion, reddish-brown hair center-parted and disappearing down the back of her cape, the hand she has around Arno so delicate Bagger mistakes her fingers for a spill of cigarettes, the red dress hiding a body that Bagger somehow feels no prurient curiosity about,

and one of the rats that was floated into the trench with Bagger and Arno lazes atop the kid's knee, as content with the kid as the kid is with the woman, and though Bagger despises rats, he finds the detail stirring, natural laws have been supplanted by a law even more natural, restored from a time before humans taught animals to fear them, and perhaps a floated insect lies happily atop the rat, and on that insect rests a happy fungus, and so on,

and despite the chortling of bullets, the thunder of heavies, the mist unbraiding into pattering rain, the bubbling mud, the heart still hiccuping in his chest, Bagger is strikingly glad that Private Bagger did, in fact, go to war, if only to witness this strange nativity, and to know, if only for an instant, what the world might have looked like if, as his father used to preach, the Tree of Knowledge had gone unplucked and the Garden of Eden had been allowed to grow into the sort of paradise Bois de Fays once was,

XVII

and Goodspeed sounds angry when he asks, to anyone, "Did you
see what she did?" and Popkin grunts, "We didn't see nothing," but
Goodspeed insists, "She flew them right up out of there and saved
them," and Popkin growls, "That was the shell that blew them,"
and Veck, astonished or terrified, asserts, "The shell hit *after* they
flew out," and Popkin snarls, a promise that if the Negro doesn't
adhere to the lummox's version, there's going to be fists,

and it's an inauspicious day when the voice of reason is Vincent the
Vulture, but that's who turns to Bagger and asks, "Who is she?,"
forcing Bagger to find his voice cringed way down in his chest, as
if fearful any reply might sink the supernatural ship that carried
them to safety better than the Lusitania, and he ekes out, "She's
him," hogwash when he hears it, so he clarifies, "I mean, she's *it*,"
no better, so he coughs mud and lets rain soothe the burn, and
says, "She's the shrieker,"

and on cue the woman's lashes flutter apart, soft acorn eyes on
Bagger, a look he can't hold, there's a burn of inadequacy he never
felt under the glares of Aquila or Hollis or Chester or even Reis,
but thankfully her eyes slide to Goodspeed, then Popkin, then

Veck, all three of whom shift enough for Bagger to think they feel the same, like sandlot kids who just hit a baseball through Babe Ruth's window, mortification wrapped in the desperate fantasy the Babe might chuck them on the chin and say, "Nice hit,"

and the woman, though, says nothing, her gentle exhale tousling Arno's hair, and Veck asks, "Can she talk?," and Goodspeed clears his throat and asks, "Ma'am, can you talk?," to which Popkin snorts, "She don't speak Yank, dummy, this here's France," and Veck asks, "Any of you speak French?," and six eyes land on Bagger, everyone's heard him belt out a frog phrase now and then, though he only does it to enervate soldiers who associate the language with pain, plus all he knows are erotic vulgarities taught phonetically by Marie-Louise, *Léche moi la chatte, Baise-moi par derrière, Suce moi la bite*, and the thought of repeating any of that to this woman makes him blush like he hasn't since boyhood,

and this makes Bagger think harder, he supposes he's picked up a few scraps, and he licks lips still salty with another man's blood and says, "Bonjour," and then, after some thought, "Commen ça va?," to which the woman only blinks, and why not, it's the kind of casual question a waiter poses of a diner, insane to ask amid the deadly drama of a trench, so he follows it up with the only other question he knows, "Comment vous appelez-vous,"

and this gets a reaction, the woman smiles, the slightest breeze across pale pink lips, and Bagger senses she's amused by the question, which embarrasses him, so he refocuses on Arno, who looks five years old, the rain on his face as soft as a mother's hair, and Bagger has the strange urge to join them in the mud, curl around them both, sleep off the rest of the war, and the dream is punctured by Popkin, "What are we supposed to do with her?," Bagger's back to the distasteful present, where he's unable to cloak his hatred for Popkin, forget French, conflict's the only language the lummox ever mastered, but Popkin answers his own question, "Reis said take care of her," and the rain goes twice as cold as Bagger feels the need for a long, heavy axe to plant in the bastard's face, he could warm his palms in the hot, spurting blood,

and before he can find an axe-like object, Veck drops to his knees, the P3 slugging noisily on his back, a pose of prayer, and whispers, "You all know what this is," audible despite the shrill of German arms, and Bagger feels that he does know, yet still wants to be told, and Veck grimaces, pained by their ignorance, and says, "Hasn't any of you heard of the Angel of Mons?,"

and that's right, Bagger *has* heard of it, even before being railroaded into the infantry, and he's always given the tale the contempt he gives all superstitious bunk dating back to Jesus walking on the water, but having been inexplicably saved from death, the door long shut to him suffers a crack, and Bagger peeks through the crack at the honeyed wonders,

and the tale every soldier's heard goes like this, it's August 1914, the war still revealing itself as a world ender, and the British II Corps, with their .303 Enfields, tries to hold a canal line in the Belgian city of Mons against the Schlieffen Plan assault of a German Army powered by artillery and esprit de corps, a futile task for Tommy until a towering angel in rippling raiments astride a white steed, hair fiery gold under a silver helmet, a flaming sword dipped in light divine, forbids the advance of a single Jerry for a whole day, for God, you see, is on the side of the Allies, and though other tales of angelic intervention followed, Joan of Arc over here, Saint

Michael over there, it's the Angel of Mons to whom the devout pray for another miracle,

and all of Bagger's long-dead beliefs come back up for grabs, seedlings of credulity, conviction, fidelity, and allegiance, the nooses that once swung from those branches gone, and this timid renaissance of faith makes him gasp, feels like being a kid again, how snuggly, safe, and smug it feels to believe in something bigger,

and Bagger fights it, he's taught himself to deny anything he can't touch, feel, and hide up his sleeve, so he says, "This is no Mons," and it's true, from what he's gleaned, Mons was a critical juncture, while Bois de Fays is but one negligible point in the ugly sweep of the Meuse-Argonne Offensive, and if angels existed, there's no reason one would come here,

and Veck declares, "No, it *needed* to be here," and bows his head, the hysteria that lives in his shoulders shaking out through his limbs, "First Lieutenant McNabb said three hundred thousand French died in these trenches," and the glances of Goodspeed and Popkin signal they translate Veck's message the same as Bagger, that the whole Woëvre plateau was a cemetery long before the Butcher Birds arrived,

and it had been good old dad who'd preached how angels, God's soldiers, always went where blood was spilled, look at the Babylonian cuneiforms depicting winged lions, human-headed bulls, scorpion people, or their biblical equivalents, the cherubim, who guard gateways between realms breached by indiscriminate slaughter, this forest might always have been such a gateway, *Bois de Fays* means *Faerie Woods*, after all, and a woodland doesn't get that name without centuries of arcane episodes, and Goodspeed's the first to puncture the shock, he steps up next to Veck, eyes bright behind pince-nez, his swamp energy enough to heat the chilly hole, and nods at the orange ribbon of a shell lobbed to the east, and says, "Those guns, there's never been anything like them, ever in history, the Big Berthas, the Sea Bags, the Jack Johnsons,"

and Veck adds, "The Paris Gun," and no one says shit to that, they've all heard of the Kaiser Wilhelm Geschütz, a barge-sized weapon with a three-story barrel that months ago pummeled Paris with two-hundred-plus-pound shells from seventy-five fucking miles away, a distance so vast the Squareheads had to factor Earth's curvature into their trajectory math, or so rumor had it,

and Goodspeed's theory has a logic Bagger can't quip aside, for if you were to forge new kinds of weapons, and those weapons flew farther and sailed higher than anything before them, it stood to reason the payloads might strike beings hovering at altitudes that, prior to the Great War, had been secure, and that one of these beings might be a goddamned angel,

XVIII

and Veck, stalwart day after day in the hostile 2nd Battalion thanks to Reis's acceptance of him, finally falls apart, the P3's lance dropped into muddy water, where it slithers off like a snake, freeing his blistered hands to cradle his face, his lock-jawed expression like a clotheslined sheet dropped into a mess of disconsolate wrinkles, tears daggering from eyes shut hard as fists,

and he sobs, "She knows," and, fuck, how Bagger hates it, he's worked so hard to excise emotion from his life, it's why he kept Marie-Louise, whom he might have loved, at wisecrack length, why he needles fellow soldiers so hard, because anger's easier to handle than grief, so he scoffs, "Veck, she doesn't know us from five big shits," but it tastes like a lie, if this woman fell from the sky, if she radiates light, if she can move men through the air, if she is an *angel*, then she has a direct line to God, and God knows all, even the Bishop believed that at the end,

and Veck blubbers, "She knows what we've done! We need to beg! Beg for mercy!" and Bagger's next wisecrack dissolves in the acid hitching up his throat, making Uncle Sam dance, for though Bagger has stewed plenty over his own pitiful plight, he's rarely pondered

the larger wrongdoing in which they are all embroiled, men of every
creed mowed down like Iowa corn,

and he thinks of *The Son of Tarzan,* Korak's jungle years spent murdering natives left and right, Arno hooting happily after each kill,
except now the slaughter seems pointless to Bagger, Korak killed
because he felt like killing, that's it, a pattern picked up by the rest
of the world, and isn't it possible the angel was shot down while
serving a summons to the human race, subpoenaed to defend the
Korak-like crimes they mistook as valor,

and Goodspeed ignores Veck and says, "I know a man in New York,
tours the continent selling medicines, he's a friend, a personal
friend, and showing off this thing? This angel? He could go big
with this. If she floated someone over the audience? Gentlemen!
There would be no opera house he couldn't fill. We strike a deal
with him, we're set up for life,"

and Bagger glances at the angel, she's watching, though it's
unclear if she's comprehending, then he squints at the beady-
eyed private and asks, "How do you propose getting her out of
France?"

and Goodspeed's too aroused to be fazed, he pivots on an underwater heel and appeals to Popkin, which makes sense to Bagger,
you get Popkin on your side, hell, maybe you can do whatever you
want, and Goodspeed says, "Well, I met a guy here too! French
doctor, down in Nancy, I sold him an engraved German bayonet,
he wanted to go into business right there. And business is what
we've got! Nancy's, what, fifty miles south? We make this deal and
we're European princes!,"

and Popkin squirms his brains and says, "You'll cut us out," and Goodspeed acts offended, "I will not," and Bagger says, "Don't buy it, Popkin, Vincent the Vulture doesn't cut anyone square," and the lummox glowers at Goodspeed and asks, "You'd split us equal?," to which Goodspeed's eyes shine with alarm, "Well, come on. It's my plan, my contacts. Naturally I'd maintain a controlling interest. That's only fair,"

and Popkin's ox nostrils flare and his moose lips curl to display apple-stem teeth and scarlet gums, and he says, "Nuh-huh. No way you get more than us," and Bagger's briefly grateful to Popkin until the lummox splashes through black water, bends over the angel, and orders, "Get up, you're coming with me," and when the angel only blinks over Arno's dozing head, Popkin fixes his Springfield's sight on the woman's face, an action so profane Bagger goes numb, Popkin's forefinger's too pudgy, it'll squeeze the trigger, and the lummox grunts, "Get up, I mean it,"

and, Veck, though, Veck reacts like his weapon is strung to Popkin's weapon, when the Springfield levels at the angel, the P3 lance splashes upward from the water, and clocks the underside of the rifle barrel, knocking it aside, and then, more or less, hell breaks loose, Popkin bleats in dumb fury and kicks Veck's sternum, but Veck traps the boot and both of them go down into trench scum, mud lapping over Arno and the angel,

and Popkin presses his knees into Veck's shoulders, pinning him, and pushes Veck's face underwater by the forehead, and Veck's neck stretches into a root system of strained jugulars as inky bubbles of air fight through ooze while his hands rip at Popkin's puttees, and yet Bagger holds still, holds tight, holding's what he does in battle, no reason to get involved, no fucking reason at all,

and the bubbles get smaller, and Veck's hands go wilder, sightless attacks, the guy's going to drown in six lousy inches of water, Bagger's seen it happen, boys too injured or too exhausted to lift their faces from puddles, and Bagger glances at Arno and sees the kid's eyelids flutter, he's going to wake up, he's going to look up, and he's going to see the real Cyril Bagger, a coward unfit for reading stories of selfless heroes,

and so what the hell, Bagger lurches and bends an elbow around the tree trunk of Popkin's neck, and the beast bellows and twists like a saddled rhinoceros, and Bagger's collarbone gets crunched against a discarded helmet, pain in bright pinwheels, and he's slammed into the water, his turn to drown, and he grapples through the gumbo of lost slickers, boots, pipes, pocket watches, bandages, rats, not a single good bludgeon among them,

and then Veck rises like a kraken, mud glopping from his open maw and sluicing down his chin like black merlot, his jaw twitching like never before, enough to rip open his cheek, and as he launches at Popkin, one of his boots plants onto Lewis Arno's knee,

and Arno wails himself awake as Veck cannonballs helmet-first into the lummox's kidney, Popkin ejecting brown batter, but even with the P3, Veck's an underweight foe, and Popkin finds under-mud purchase and slings Veck toward, well, Bagger doesn't see, because Bagger's juking toward Arno, the kid's clutching his knee as Bagger loops him by the armpit and dives both of them into the safety of a cold clay wall, and Bagger knows his noises, the snap of a rifle strap across rain-sogged drabs, the metallic joggle of a bolt handle, either Popkin or Veck has gained the upper hand, and when a soldier out here gains an upper hand, two things reliably follow, the cough of a cartridge and the whine of death, and Bagger wraps himself around Arno while noting he could have just run, just left the kid behind, maybe it's the influence of the,

and before he can finish the thought, Arno points and yells, "There!," and Bagger orients his eyes into the needling sheets of rain, there will be no outfoxing a third trench mortar, its grim reaper finger selects you to die and you die, and Bagger's luck has run up a tab his flesh is overdue in paying,

and so he's surprised to instead see Goodspeed spidering off the top of a trench ladder, the only ladder in sight, and rolling onto an elevated island of incinerated turf, while Bagger and the others tussled like Korak and the baboons, Goodspeed just took the fuck off, but that was the Vulture for you, three steps ahead and always hoarding the most valuable treasure,

and though Goodspeed isn't strong, the angel has a canteen weight, and with a final heave, he shifts her from the ladder into his lap, and Bagger's so dumbfounded that Arno weasels away, vaults the trench water, and grabs for the angel's dangling ankle, begging Goodspeed too softly for Bagger to hear, a useless effort, Goodspeed simply lifts the angel up out of the kid's reach,

and Veck, reptilian with mud, sputters, "She's not yours," and Popkin, hacking foul water, says, "I'm warning you, Goodspeed, don't you fucking leave us," and for a few seconds Goodspeed looks cooperative, as if ready to tell them they can all reconnect post-armistice, where he will parse out their earnings, all promises kept,

and then, ah, fuck it, Goodspeed drops his mask of dopey earnestness and lets a long, wicked grin eel outward, so long it threatens to detach everything above his jaw, and with the angel draped over his thighs as if for a spanking, he takes hold of the ladder and lifts it out of the trench, easy as can be,

and like that, the rest are cut off, and Bagger hustles in hopes he can leap and snag the lowest rung, but everyone else is closer, and Arno jumps, and Veck jumps, and Popkin jumps, the tallest but still a foot shy, and Goodspeed watches from above in giggling delight, the same way, Bagger wagers, he watches a rabbit suffering in a snare, and if Bagger hadn't lost his rifle in the trench-side miracle, he'd spray Goodspeed with blazing lead, though Popkin, a more frequent firer, knows better than to bother, Goodspeed could roll out of view in half a second,

and knowing he's beyond their reach, Goodspeed untwists his lizard body and stands before a brass sky flowered with explosions, chuckling so hard it sounds like hiccups, the angel limp as a bath towel in his arms, and he gazes down at her, chuckling, chuckling, and with two fingers pinches the robe hood and lifts it entirely off her head,

and maybe it's the low angle, maybe it's the smoke saturated in dusk's amber, but the light coming from the angel's face is now joined by something else, floating a few inches off the crown of her head, a golden ring as faint as dust, and if there was any doubt in Bagger's mind, that doubt is gunned down, the ring is a halo, a fucking halo, the woman's an angel, all right, a proper angel, and Goodspeed lords down through his pince-nez, tips his helmet, and says, "Bon voyage, boys! I'd like to say we'll meet again, but we all know that's not in the cards. Not even the kind of cards you deal, Bagger! You'll see my Theda again, though,"

and Bagger notices he calls her *Theda*,

and Goodspeed continues, "You'll see her in newspapers and film reels, and maybe in person, too, if you can save up the scratch to buy a ticket. If you do, rest easy that a hefty portion of the ticket price went to good old Private Goodspeed. Though I'll have dropped the rank by then. Sir Goodspeed. *Lord* Goodspeed. Has a nice ring, don't it? I'd say look me up, but that's assuming any of you surv,"

and there's a great flash of light like the sudden death of the sun, a noise so loud it's silence, it's that third minenwerfer Bagger has been expecting, fired by Jerry, who, after Goodspeed uncovered the light beam of the angel's face, had a direct target to shoot at, and the shell lands just north of the trench, a near miss, but it's followed by a wallop of sweltering wind that squalls a blue blur of shrapnel over the trench top, and with a swift, moist *snick*, Vincent the Vulture Goodspeed is cut in half just below his ribs, neat as a holiday fruitcake,

XIX

and there's no fear, fear requires understanding, there's only awe at how fast the rules of the game change, the legs half of Goodspeed teeters backward, the torso half tips forward into the trench, and Arno, directly below, wiggles away like a trench rat, and Veck parries back with the P3 lance like a saber, and Bagger's just too far away,

and so it's Popkin who plays valet to the gruesome luggage, Goodspeed's head still grinning, mouth still chuckling, arms spasming around Popkin's neck, a better brother in death than in life, and the lummox is bowed by the weight until Goodspeed's organs begin unwinding from the chest like a bolt of fabric,

and the angel rolls down onto Arno, the kid's huddled back breaks the fall, and Bagger skids to his knees in the black porridge and folds her into his arms, loath that one drop of mud might sully the red dress and blue cape, and he's shocked, but also thrilled, at the singing of his skin and the chiming of his bones, the full-body exaltation to have her back, Alleluia, he's whole again just as Goodspeed is halved,

and the German fusillade unrolls over the trench, a blanket of yellow flame, each tendril a hissing viper, something chemical in the mix, the steel of Bagger's helmet going ice-hot against his scalp, and he crawls away on two legs and an arm, the other arm toting the angel, an elbow all he's got left to whack Arno on the ear, get moving, stupid kid,

and Bagger launches to his boots and glances back to see Goodspeed's bodiless legs, way up above, drop to their knees and tip forward, the pelvic bowl pouring steaming intestines into the trench, while Goodspeed's haversack, bisected by the same shrapnel, pours salable goodies like signal whistles, pocket watches, insignia pins, campaign bars, and division patches, though the last item to tumble is none other than *The Son of Tarzan*,

and the book is inches from the hot offal when a hand plucks it from the air, Veck's hand, and Bagger doesn't know if Reis was correct and Veck is the finest Butcher Bird of all, or if he simply wants protection, Veck holds the book alongside his face and fire gnaws at it, the largest word on the cover promptly sizzled away to *TARZ*,

and here come the Boche, their hounddog blood bullwhipped by the smell of miracles, but the advantage of the Company P relics is that there's only four of them, five with the angel, but to maintain those odds they need to move, so Bagger sprints down the trench, each footfall detonating a six-foot geyser of mud, and when he takes a southward turn, his side vision catches Arno, Veck, and Popkin in pursuit, their own cracking footfalls indistinguishable from Gewehr rifles,

and still Bagger believes he can hear Vincent Goodspeed's lunatic giggle, you fools, giggle, you suckers, giggle, you doughboys all too ready to give up your dough, you'll join me in hell soon enough, giggle, giggle, and Bagger goes harder, if only to outrun the giggle, no fucking clue where he's headed, he's spent less time inside trenches than anyone, he tries to keep war's false sun at his back, zigging right, zagging left, fleeing Jerry like he's heard you ought to flee alligators,

and abruptly Bagger's scaling the ramp of a trench exit, out of dank sewage funk into a troposphere of hot ash that burns a cigarette cherry into his every bronchiole, they are out in the open, boots scrunching through scorched grass, sitting ducks until Arno catches up and throws the hood over the angel's face, hiding the halo, blotting out her illumination, and everything goes dark, like they have been stuffed into a giant's pocket,

and Popkin gasps, "Woods," but Veck gasps in dissent, "Stay by the trenches," and Bagger thinks he agrees, if they get lost in the woods, lost from the 43rd, they will be a whole new kind of fucked, they will be the deserters Goodspeed wanted them to be, so Bagger hunkers down, the angel held to his chest like a baby, Arno shuddering close,

and he shouts, "We stick to the trenchline and we'll run right into the division," to which Popkin sputters "With her? You just want to hand her to Reis?," and Bagger snaps, "Goodspeed lied! There's no doctor in Nancy!," and Popkin says, "I don't give a shit about any doctor! That girl belongs to me!," and Bagger's astounded all over again by the lummox's entitlement,

and more astounding is his willingness to fight Popkin over the angel, a devotion he's only ever heard from new parents and young lovers, the two biggest categories of sucker that exist, but now he gets it, it's a release to feel so strongly, this is the point of a purpose, the purpose his father wanted for him, the purpose Uncle Sam wants for him, too,

and before he can tell Popkin how many inches to shove it, Veck asserts, "She's mine," which draws flabbergast all around, what is wrong with this Negro, and Veck gestures in frustration and says, "You can see she's mine, you can see it with your own eyes!," and though Bagger doesn't have the first fucking clue what Veck means, he finds the same sense of possession in each man's face, even Arno's,

and the truth is, Bagger feels it, too, he envisions his fantasy farmhouse again and this time the angel's there, too, they live together, nothing romantic, a blissful harmony, and he thinks of the last passage he read in *The Son of Tarzan*, further ahead than what he's read to Arno, *He did not even wonder that he was unafraid, for his mind was entirely occupied with thoughts of another's danger*, meaning the girl Meriem in the book, but for Bagger, here and now, it's the angel, the angel,

and so he yells, "We need to keep our fucking heads and get this girl back to the division. This is bigger than us! Bigger than Reis! Bigger than John Fucking Pershing! This girl needs to go to the President. All of us know that!," and the others stare at their boots, to voice opposition would be to expose themselves as Benedict Arnolds, although Bagger doesn't want to give up the angel either, he wants the farmhouse, not the 43rd, but right now he needs to get these fractious fucks out of Dodge and he can't think of a faster way,

and so he says, "We'll take turns carrying her," like she's a burden, when they all know it's the opposite, at least this way they will each have to suffer one another's watchful suspicion, the glared warnings that if they try to ferret away the angel like Goodspeed, they will be violently stopped,

and another minnie blows the trench they just exited a hundred feet into the air, and Veck, as usual, dives for cover, face clenched, body in total contraction, while the rest of them Cossack squat to their feet and run,

and Bagger darts for a fringe of timber, a compromise, not the woods, but not the open trench either, and hears the other grunts follow, Veck included, because if there's one thing the four of them agree on, it's that possession of the angel elevates them to a higher rank, and if they can just stay alive, their days as Company P's ingrates are finished,

XX

and because fairies don't recognize straight lines, those feeble attempts to tame a planet reliant on disorder to tender magic, the men's trek through Bois de Fays is a vine of arboreal improvisation, hills too treacherous, underbrush too thick, rosettes of thorns to be avoided, sharp ravines not worth fording, and areas razed so treeless they are avoided by soldiers as rabbits avoid an open dell, and in such black hash, Bagger can't sustain a consistent direction, only platoon leaders are issued compasses,

and sallies from the timber are unavoidable, first they end up in a ghost village, each obliterated building honored by a chimney headstone, dead dogs everywhere, fetid with the stench of cordite and rot, and then they end up back in fungal trenches, one so bygone it's staffed by Huns chewed to skeletons by rats and maggots, cobwebbed figureheads of futility pointing future generations down the same useless paths,

and it's only the combat jolts to the west that keep Bagger's squad from digging foxholes, any Jerry who witnessed the angel's radiance is unlikely to halt in pursuit of it, so onward they march, between reels of brand-new barbed wire, around a spiral staircase to nowhere, past an observation post disguised as a haggard sycamore, and though all marches aggravate, this one's especially shit, for Bagger's the de facto leader now, how the fucking fuck did that fucking happen, for the first time in his life he's dying for an authority figure, his goddamn kingdom for an asshole to shout, do it this way, do it faster, do it better, Bagger can't get the men to form a simple skirmish line to find the best avenue of advance, of course he can't, he won't let whoever has the angel out of his sight,

and because the angel hasn't proven she has the ability, or maybe the desire, to walk, the men keep carrying her, and each fellow goes about it different, Popkin's drooly, lascivious stare, Veck hulking his arms like he's protecting a baby, Arno mooning like he'd rather the angel carried him, while Goodspeed, by Bagger's recollection, had carried the angel like she was a slot machine that would never quit paying out, all of which makes Bagger wonder how *he* holds the angel, all he's certain of is that he *knows* her and she's inspiring something inside him,

and when a man isn't carrying the angel, his anxiety extrudes like pus, Popkin so desperate for tobacco he takes a dead maple leaf, strips it, tucks the shreds into his lip, and ptooeys unsatisfactory green spit before perpetuating the cycle, wood ferns, pine needles, club-moss, finally birch twigs, and Bagger is cursed to glance at Popkin right when the lummox spits out the woody bolus, along with two of his eroded teeth,

and Arno, in his angst, picks lice like it's his first day in France, they all have lice, bred in every seam of every item of clothing, little fuckers that suck blood all day, all night, a microscopic war raging beneath the bigger one, and Arno slaps, and pinches, and runs matches over seams to hear the buggers pop, until Bagger smacks the back of the kid's head to remind him he's only making it worse,

and Bagger's compulsion is worse, he's got it in his head that every dead Jerry they pass might be faking it, there's countless stories of dirty Fritzes doing just that, so Bagger's taken it on himself to stab each corpse, and because he and Arno lost their bayonets in the trench collapse, he scrounges up an old pitchfork and pitchforks every carcass he sees, doughboys included, who can say they aren't Jerrys in disguise, and soon the squishing stab is the beat of his struggling heart,

and it's Veck whose reaction to the angel is the most disquieting, only a few miles into the march Bagger noticed Veck studying an old bay nag pulled apart by shrapnel, nothing unusual there, last Bagger heard, the going estimate was seven million horses killed in the war, a number that makes him believe that, should the war birth ghosts, they will be of the nickering, neighing sort,

and Veck shooed flies and picked up the horse's severed head, then reached into the open neck and began extracting its contents, the pale trachea, the brainstem like a malformed fetus, the huge red salmon of a tongue, handfuls of purple muscle and gray cartilage, all the while Veck, suppressing a smile like he was preparing a gift,

and when it was Veck's turn to carry the angel, he completed his work by avulsing the horse's eyeballs and putting its head over his own head, over his actual fucking head like a mask, the bay's ears flapping with Veck's chuckles, and though Bagger was anxious handing the angel to a man in a horse head, Veck exuded such uncommon frivolity that Bagger laid her in his arms and watched him wobble his horse head at her, making neighs, shoulders shaking with laughter, to which the angel returned her cryptic smile,

and so the strange band footslogs, drained and starved, across a pitted, plundered country, one man, one beast, one boy, one centaur, and one angel, pitchforking corpses, chewing up the world, drinking only from puddles with frogs, actual amphibial frogs, not Frenchmen, because frogs don't wallow in poison water, unless they, too, have death wishes, and only occasionally do these puddles bob with kerosene globules, which taste bad but make Bagger feel like a machine, keep rolling along, keep rolling,

and it's in these hours and through these travails that the haloed woman entrenches her sorcery of compassion, which solidifies the men's devotion to making her belong to them, no, to *him*, only *him*, like when Popkin says he'd smother his mother for a real smoke and there, a minute later, centered on a chunk of sandstone right in their path, lays a pack of Lucky Strikes, spiffy in cellophane,

and when Arno gets a nail through his tattered boot sole and gasps and goes pale as Bagger pulls it out, two inches of rusty iron slicked with blood, and Arno hugs the angel's leg as Bagger removes the boot to assess the wound, only to find there is no wound at all, not even a scratch, the blood source whisked away on angel feathers,

and when Veck comes across dead kittens, the whole litter mashed by a wartime wheel, all that feeble sweetness mangled, eggy little organs expelled from each yowling mouth, it's too much for Veck to take and he dabs at the horse head's eye holes like they are the eyes that are crying, until one of the kittens, dead thirty seconds before, Bagger swears it, wobbles up on foal legs, shakes itself of filth and gore, and scampers away, and despite these maybe-miracles performed on each man's be-half, never does the angel alter in comportment, except once, five hours into their hegira, when Popkin hurls a rock at a field mouse and hits it, and woofs with victory, and dangles the mouse by its tail over his mouth, impatient for its demise so he can chew it whole, and Bagger glances down to find big tears rolling down the angel's cheeks, so heartbroken at the pest's murder that Bagger catches his breath, no, he's not a machine after all,

XXI

and though the angel is carried like Hestia's flame, night falls anyway, and the men, wherever they are in Bois de Fays or Bois de Dannevoux or Bois de What-the-Fuck, are dead in their boots and stymied by a honeycombed terrain that makes Bagger feel in service of a diabolical queen bee, and stymied as well by blimps of fog concealing what could be two million more Germans, so they grunt their agreement to stop for the night,

and when a French 155mm howitzer materializes through the fog, derelict with rust, spoored with forest growth, wheel spokes ligamented with weeds, twenty-foot cannon slanted like a playground slide, they know their chances of finding better protection from the rain are roughly zilch,

and Bagger's low mood sinks lower when he sees from forty yards off that the space under the howitzer is occupied, a man sitting cross-legged before a miserable spit of fire, no telling if he's friend or foe, might not matter if he's edgy and armed, and most men out here are both, which means skirting the howitzer is the smart move, but also means more hiking, more mud, more rain, and the dull looks the foursome give one another tabulate the consensus of no fucking way, and right now it's Veck who carries the angel, something none of them loves, not with Veck's red eyes pitting the horse's black sockets, and though the horse-man doesn't seem likely to gallop away, who the fuck knows, so Bagger tells Arno to wait with Veck and scream bloody murder if he tries to leave, a better option than leaving Popkin, Bagger's gambler senses tell him it's an even break the lummox would slay Veck and take the angel,

and that leaves Popkin to go with Bagger to the howitzer, he can't think of a worse sidekick but the pickins are slim, so they slug across a slipskin turf the Great War peeled from the planet, Popkin lugging his Springfield, Bagger waving a banner of puttees to signal peace, and it's a positive sign that the man, upon spotting them, keeps eating,

and that good sign seems less so when Bagger and Popkin reach the howitzer to find the man devouring a cooked rat, his face glazed in crackling fat,

and that's not even taboo, not an hour ago Popkin tried to get Bagger and Arno to use their bloody toes to attract leeches, then use those leeches to attract vermin, but this man grins, big moth-gray teeth, and hoots, "Oh, ce sont les américains!" and unjoints upward and bonks his head on the howitzer's underside, which knocks his cap from a balding pate mottled with the corpus delicti of previous bonks, a risky habit in the French army, which the man's pigeon-colored overcoat, tunic, and breeches identify him as part of, poor bastard,

and the man springs to flagpole stance in the rain, scabbard swinging, and salutes with his non-rat hand, a hand lacking Chauchat or Lebel or Hotchkiss or Berthier, instead armed with Pinard, the manure-tasting so-called wine issued to French fighters, this fellow has a full bottle, less so after his salute spills a glass's worth, which he licks from his chin, snorting amusement,

and Bagger glances at Popkin, this poilu's as blotto as the day is long, but seems so harmless Bagger's tempted to beckon Veck and Arno, Pinard and Rat du Jour all around, but Popkin jabs his thumb at Germany and says, "Take a hike, Frenchy, we need to bivouac,"

and the soldier's tipsy grin plunges into a frown so harlequin Bagger thinks it's a joke until the man snatches the handle of his sword but struggles to extract it from the leather scabbard, he grunts and tugs and curses while Bagger and Popkin stand there getting soaked, whereupon the two-foot blade dislodges so abruptly the soldier staggers sideways and nearly falls, only to plant his feet, point his blade at them, and shout, "Mind that tongue, blackguard! Soit!,"

and Popkin simply hitches up his Springfield, which makes the poilu gasp as if shown an obscenity, whereupon he starts swinging his blade in off-center figure eights until the effort trips him backward into the mud, from where he laughs up into the sky, opens his mouth, and starts drinking the rain like it's better than the pinard, which it is,

and Bagger nearly agrees with Popkin, it'd be easier, and drier, to murder this fool, but instead Bagger wipes his face and says, "Look, Frenchy, what's your name? Comment vous appelez-vous?," to which the soldier sirens, "Oui! Frenchy! Frenchy Franchouillard, this is the name for me! Soit!," and Bagger has a hunch this soldier, an officer according to his sword, has gone AWOL, and in more ways than one,

and Bagger sighs, "Don't make this hard. We've had a rough goddamn night,"

and Frenchy Franchouillard sits up with automaton speed, widens his eyes, places a hand to his chest, a burlesque of concern, and coos, "Rough night, is this so? Poor, poor doughboys. Two or three months you spend in discomfort, Je suis désolé," and then his eyes go gimlet and his smile warps into a snarl, "Four years we die in mud. Waiting for les héros américains to look up from their baseball mitts and Cola-Cocas,"

and Popkin throttles his rifle and gets closer, "Ain't our fault you can't handle your business, frog," and Frenchy Franchouillard drops both rat and saber to clap his hands in sarcastic appreciation, and Bagger feels his own fingers twitch in want of a weapon as the poilu sings out, "Bravo! Here the doughboys come, just as we grenouilles have finished les Allemands for good,"

and Popkin impresses Bagger by knowing that's how the French say *Germans*, the lummox sputters with trench mouth viscosity, "Finished? You cheese-stinking drunkie? You ain't noticed how Jerry's shelling the shit out of us?," to which Frenchy Franchouillard twirls the sword he's no longer carrying and begins the painstaking process of getting back onto his boots, what's left of them, the peeling soles, the eyelets enucleated, the leather tongues as rotten as Popkin's,

and the poilu jeers, "La Boche was fichu in March! Ludendorff could have taken Amiens and then, qui sait? But les Allemands always wants his schnitzel and sauerkraut both. So he splits his armies in three, chop chop chop, and tries to take everything at once. C'est la vie. They say Ludendorff is, how do you say? Maniaque? Everything must be tidy? War is not so. So Allemagne falls. Adieu la guerre à l'outrance. Now France and Britain have only to round up the Les Boche livestock,"

and Popkin raises his Springfield to the level of Frenchy Franchouillard's knees, "France and Britain and *America*," growls the lummox, a freshborn patriot, but his face purples when the poilu snickers, swipes up his sword with surprise aplomb, and whirls it theatrically, bisecting raindrops with enough élan to make Popkin back away, the French always could hold their liquor,

and the officer holds his saber perpendicular to the ground, a musketeer pose to match a musketeer tone, "Les américains hatch like maggots on the corpse. But it is my corpse, you see, dear doughboys, and I am not so happy to have all this worming about. It is not fighting America wants. Not glory. Not la dignité personnelle. It wants spoils, only spoils,"

and Popkin directs the Springfield at the poilu's face and says, "Frog, I'm gonna shoot you," but Frenchy Franchouillard's smirk is for Bagger alone, the man might be drunk, but he knows which doughboy's haversack carries all the brains,

and the poilu mutters at Bagger with astonishing odium, "You know nothing of courage. Nothing of despair. Nothing of pain. You are children who arrive late to playtime believing there are games yet to play. Non. The games are over. And we have all lost, mon frère," and Bagger inhales to tell this frog to can it, but instead chokes, a hot shock,

and because Frenchy Franchouillard spoke of maggots, Uncle Sam hatches his own in Bagger's lungs, and a fly swarm fills his chest, the tickling shivers of a thousand palpitating wings, a cold roll of housefly thoraxes up his trachea, that's how hard the shame hits, for the poilu is right, American suffering is a stubbed toe next to what befell the French, and Bagger tilts his face to the rain to cool the fever, to keep the bugs from exiting in a visible cloud of disgrace,

and he gags to Popkin, "Don't shoot him,"

and Popkin's stupid, but less so in matters of violence, he assumes that, by nixing a noisy bullet, Bagger authorizes anything else, and through his choking, Bagger hears the clatter of the Springfield barrel disarming the officer of his sword, followed by spongier noises, a body into soggy ground, a kneecap cracking ribs, the eggshell shatter of facial bones, and the knuckle drub, wetter each time, of fists into flesh, fists into flesh,

and that's it, Bagger vomits up what feels like a jellyfish with a gasoline kick, one spark and he'll be as torched as the dinner rat, but once he's regurgitating, he realizes this is his chance to get Uncle Sam out of his system for good, so he retches hard, inhales, retches even harder, timed to each soggy crack of Popkin's fists, until there's only the whistling, glottal giggles of Frenchy Franchouillard,

and by the time Bagger's sinuses are voltaic with scalding acid and his throat bruised from esophageal exertion and his lips drizzling blood because there's no puke left to puke, he looks up through tear-dunked eyes to see Popkin lift the officer to his feet by his blouse, walk him a few yards into the rain, then shot-put him away,

and yet the poilu's nimble feet keep him upright, he doesn't stumble off so much as foxtrot, he's even got his cap back on, which he tips to Bagger as he fancy-foots backward, such fortitude, so much élan Bagger's bones bake with jealousy until he's fevered with Popkin's patriotism, the U.S. *will* win this war, they *will* be the victor no matter how many weary and weakened nations need their faces punched in,

and when Bagger coughs more blood, Frenchy Franchouillard laughs from the darkness, "Le Pauvre! Is it the plague? The Spanish plague? Or are *you* the plague, mon frère? Soit!,"

and Bagger roars, "Get the fuck out of here!," which only sets off more coughing, which only reveals the coy tease of Uncle Sam's wings, the shamefly's still there, which only makes Bagger more desperate for the angel to fix his guilt, fix his cowardice, fix the remorse, fix *him*, at last, no matter what else he must disgorge,

XXII

and the four scalawags of Company P hunker beneath the French 155mm, downcast and dissolute in the stoning rain, twenty-four hours since they had them any chow, their attempts to get the angel to miracle them some porterhouse steaks having flopped, seems like her conjury doesn't work like that, so they use the lull to see what vittles survived their hasty retreat,

and though Bagger and Arno lost their bags in the trench collapse, the kid managed to swipe two haversacks along the march, and Bagger salivates upon finding inside the first one a rations tin of corned beef, potatoes, and biscuit, which he gives to Arno as he can't bear to see the kid paw through the second sack, the one crunchy with dried blood, which ends up holding a largely unspilled cup of corn willy, smells all right to Bagger, so he gets finger-spooning,

and though the Butcher Birds were taught to eat separately after Jerry vaporized ten supping soldiers with a single shell, the battle din is as soft as it's ever been, so it feels safe enough, the most hostile force is Popkin glaring at Veck while gnashing a butter pat, though Veck's oblivious, he's trying to amuse the angel by pretending to chew his chocolate bar through the horse's mouth before sneaking it up the neck, and with cheeks full of a dead man's dinner, Arno asks Bagger to read to him, and Bagger checks Veck, skeptical the man speaks anything but horse, but Veck takes *The Son of Tarzan* from his pack and tosses it to Bagger's lap, which draws a sapped smile from Arno, the kid knows the drill, he shovels himself a funk hole beneath the field gun and tucks in, a sight that makes Bagger oddly weepy, how adapted to dirt all of them have become,

and once Bagger opens the book, he realizes it's too dark to read it, and glances at Veck, who returns a long, steady, in fact horse-like stare through the nag's fist-sized eyeholes, a silent reminder a horse can kick your fucking head off if it wants to, so Bagger nods his appreciation and Veck guardedly hands over the angel, her half-lidded eyes as calm as milk, smiling drowsily at Bagger before he lowers her beside Arno, who instinctively curls into her side,

and Bagger tents her hood so her brightness is enough to light the book's pages, whereupon he finds the lattermost folded corner, clears his throat of corn willy, and commences chapter 19, "'Behind them Korak emerged from the jungle and recovered his spear from Numa's side,'" and Popkin takes a rip of bacon and snipes, "Keep it down, shit-hole, or I'll eat you next," the lummox didn't appreciate Arno getting the angel without a vote,

and Bagger stops reading only when he notices Arno's eyes are closed, but it turns out the kid's not quite asleep, he sighs and nuzzles into the angel and asks, with a disturbing calm, "We gonna die out here, Bagger?" to which Bagger forms a weary, mud-caked grin and replies, "Maybe we already did," delivered as devil-may-care gag but feeling more like a lonely arctic wind, and it's the book's flimsy paper cover and coarse pulp pages that make Bagger's palms itch for the soft luxury and aromatic assurance of his father's red leather Bible, but when he moves to find it, he realizes he doesn't have it, it's in his haversack and his haversack is twenty miles back in the trench,

and Bagger's chest seizes and his mind flashes back, two months after the Bishop's body filled with seawater, the day Bagger itemized his dead dad's apartment, how each of the leavings felt like a piece of the corpse that never got buried, china dishes as teeth, pewter silverware as bone, heirloom sheets as wrinkled skin, Bagger could have inherited all of it, enough physical weight to force him to stop hustling and settle down, but a burial was a burial, so he boxed everything for sale, kept nothing,

and why not, he already had the only enchanted item, the red leather Bible, except now he doesn't, he fucking lost it, he wants to rocket to his feet and go careening back through the Argonne to find it, it will glow red through the trench clay and beat like the Bishop's heart, but no, it's gone, just like his father's gone, leaving only the shamefly, which has more reason than ever to shame him,

and Bagger butts his skull against the bottom of the howitzer, like Frenchy Franchouillard, but on purpose, for he's the dumbest fuck, no fucking good at anything that matters, all the naysayers were right, he's never been responsible enough to be the keeper of anything good, and Bagger looks down at Arno and the angel, the greatest goods he's ever needed to keep, and he knows, in the hole where his heart used to be, that he'll fail in keeping them too,

XXIII

and the horizons bruise with muted but supercolossal orange flashes that demarcate tracts of mutilated tree trunks, en masse they look like creeping squads of gnarled gnomes, most of them prune black but a few broken open to sapwood so shocking white they look like combat nurses in unblemished dresses, standing in the foggy rain, plotting amputations,

and when Bagger, aching for sleep, finally turns over for comfort, reluctant as he is to let the angel out of his sight, he finds himself staring into the eyes of the horse head, not a fun jolt, Veck laying just a few feet away, while Popkin snores from beneath the gun's front wheels,

and Bagger, once his fright cools, hesitates to ask Veck to take the damn thing off, it's the only thing yet to soothe Veck's shakes, he's acting almost normal if that's a word you can apply to a guy wearing a severed horse head, but Bagger's never going to get any shut-eye with that thing ogling him, plus the flesh is starting to ripen, so he hisses, "Veck, take that damn thing off,"

and as much dignity as Veck has shown, he's not to the point of disobeying reasonable requests from fellow doughboys, and his hands creep upward and slide the head off until it rests beside the P3, revealing a face that lacks any equine tranquility, brown eyes darting, cheeks pinching,

and right as Bagger closes his eyes, Veck whispers, "Bagger," and Bagger ignores it, but then it's "Hey, Bagger," and Bagger grinds his jaws and glares a warning at Veck, though it's hard not to feel for the guy, sweaty despite the cold, wide awake like someone who thinks the world is out to get him, and in Veck's case it probably is,

and Veck licks cracked lips and says, "She's granting wishes," and Bagger flips the bird, thinking of those porterhouse steaks she didn't deliver, but Veck says, "You're telling me you didn't wish to be saved when that minnie dropped, you and the boy?," to which Bagger only stares because he can't remember, and Veck says, "And Goodspeed. She took care of Goodspeed, right? You saying none of us didn't wish Goodspeed gone?," and Bagger keeps staring, for as little as he cares about unity, it still feels dicey to admit you wished a fellow soldier dead,

and Veck rolls onto his back and sighs dreamily, as if indulging in a velvet starscape instead of the oily underbelly of a 155mm gun, and repeats with smug anticipation, "She's granting wishes," and Bagger resists asking the follow-up Veck is begging for, but the silence is too absolute, the kind you only get when a whole forest is erased by war, so he hisses, "Fine, tell me your stupid wish already,"

and Veck, patient bastard, draws an inhale so long it might have traveled the full length of a horse's snout, his eyes bright as flaming petrol but strobed by that pesky facial tick, and with a hush he replies, "If you asked before France, I would've said my family,

I wished good on my family, something like that. But after all I seen?," and he shakes his head once, a crack of neck, a crunch of soot, "No, sir. What I'd wish now is for revenge,"

and Bagger knows he best be vigilant after hearing such an oath from a Negro, but Veck only burps, and his eyes water, and he's briefly handsome, and he says, "What they say about the 368th is all lies," a claim that makes Bagger uncomfortable, so he replies, "No one says shit, we're busy fucking up a war if you didn't notice," but Veck ignores him, it's clear he's heard the same slanders as Bagger,

and Veck says, "They set us up to fail. We shoulda known. We were dumb not to. It's just we were treated all right at Camp Meade. Frenchies were good to us, too, treated us square. But then they carved us out of the 92nd and strung us between the 77th and the French, no idea who's leading who. When H-hour came, they pushed us into woods nobody'd bothered to shell. Still had all its barbed wire. We didn't have wire cutters. We didn't have maps. We had to use what lanes we could. Made us sitting ducks. We were turning into puddles. Damn right we ran, no different than the 43rd running today, except the 43rd will get a second chance. You're in the 368th, one chance is all you get,"

and Bagger feels like he's being blamed and it pisses him off, because hell, he's got a goddamn angel two feet to his right, a goddamn living miracle who wouldn't be here if not for his goddamn American heroism, it's not fair he should be pissed off about jack shit,

and so he says, "Well, Veck, you said yourself you shoulda known. No one put a gun to your head and made you volunteer," though the second Bagger says it, he pictures the Selective Service form he was forced to sign and the tiny text printed in the lower left, *If person is of African descent, tear this corner,* how all those little corners must have collected on the floor like spent cartridges,

and Veck breathes low, and steady as a river, "You want better for your family, you got to prove you *are* better, then maybe they give you what they ought to gave in the first place," and Bagger wants to ask who *they* are, but is afraid he'll end up being blamed again, and even more afraid he deserves that blame, maybe it's best to calm this private down,

and so he asks, "You got a big litter of kids at home or what?,"

and Veck's face crimps like he's hit with a hurled pebble, the worst tick Bagger's seen yet, but he manages a reply, "Got a wife and a little girl, Naomi. Loves everything. Animals, especially. You saw her yourself," a crazy offhand claim that makes Bagger's incredulity soften to pity, the man's falling apart, wearing a horse head is saner than seeing a phantom Naomi ghosting about the Argonne,

and Veck continues, normal as can be, "Guy like me, you got to prove everything. Prove you deserve to work the job you work. Prove the pay you get should be as much as the next guy. Prove you deserve a home. When men break your windows, prove to the police they should go after them, not you. Prove to the bosses you're better than the other guys that look like you, but don't let those other guys know you said it or you're going to lose some teeth,"

and Bagger says, "Like dogs fighting," and Veck laughs, "You think we're dogs? Well, how about this? Your people are rats. Look around, Bagger. Don't see a whole lot of dogs, do you? Rats, though, they everywhere. They ought to call it War of the Rats," and Bagger blinks, "Did you just call me a rat?" but the insolent bastard has moved on,

and Veck's whisper is the shiver of stirred syringes, "Soon as white boys started shipping out, they started hiring us for you all's old jobs," and goddamn it, there it is again, the blame, "Who's *you all?*" Bagger challenges, and Veck, haughty bastard, replies, "The rats," before continuing, "And there were riots. They chased us out of a factory with guns. Forty dead men that look just like me. A fellow starts doubting the point of fighting for a country who won't fight for him," and Bagger goes so cold the only warmth inside him is Uncle Sam,

and Bagger asks, "That's who you propose revenging on? The whole damn country?" and the answer is a shush of fabric and an uncrinkling of paper, then the slog of Veck reading aloud in the dark, "'Can you go into a restaurant where white people dine? Can you get a seat in the theater where white people sit? Now, this is all different in Germany, where they do like colored people, where they treat them as gentlemen and as white people, and quite a number of colored people have fine positions in business in Berlin and other German cities,'"

and Bagger can't believe his fucking ears, "Jerry air-drops that shit just to stir you people up," he says, but as soon as he says it, he feels off, he's never defended the U.S. Army in his life, the only side he's ever fought for is the side of Cyril Bagger, which sort of puts him in league with Ben Veck, them versus the institutions that made them pick sides in the first place, when one need only look at this genocided forest to know they failed, not as an army but as a species, and it's whiplash to consider the end of the world alongside the new beginning the angel augurs, and Bagger pictures France's deepest craters cracking open to unleash new varieties of predators, pig-faced superwolves out to avenge their earthside cousins who lost everything when humans bombed the holy fuck out of their habitat, superwolves that even now pad toward the howitzer camp, snorting, growling, wait, no, that's just Popkin snoring,

and so Bagger buries the speculation of what wish he'd ask of the angel, the same way he's buried hundreds of American dough-boys, and his final shovel-pat on the grave is diverting Veck with flattery, "Well, shit, Veck, Lady Liberty must think you've got something going for you, else they wouldn't have attached your sorry ass to the illustrious 43rd,"

and though the compliment comes out less complimentary than intended, the spark in Veck's eyes blooms like P3 fire, and he smiles, teeth so bright they don't need the angel's light, and he says, "Don't reckon I'll ever forget seeing little Arno come into Marbache waving a letter he wouldn't give to nobody but the captain. So dunked in mud we didn't know if he was friend or foe or what,"

and Veck goes dreamy again and, still goddamn handsome, says, "When I heard the order, all I thought was how proud Naomi would be when I told her Major General Reis chose *me*,"

and there it is again, the pride of being selected all that's keeping Veck going, proof that he's valued in France as he never was in the U.S., and the truth is, right now Bagger needs Veck to keep that pride going, what with Arno reverting to the child he is and Popkin not to be trusted, so Bagger rolls over in his funk hole and replies softly, "Naomi will be as proud as a flipping peacock,"

and exactly when Cyril Bagger became such a delicate fucking listener he's got no idea, maybe the extra ear is to blame, the ear that got splatted onto his cheek all those hours ago, maybe it took root and sprouted an eardrum, maybe it carried the worst curse in the book, the curse of giving a shit, and before Bagger can decide if that's baloney, a bomb of exhaustion hits like the last three shells didn't, he's pounded into the ground, gone like a gasp, only not rapidly enough to elude Veck's final whisper, as faithful and haunted and sweet and deranged as anything Bagger's ever heard,

and what Veck says is, "Oh, she is. She's proud. Aren't you, Naomi, baby?," as if the little girl is right there beside the field gun, screened by fog, laughing into her hand, a clever stowaway bemused by her own overseas trick,

XXIV

and what Bagger dreams of is chickens, not for eating, that would
have been nicer, but rather for brutal profit, a cockfighting derby
he ran in Cedar Rapids, fall 1915, a battalion of cockerels with
the youth of drafted soldiers, the steadiest dough he ever made,
men in hats paid to enter the tent, paid to buy smokes from the
girl Bagger hired, paid to bet on their favored gamecock, paid for
booze to dull the ache of defeat,

and defeat most of them suffered because Bagger, the Sioux City
Sharpie, rigged the results, stage-painting wounds and cracked
beaks on birds that were actually remorseless killers, attaching
sharp blades, gaffs they called them, to certain roosters' ankles to
guarantee they'd fight till the ring was a bloodstorm of feathers
Bagger had to peel from his face,

and he learned to hold his nausea long enough to pad his pockets
in paper and coin, the usual routine, really, ignore the revulsion,
Bagger, ignore the blood, ignore the death, and die the gamecocks
most surely did, muscles too herniated to be eaten afterward,
though in this dream, Bagger's the one on the menu, roosters
waddling up to him, gaffs outward, beaks herky-jerky, pecking off
wads of his flesh while the angel watches in cryptic contemplation,

and the cockfight carnage transforms into photoplay reels of basic training in the Tennessee swelter, the whole thing laughable, Camp Winn officers teaching battle techniques they picked up in Cuba and the Philippines, irrelevant to what waited in Europe and the recruits knew it, all they did was march and drill with cut-out rifles sawed from wood, though when it came to close combat training, soldier versus soldier, Bagger was ready, he had a gaff on his ankle, secured there by his father,

and he cockfought the shit out of his fellow recruits, it was easy, all you had to do was go literally insane,

and Bagger wakes up fighting like his angriest rooster, claw and beak, scrapping for his very life, no idea who he's going after, only that the gaff won't let him stop, and in the furor he gets skin under his fingernails and tastes sweat and blood, good signs he's striking true, but the instant he breaks free and tries to stand, his skull whacks the field gun's belly again,

and he's out, gunpowder black, entombed in lurid shock,

and new hands, eager ones, lift and shake him, Bagger's eyes banking from howitzer black to mucky morning gray to Veck, the actual Ben Veck, not the horse-man, his bugged eyes, one of them newly swollen, only inches from Bagger's own, mouth moving in shouts Bagger doesn't hear, he's busy discovering blood smeared from his sore lips to his aching cheek, evidence of being socked in the mouth,

and Veck's voice breaks through, "He took her! Bagger, he took her!," and Bagger tries to reply but as a gamecock can only squawk, so he wings Veck aside and pivots on a knee to check behind him, and straightaway finds that it's true, the angel's gone, nothing lights their camp but the thin gruel of dawn,

and in that gruel lies Arno, pupal in his funk hole, skin sky-colored, hands crawling over a neck spouting cherry jets of blood,

and for one second, or for a thousand years, Bagger can only stare as Arno gurgles and chokes, his boot heels carving through clay, torso in arhythmic writhe, olive drabs watermelon-striped with his own blood, look at it all, babbling through the kid's fingers, the kid, the goddamn age-fibbing orphan, and the main regret that overtakes Bagger is the climax he contrived *The Son of Tarzan*, in which young Korak falls to Tarzan, the kid's going to die believing that injustice, and the shamefly inside Bagger swells to the full size of top-hatted, bearded Uncle Sam,

and Bagger hiccups to life, looks for a bandage, pats his own person, overcoat, blouse, puttees, everything filthy, so he rips a gunnysack, crunchy with frost, from the howitzer, where gunners of yore left it to cool the 155mm barrel, he has to hope weeks of rain cleansed it of munitions toxins, Bagger knee-walks to Arno's side and boxes the kid's slippery hands out of the way, and thereby glimpses the wound, outer skin ragged, muscles prolapsed, silken with pulsing blood,

and Bagger presses the gunnysack to the neck and screams, "Veck!," and screams, "Veck, get over here!" and screams, "Veck! Veck!," and then Veck's there, gamy horse head back on, but Bagger's got no time to complain, he grabs Veck's hand and slaps it over the gunnysack, demonstrating how hard to press, then snags Veck's mane and tugs it so the horse's forehead meets Bagger's and he can bore into Veck's eyes through the slimy sockets, and he shouts, "Take care of him!," verbatim the same mission Reis gave them, and muffled through horseflesh, Veck cries, "I can't do anything for him!," to which Bagger roars, *"Take care of him!,"* and rolls from beneath the howitzer into piercing needles of rain, electric with loss but voracious with rage, there's only one type of weapon that punches a hole like that into a body and that's a bayonet, and bayonets attach to rifles, and only one fucker in their party still has a rifle,

and Bagger looks from the hog wallow where Hugh Popkin slept to the muddy bootprints where Hugh Popkin fled after knocking out Bagger, socking Veck, and stabbing Arno, who would have clung to the angel with all he had, and Bagger bolts after the prints, rain going horizontal, the whole Meuse pelting the back of his throat, all of France a moontide smear as Popkin's bootprints vanish into trampled weeds only to reappear on the bare faces of a rock, or a duckboard, or a helmet, or the shoulders of a dead Jerry,

and not once does Bagger slow, to slow would be to think too hard of Arno, who will be dead before Bagger makes it back, dead not despite his goodness but because of it, like poor old Job in the Bishop's sermons, and though the kid's death should feel no different than any death Bagger has witnessed, it *is* different, it feels like Bagger's life, too, hinges on this sprint,

and if he can't catch Popkin, he can't catch himself from the distance he has fallen, and then there will be no point in surviving long enough to go home, there won't *be* any home, the Iowa corn stalks will slash him and the rich soil will rebuff him, it's only in this wet, windblown instant that he understands the angel as the only buckle that belts him to Earth, an Earth that, four years ago,

was pleasant but is now unlivable, all due to the loss of one parent-
less, homeless, worthless, perfect little bastard kid,

and Bagger might collapse and become a shrieker himself if he
wasn't so sure he was going to catch Popkin, the lummox didn't
leave behind his gear, which means he's traveling at a sluggardly
doughboy pace, that's why his bootprints swerve into a village,
cobblestone roads conceal prints better than mud and buildings
offer lots of hiding places for a man and his kidnapped angel,

and this is despite each building having been reduced to a couple
walls bracketing atriums of broken stonework, an architecture of
subtraction that transforms the village into an absurdity of brick
porticos, pergolas of twisted steel, doors leading to nothing, stair-
ways to nowhere, windows that open to the bleakest vistas, there's a
roofless church, there's a bombed town hall surrounded by ejected
seats, there's what was either a hotel or a brothel, the only excuses
for the charred mattresses cast about like beached fish,

and two townsfolk marbled in mud look up from where they balance rocks atop sticks for some reason, and scurry through the rain
at him, an old man with a mustache the size of his arm, and his
wife, who holds in her apron what appears to be a dead cat, and they
run up to Bagger, who waves them off, the couple looks as shell-
shocked as Veck, and you don't know what people like that will do,

and the husband jabbers French that Bagger interprets as begging, so Bagger repeats, "Affaire militaire," a handy shibboleth he
picked up from First Lieutenant Hollis, easy to memorize because
it rhymes, only for the old woman to take the dead cat by the back
legs and start pummeling Bagger with it, the sodden little corpse
squishing with every strike,

and Bagger catches the cat in his hand, wrenches it from the wife, and throws it like a football into a drift of burnt mail in front of a destroyed post office, and the wife screams and chases it, while the husband keeps on jabbering with breath so foul Bagger looks straight at him, and the pleased husband grins, showing the mouse tail stuck between his front teeth, which makes Bagger realize those rocks and sticks were deadfall traps, this old couple has been living off squashed mice,

and Bagger sees a broken-down army ambulance, a red cross painted on its canvas carriage, but has no intent to investigate it until he hears a plea coming from it, the same plea that cajoled him to join Arno in No Man's Land, *Save me*,

and he halts so hard the snap of his boots resounds off what few walls still exist, and he peers through the rain into the black void of the truck bed, the metal bars of a bunkbed cot all that's visible, and the old man notices and shuts up, and the single-note song grows even clearer, *Save me, Save me*, before the ambulance interior yowls as feet clump across the thin steel,

and the light from inside turns raindrops into fireflies, and only brightens as the source grows nearer, and then, like a tank crunching from Argonne fog, the lummox appears, silhouetted in the glow, the Springfield's strap over his right shoulder, the barrel aimed loosely at Bagger, Popkin's hard-on visible through his trousers below the angel he carries, who is startlingly naked, head tipped back, halo vertical, body alive in coruscation, a minor god created to illuminate this one shitty village forever and ever, amen,

XXV

and this means Popkin hasn't imitated Goodspeed by taking the angel off to barter, what he's done is strip the angel of her red dress and blue cape inside a truck stinking of coagulated blood, putrid bandages, and the sweat of the doomed, with Popkin's sweaty drabs next to be stripped, why not, no one was around to intervene but a couple of elderly mice-eaters,

and though Bagger has known Popkin as a beast for months, this turn makes Bagger's hindbrain throb, lusting for the angel is sick, worse than pedophilia, Bagger's never even thought of the angel as having genitals, though she must, she has nipples, she has pubic hair, and Bagger's anger at Popkin fireworks into sputtering fury,

and so he strides at Popkin, his lack of hesitation catching the lummox off guard, and though the angel weighs little, rebalancing her in one arm is tricky, she's rolling shoulders, rolling hips, flopping arms, flopping legs, and in two seconds Bagger has closed to ten feet so Popkin simply drops the angel, who hits the ambulance floor like a sack of potatoes,

and up comes the Springfield on its leather sling, carving through rain, and though Bagger's had guns pointed at him before, this is the first time in France, where he's seen what a .30 caliber can do at close range, the barrel's foresight like the steel-rivet eyes of the snake he once bumped into at Lake Zabriskie, and Bagger halts on wet cobblestone, arms to his sides in the universal plea for dispassion,

and Popkin's eyes have the greasy sheen of a dead fish as he bellows over the rain, "None of your business, Bagger," and the part of Bagger forever allegiant to his own welfare agrees, all he's got to do is hump back to the 43rd, dig more latrines, bury a few thousand more corpses, and get back to fleecing fools along the Mississippi,

and he's ready to do just that when he thinks of Tarzan again, maybe it's the junglelike deluge or maybe it's Popkin's great-ape size, and if Bagger's learned one thing about Tarzan, it's that he never turns away, never abandons a weaker party, and if Bagger wants to give Lewis Arno the send-off he deserves, this is how, be Tarzan to the kid's Korak just this once,

and so Bagger shouts, "Do this and you'll regret it," and a smile as miserable as a broken twig surfaces from the chub of Popkin's cheeks, gums as red as clown noses, gray teeth draining caramel drool, and he angles his face so rain strikes it straight on and washes mud down his neck, and closes his eyes like he's luxuriating in a bath, and says, "No one tells the rain it'll regret falling. I'm gonna be the rain, Bagger. I'm gonna be the storm,"

and Popkin's never talked like this, to say the fucking least, so Bagger squints through the downpour to see if the lummox has suffered a head injury, but instead Popkin has a look Bagger recognizes from his father's congregation, he looks goddamn empowered, and Bagger's gut constricts with the notion that Popkin, otherwise destined for a life of hillbilly irrelevance, believes inter-course with an angel will elevate him to godlike status,

and Bagger thinks mad thoughts, what happens when an angel is infected with the clap, do the heavens rain fire, do flowers release poison pollen, fantastical terrors already indigenous to the Great War, which makes Bagger wonder if a whole brigade of angels has fallen to Europe's battlefronts, loaded with sicknesses holy enough to bring down the human hellions,

and Bagger shouts, "You're not the fucking rain, you fucking jack-ass, you're a shitty fucking private who doesn't know his rifle from his pus-oozing dick," and the single wrinkle that clefts Popkin's forehead tells Bagger the jab has landed, the lummox's eyes clear a bit and he says, "You want her too. But she's mine,"

and because the rain's so thick, Bagger can fake a stumble to get closer, eight feet away now, and he distracts from his advance by saying, "Stealing her doesn't make her yours, you dumb side of beef. If she belongs to anyone, it's me and Arno. We found her. We rescued her. And she rescued us, remember? She doesn't give a shit about you,"

and Popkin's forehead goes into full furrow, and here comes the toddler frown, and he simpers like a boy whose birthday party is being ruined, and he says, "She let me hold her hand. She let me touch her hair. She loves me, Bagger. You don't know. Just because she don't put it in her letters don't mean it's not true,"

and Bagger's really fucking confused until a needle of clarity sliv-ers in, and Bagger slops rain from his face and shouts, "Effie? You think she's Effie Weffie?," and Popkin goes pink, and he gets that snorting-bull look, and he cries, "She's mine, Bagger! Stay away!," and Bagger laughs, he can't help it, he can't believe what he's hearing, "Popkin! You fuckwit! That's not Effie,"

and Popkin's pink goes red, and the Springfield's bolt action rattles back, and he spits, "Get her name outta your mouth!," and Bagger recoils, doesn't like the gun's snake-eye trained on him, so he holds out hands to ward off any rash triggering and yells, "Popkin! Fucking listen! Effie's back home! Back in whatever shitheel town you come from!,"

and Popkin bellows, "This is the last time I'm warning you, Bagger! All you ever do is trick me! But this ain't no blackjack! This is my girl. She came all the way to France to see me. That's love is what that is! You can't tell me it's not!," as the rifle butt lodges harder into his shoulder, he's really going to goddamn shoot,

and it shouldn't surprise Bagger, the lummox already mortally wounded Arno, Bagger only regrets he didn't move fast enough to stop him either time, there's no point even trying to hide from the bullets, not in this mud-and-rubble slurry, all he can do is lock his jaws and wait to learn what millions of soldiers already know, how it feels when your innards meet iron,

XXVI

and then he explodes in sobs, not Bagger, not Popkin, but the over-
looked third character, the old husband, and the soldiers break their
face-off to watch the old man limp at the ambulance, mustache
spread broadly above over the outlandish diameter of his sudden
smile, mouse tail flapping from his teeth, blubbering in disbelief,

and the scamper is so unexpected that the old man makes it all the
way to the ambulance, hands grasping inches from the angel's hair,
but at the end of the day, he's only an old man, and Popkin redirects
the rifle a few inches, nothing simpler, and shoots, no visible burst
of light because the angel's light absorbs it,

and the back of the husband's skull explodes open like a broken egg,
raindrops going red as they are impregnated with blood, while the
cobblestone is splattered by brains like thrown mustard,

and though the report is loud, Bagger knows from experience that
rain dampens gunshots too much for the farmer's wife, wherever
she is, to hear and come running and discover her husband, the
last person she has left in the world, dead, and it's a good thing she
doesn't, the man's body tips backward and falls, the fractured skull
splooshing as it shatters against stone,

and the whole thing takes three seconds, the first two of which Bagger spends immobile with shock, but that third second is all he needs, he darts forward, wraps his arms around Popkin's shins, and pulls, the lummox's boots sliding off the slick truck bed and into the air, which punts the angel to the ground as Popkin's shoulder blades slam to the bumper, both his helmet and the Springfield knocked aside, clattering off cobblestone,

and Bagger drives the meatier man to the hard road, and how strange it is, he thinks, that he's finally engaged in hand-to-hand combat, and it's not even with a Hun Heinie Boche Fritz Jerry Squarehead,

and Popkin gobbles in startlement and pain, and Bagger wants that rifle, but he's afraid he'll die if he turns away, so he rolls to his knees and rabbit punches Popkin in the nose, blood bursting fast and short like a stomped tomato, Popkin blinking, stupid and childlike, but when Bagger unleashes a second fist, the lummox's big hand springs up and catches it like a baseball in a mitt, then grips that fist like the head of a gearshift and flings Bagger all the way off,

and Bagger rolls and rolls, each cobblestone a clawing crustacean until he brakes himself and pushes to all fours only to be hurled back down, Popkin's full weight on him, the smothering mode of combat he used against Ben Veck and Frenchy Franchouillard,

and Bagger's nose is smashed flat to the road, lips split between teeth and stone, breath vacuumed out, he's emptied and gasping, the lummox's weight like grave soil, the big belly a bag of wet cement, the hard-on like a revolver jabbing Bagger's kidney, and there's a fist to the back of Bagger's head, he hears the skin of his forehead pop open against cobblestone, then a fist to his left side, ribs squealing, lungs beneath spasming from the blood loss of ruptured vessels, and then the goddamn animal bites him, right on the scalp like a bat, and over his own confounded blat Bagger hears Popkin rasp, "You don't touch my girl, you don't ever touch my Effie,"

and Bagger believes he could talk his way out of this friendly fire if his mouth wasn't full of blood, he'll be dead before he can get out a single word, so he reaches behind him with both hands, and though Popkin slaps away the first, the other finds a rogue puff of hair on Popkin's head and yanks it,

and the lummox honks like a goose and tries to pull away, hard, riding Bagger like a sled before Bagger's hand makes a tarantula hop from Popkin's tuft of hair to the scalp itself,

and the chemical gas scar tissue feels like it's always looked, a custard that has formed a delicate skin, seeded with scabs where Popkin scratched, and that's what Bagger does, he scratches, all five fingers pierce the filmy skin and drag along the skull like the plows of Iowa cropfields,

and when the fingers submerge in hot quags of blood, Popkin goes rigid, orgasmic in agony, and his punches stop, and his breathing arrests as he tries to vocalize his pain, and Bagger digs a boot toe between two cobblestones and heaves, and the lummox tips like a paper boat and goes down with a thwack,

and Bagger army-crawls, hips wagging to dispel arms that don't even try to stop him, and he crouches, all he can manage, his vision swirls and muddies, there's blood in his eyes, it's coming from the cold sting on the top of his head, Popkin's bite, and Bagger staggers in an oval, wanting the Springfield but everything's reeling, until Popkin finally unleashes a long, guttural groan,

and Popkin's on all fours now, he'll be lethal in seconds, so Bagger stumbles half-blind into the rain, hoping to find the rifle by blundering into it, though, hell, at this point he'd take the wife's dead cat, and he does kick something dead, but it's only the husband, his open mouth so full of rain only the floating tip of the mouse tail is visible, and if Bagger can see that, his vision must be sharpening, he plants his feet, yes, the Springfield's under the ambulance,

and it's too late, Popkin's up, fists gyring like two filled buckets, groan broadening into a woolly mammoth roar, and he tilts his head to find Bagger, blood cascading down the lummox's face but quickly thinned by rain, achieving permanence only at his uniform's collar, the red ring of a diabolical jester,

and Popkin charges Bagger, boot after leaden boot, and Bagger backs up, trying to think through the ringing pain, but there's no time, so he runs, but he can't run far, he can't leave the angel, so he runs toward the closest structure, a single standing wall, two stories high with iron bars over the upper windows, a former jail, how darling, as if any of the village's past malefactors could rate alongside this fratricidal dolt,

and Popkin closes in, inevitable as a combine, and Bagger tries to lift a brick but his balance is funky and, fuck, it drops from his numb fingers, he's going to have to fight, finally, and right fucking now,

and when he puts up his dukes, it feels as silly as he always imagined, and Popkin must think the same, his loose, spitty maw bends up at the corners, he's so close Bagger can see the trench system of his scalp, Bagger must have raked it to the bone, and if that didn't stop the lummox, he can't imagine what will,

and Popkin swings an arm like an elephant tusk, clumsy, easy to block, but also really fucking heavy, Bagger is walloped sideways, barely staying upright across the rubble, and Popkin lumbers after him at a heavyweight's pace, eyes leaking blood, mouth gouting the same, and Bagger drearily accepts he has no plan but to take the brawler's hits and hope for the bell,

and it only takes until Popkin's second punch, which launches Bagger against the jailhouse wall, which crunches unhappily and haws like it might fall, for Bagger to realize no bell can save him, the lummox will never tire, he's not even the lummox anymore, he's one of the landships that staved like barges through the Western Front's mud,

and Bagger wonders if this landship runs on angel fuel,

and it's then, with knuckles cracking inside tire-sized fists and trench-mouth slime sheeting from busted lips, that Popkin takes a step that puts the angel's light directly over his shoulder, and rain and light combine as they always have and form rainbows, rainbows like Bagger's never seen, arcing east, ribboning west, stairstepping one to the other, an infinite quilt of colors that's the most beautiful thing imaginable, and it's strictly for him, Popkin can't see it and the old husband is dead,

and Bagger suddenly feels dry, and clean, and refreshed, and it's funny how these pleasant feelings clamp a metal ring over his ankle, it hurts but he loves it, too, which tells him *she's* the gaff, the angel's the gaff, and that claw digging into his tenderest flesh tells him that this here is a cockfight, and he's seen enough cockfights to know little cockerels, properly gaffed, can tear apart the biggest roosters,

and Bagger fins his hand, so much quicker than the rooster, and shoots it outward, *gaff*, right into Popkin's left eye, and Popkin wails, and jerks away, and heaves one of his anvil fists, but he's off-center and it whiffs past Bagger close enough to flutter his nose hairs, and Bagger fins his other hand and pecks his fingers into Popkin's right eye, *gaff*, another wail, and Popkin's hands cycle in small punches near his face, trying to keep Bagger away,

and every stab into his ankle is the angel cheering him on, an odd thing, really, brutality celebrated by a heavenly being, but damn if it's not more bracing than any bugle, Bagger rears back, his eyesight as level as a German blockhouse, and kicks Popkin in the balls, probably so gonorrheal they burst, and Popkin moos with groping rage while the rainbows scintillate like fish scales, Private Bagger unbound, unstoppable,

and Popkin keeps swiping but Bagger dances around him, the rainbows out of sight now but that's all right, he watches Popkin clobber the freestanding wall, left, right, left, right, leaving feathers of blood, the wall beginning to bend like leather, and here, several feet from the wall, the jail-yard rubble is smaller, easier to wield, and Bagger grins as he bends to pick up a rock, wait, no, there's a better rock, it's got a nice sharp edge to it,

and it's that flare of greed that does him in, as Popkin, full of animal surprises, kicks backward like a horse, a boot heel connecting with the underside of Bagger's chin, and his jaws clap shut onto his tongue, slicing off a narrow ribbon, and Bagger's head rockets back, he's thrown for a literal loop, wholly airborne, and lands on cobblestone straight as a board, head, shoulders, hips, and ankles all hitting at once, his own ghost ejected from his nostrils,

and with his skeleton too numb to move, that's all she fucking wrote, Popkin unfolds to full height, Bagger's got no feeling in his hands, and Popkin turns, Bagger can't speak, and Popkin opens eyes, filled with blood, opens a mouth, filled with blood, extends two arms, filled with blood, interlaces his fingers into a swingable mace, filled with blood, raises the joined fist over his head, filled with blood, and flexes his whole body, filled with blood, to deliver the death blow to Bagger, shortly to be filled with blood,

and *I'm sorry*, Bagger thinks to the angel, *I'm sorry*, Bagger thinks to Arno, he'll never get to be someone else's gaff, which makes him surprisingly sad,

and the least he can do is not look away as he's done before, so Bagger opens his eyes to stare death down, it might take several dozen blows before shards of Bagger's skull puncture his brain, and that's how he notices a caliginous shadow, darker than the rain, pulling toward Popkin as a nightmaring child pulls close a blankie,

and it's the wall, it's tipping,

and Bagger balls his body up and covers his head as bricks hiss and growl and boom and finally sing, a crashing chorus by some vainglorious German maestro, and Bagger feels the shadow splash over him, as cold as cannonballing into a lake, and like a cannon-ball he rolls away as the falling bricks begin to explode, the wall delivering jailhouse justice even in final collapse, stone turned shrapnel that Bagger absorbs, still rolling,

and the time when loud noises were merely loud is so far in the past Bagger has to strain to recall them, the landslide hiss of half-ton lots of coal dumped in metal carts, the nerve-chiseling peals of streetcars along corroded tracks, the marrow-deep thunderclaps of garment factory manglers, the choking shotguns of backfiring Model Ts, while here in France, each truck and gun and shell and angel *howls*, a race to the finish line of deafness,

and somewhere inside it, Bagger hears the dice-bag scrunch of two hundred bones obliterating in unison,

and only after the last pebbles whisper into their favored crannies can Bagger think again, and his big idea is to open his stupid eyes, which he does, and he sees a raft of rain arrows fired from a sagittarii of holy archers, a soggy debauch of dead roads and buildings and humans, and a foothill of brick that fell so close it coated Bagger in a pale dust that the rain is turning to grime,

and thick tongues of blood extend from the foothill ten feet in every direction, Hugh Popkin reduced to a red rose pressed between the pages of Effie Inez Barbeau's diary, he's deader than anyone's ever been dead, and Bagger is caught off guard by the sympathetic thought that old Effie Weffie might at long last feel affection for her lovelorn lummox,

XXVII

and Bagger takes to his knees, then feet, then weaves toward the ambulance, easy as jumping jacks on horseback until he relearns bipedalism and reaches the angel curled beneath the truck, bright as a fireplace, and crawls into the stinking carriage and collects the red dress and blue cape from floors crusted brown with spilled blood, and under the truck re-dresses her, guiding her limbs through the garments as one does a toddler,

and then he slumps in the truck's oily underworld, as tired as if he has buried a hundred men, not just one, and the angel blinks at him from his lap, skin especially clean and soft next to the mud crusted to his hands like curdled bile, and that's the emotion that surges, bile, he's worked so hard carrying her from the battlefield wire, pursuing her into this village, rescuing her from Popkin,

and he demands, "What's wrong with you? Why can't you walk?," to which she only blinks and smiles, and now, for the first time, the smile grates him, so he jostles her and says, "You're not wounded. You're *not wounded.* Is walking not something angels know how to do?," and that's how it comes to him, she has no wings, a halo but no wings, and a long icicle slides between his ribs, everyone knows angels have wings, even if they'd been blown off by artillery, there would be snapped feather shafts and busted scapulars, he's watched enough gamecocks get eviscerated to know how tenaciously wings hang on,

and Bagger persists, "Why won't you answer me?," to which he gets nothing, so he taps his bloody tongue with a filthy finger and orders, in quasi-French, "Par-lay," to which her lips part as if she has only the vaguest sense of his wishes, and he spits mud and blood, the heat of his anger enough to steam the falling rain, and he says, "I saved you. Haven't I twice now saved you? Don't you owe me something? A word of fucking thanks? Your name? Something?,"

and after Bagger receives precisely jack shit, he can't stop his demands from growing in volume, "Can't you talk? Can't you hear? Are you deaf and dumb?," which feels possible, it would explain a lot, and he takes her shoulders and shakes her, and when he discovers he has nothing more to ask, shakes her even harder,

and her silky copper hair bounds like sparks from a crumbling fire, and with every new shake, her collarbones articulate, and Bagger feels the delicate twigs of her arm bones, she's sure built like a regular woman, and therefore must be able to feel pain, and Bagger wants to use that, wants to shake her till it hurts, the idea's exciting, pain's a language they can share, the universal language, and out here, you grow fluent fast,

and what if Honest Abe knew what he was talking about when he'd coined *the better angels of our natures*, what if he meant it literally, that our judgment at the holy gates is based on how we treat angels when chancing upon them, maybe your angel looks like a woman in a red dress, maybe it looks like a puppy, as long as the being is defenseless it serves as a test of benevolence, maybe that's what's happening, Cyril Bagger is being fucking tested, drilled in empathy as he was once drilled in warfare,

and all Bagger knows for sure is five soldiers were assigned to take care of the shrieker and three of those soldiers are dead, and those deaths didn't come at the hands of Jerry, they came from this shining woman whose one major miracle was only witnessed by a few men whose observational abilities were compromised, and not to be trusted to begin with,

and so maybe the angel is nothing special, nothing at all,

and so he chooses the only choice that's ever made any sense to Cyril Bagger, the choice to make no choice at all, he grabs the blue cape, crawls out into the rain, and drags out the angel, no, the *woman*, the regular *woman*, and with a grunt hoists her into his arms and covers her radiating face with the sopping hood, so he doesn't have to see her, doesn't have to think of her,

and Bagger doesn't point himself back west, there's nothing west but a hysterical Ben Veck and a dead Lewis Arno, but rather east, toward the Butcher Birds and Major General Reis, the head butcher, the only butcher at the paygrade to deal with this, and right now that's all Bagger wants, dump the problem, get back to self-protection, get his ass home,

and as the sun ascends with all the beauty of bullet-pocked canteen, Bagger stomps past Popkin's burial mound and wends from the village along a skinny dirt path until the path vanishes at a half-mile battle scar scribbled across the plain as if by a giant-sized schoolboy,

and so Bagger veers northeast into a bronze sky, over a steep hill perfectly preserved but for the biplane squashed into its side, identifiably Reichstag from the Iron Cross on the tail, a plane Bagger considers pillaging for rations until he glimpses the pilots' barbecued remains,

and then it's over the crest to a downhill grade slapdash with forty-some bodies, all of them named Jerry, they had been fleeing when death swung its scythe, the men's corpses grouped in patterns like a language only readable from the sky, maybe that's what the barbecued pilot was up to,

and though these signs make Bagger hesitate, he doesn't stop, Tarzan and Korak wouldn't stop, he hitches up the woman and descends, stepping around bodies like he used to dodge cow patties in Iowa pastures, though in doing so, there's no avoiding the faces, skin of blue leather, lips berried with rot, the whole platoon white-bearded by frost,

and because Bagger's good at games, he invents a new game, an honest game, he calls it Think of Anything Else in the World and it goes like this, you see something atrocious and you let it remind you of something nice, for example, here's a soldier with nothing left of his neck but a soft flap of flesh, so he says to the woman he carries, "Looks like the back of a lady's knee, nothing prettier, if you don't mind me saying," and Think of Anything Else in the World round two involves two hands, just two hands lying in the dirt like a pair of white mittens, and Bagger doesn't let himself down, "Look like two sunflowers at the end of summer, when they get all pale," he says, "but I still like the look of them, don't you?,"

and Think of Anything Else in the World round three involves a Jerry so well cooked, Bagger can't stop his traitor stomach from growling, so he focuses on the lung that hangs from the man's open chest, inflating and deflating in the wind, and tells the woman, "Looks like laundry in the breeze, and smells like it, too,"

and Think of Anything Else in the World gets easier every round, a skinny pair of legs are two birchwood baseball bats, the gap where a man's nose used to be is the precise contours of a succulent pear, the big black liver lying there is a leather purse straight from the Marshall Field racks, he can nearly detect the perfumed tickle of forgotten affluence,

and when the massacre is behind him, Bagger laughs, a noise absurd enough to make him laugh again, and he wonders if he's gone the way of Veck before deciding he doesn't give a shit, madness is a gift, and he guffaws the guffaw of the all-American types who, back home, always avoided him, and here in France all got snuffed out pretty quick, and now he's joined their cocky ranks, maybe he's not a shirker after all, maybe he's been a proper soldier the whole time,

and he lets the super-soldier scenario play out as he drinks rainwater from tire tracks and plods into a patch of verdure slashed by rampaging troops that might have been Company P, suddenly he misses those guys, wait till they get a load of the new and improved Cyril Bagger, he had a shrieker to save and goddammit, save her he did, such a fine surprise that even old Bishop Bagger will sit up from whatever cloud he's claimed with Bagger's mother, and look down, and finally feel something akin to pride,

XXVIII

and the fantasies put a real spring in the old step, a spring that gets springier when Bagger hears the mechanized chug and brook babble of a battalion, he tries to speed up, but the woman's limbs start catching on every branch, bush, and bramble out there, which forces him to slow down, whoever this lady is, Bagger can't deliver her to Reis covered in nasty red scratches,

and while he's mincing through thorns, he picks up unfamiliarities in the noises, the gears of machines hoarser, the mutters of men a pile-up of consonants, and Bagger's forced to accept the truth, these aren't doughboys up ahead, this is Jerry, and Bagger gives the woman in his arms a careful study, for it was her meddlesome limbs that prevented him from prancing right out in front of the Reichstag Army,

and Bagger slithers to the burnt relics of the forest edge and hunches behind the squat metal silo of a toppled Fahrpanzer, a stationary German tank, and the woman sighs, the way a mother sighs at a child who insists on playing in mud, and Bagger peeks out at a terrible sight, a hundred stormtroopers moving across a field sludged by a demolished drainage system and lumped with American and German bodies, and, sure, it's disquieting seeing so many Sturmtruppen, for once not candlelit by machine guns or leaping like demons in a minenwerfer scarlet, but more than that it's eerie, these Germans don't look particularly alive, they are wights who hold their Mausers at the lowest point of their straps like slack jaws, while their boots drop and scrape like pistons and gears,

and moving just as painfully are the machines grinding through the morass alongside them, steel-wheeled due to Germany's rubber deficiency, munitions carriages snagged in peaty bogs, Mörser howitzers cleaving through black mucilage like dinosaurs, mounted Maxims coming apart with every bounce, antiaircraft guns so mired in winter's resin that stormtroopers beat it to put it out of its misery,

and galumphing among them like a processional elephant is an A7V, tumid with clay, sickly with chemical corrosion, its ten-thousand rivets the excrescence of a terminal disease, the tank's seen too fucking much, it trembles like Ben Veck and cries a petrol storm, this advance the last it will ever make,

and Bagger's got no choice but to sit and wait, and wait, and probably wait some more, it's going to take all damn day for this company to pass through a battlefield so fresh it still coughs phlegm of flame, they aren't even collecting the German dead, only the dog tags, or at least that's what it looks like from the dead men's collars, all of them ripped wide open,

and some of the dead must be Bagger's fallen brethren, caught in enfilading fire, which means the 43rd is on the run, but also means it is nearby, Bagger has almost caught up, and as soon as this frangible stream of overextended Huns dries up, he'll be able to cut behind them, refreshed and rested, and all the food and water he wants for will be waiting, along with the accolades, the acceptance, the everything,

and so he ducks behind the Fahrpanzer, covers himself and the woman with his overcoat, and crooks his neck to fill the makeshift sleeping bag with warming breath, he even closes his eyes, why not, these stormtroopers lack the energy for a single step outside their chosen drudge, he'll be safe here till he wakes up, how about that, the first time he's felt safe in France and it's fifty yards from the German elite,

and the last thing Bagger hears before descending another hill, this time the hill of sleep, is another of the woman's sighs, this one a tut-tut at a birdbrained decision, as if to say, Cyril Bagger, now there's a real dummy, but one she can't help but like,

XXIX

and when Bagger awakens, Veck's sitting right there, facing him, elbows on knees amid the rhinestone motes of snow, sawblading his jaws through cooked pigeon, black crisp hissing down with every bite, and it's a mark of how ravenous Bagger is that his first thought isn't *Shit, is that Veck?* but rather *Give me some of that bird,*

and that's despite the bird still having feathers, which means either Veck never learned to properly pluck or he just found the pigeon torched like that, probably tastes like crude oil, not that it stops Bagger's salivation as Veck sucks the bones clean, then chews the bones, then licks his fingers,

and Bagger feels he could watch all day, it's better than any photo-play anyone could devise, and only when Veck tosses the last denuded bone does he notice Bagger peeking from the tented over-coat, and Veck doesn't look startled, doesn't look anything, doesn't even look like he enjoyed the pigeon or was especially aware that he'd been eating it,

and Bagger says, "Hi, Veck," and his visible breath applies an opaque dream over Veck's already opaque face, and the flamethrower oper-ator just sits there, still as Buddha, tongue mining molars for bird bits, and it's only because the lights of Veck's eyes are so dulled that Bagger recognizes what kindly eyes they are, he's unexpectedly grateful they were the last eyes Arno saw,

and to be certain, Bagger asks, "The kid?," and Veck's granite stare is the only reply necessary, and Bagger's cored all over again,

and he manages, "You bury him?," and Veck licks lips glossed with pigeon fat, as if debating whether Bagger is capable of understanding, before shaking his head, to which Bagger hastens to nod, he wants Veck to know he doesn't blame him, no Yank out here has buried more men than Bagger, and he knows it's pointless theater, one day when the Argonne grows back, it'll grow back *through* doughboy skeletons as capably as *from* them,

and Bagger realizes Veck has quit shuddering, absolutely quit, he's as steady as, well, the only steady thing out here, which is the dead, either something's cured Veck's shell shock or the opposite, something has pushed him to a place where madness has burned into vacancy,

and Bagger's about to ask Veck how he tracked him down, when Veck removes a small note from his coat that, when he unfolds it, shows every sign of hellish deliverance, water-rumpled, mud-pimpled, half-sullied with a brown stain Bagger identifies as blood, and Veck holds it out like he didn't hold out a morsel of pigeon,

and Bagger takes it and squints at it, blood has made the typing illegible, only the pre-printed header is clear, U.S. ARMY FIELD MESSAGE, some communiqué between officers, and there's enough sharp Vs for Bagger to understand the note is about Veck, must have something to do with Veck's original reassignment to the Butcher Birds, and because Arno was the runner who did Veck's ferrying, Veck must have found the note folded into the kid's clothing, and Bagger feels a stab, because sure, he would have preferred *The Son of Tarzan* as a memento, but here's an item Arno felt was important enough to hold next to his heart,

and hearts, though, they bleed, and Bagger realizes the blood on the paper is Arno's, he's touching the kid's blood, and he freezes, he doesn't know what to do, drop the note like it's on fire, or thrust it back at Veck, or apply it like a bandage over his own heart, so he looks at Veck, perhaps for guidance, and Veck only tightens his eyebrows to tell Bagger to look harder,

and Bagger does, and there it is, hidden in the blood's deepest brown, words that, had they been typed, would have been lost, but they are penciled in the fanciful cursive that could have only come from Lyon Reis, a nine-word oath the major general wanted Arno to deliver to whatever charming château housed Army HQ, and once Bagger reads it, there's no doubting why Arno never delivered it, the kid, after all, always had a soft spot for old Veck,

and the note reads, *I SHALL NOT FORGET YOU SENT ME A NIGGER*,

and so what, it's a word Bagger's heard all his life, fashionable among gamblers, surely Veck hears it so often it no longer penetrates his helmet, but when Bagger glances at the man, who is not, in fact, wearing a helmet, he gets the impression this particular shot traveled all the way into Veck's brain, destroying whatever parts still pumped pride and circulated self-respect, and Veck opens his coat, and Bagger perks up, maybe *The Son of Tarzan* is next, but Veck only takes the coat off, bizarre behavior in the frigid woods, and worse, takes no care to fold it atop something dry, he drops it right in the mud, so idiotic that Bagger snaps, "Watch it, dummy," even as he abruptly has an awful realization,

and it has to do with the reverence with which Veck spoke of Reis while the rest of the squad lambasted the prick, *He chose me* as they hurried along the front, *He chose me* as they hunkered by the howitzer, but this memo reveals it's all bullshit, Reis didn't choose Veck, he didn't give a fuck about Veck, turns out Reis considers Veck to be the biggest middle finger HQ could have possibly given him,

and come to think of it, that's probably why Reis kept plunging Ben Veck into harm's way, not because he thought Veck had the makings of a hero, but because he wanted Veck to die so HQ would send him a second Negro, then a third, a long, murderous game between rival officers with the men of the 368th as disposable pawns,

and Veck removes his blouse and skins off a filthed undershirt, becoming less olive by the second, his brown torso gleaming oak, sprigs of chest hair bedraggled by sweat, and Bagger says, "Hey," all the brilliance his mind can muster, and Veck stands, plants a foot on the Fahrpanzer cannon, and removes his right trench boot, rotted laces rupturing like scabs,

and Bagger, brilliant again, shouts, "Hey!," and with both boots off, Veck starts on his puttees, the leggings unraveling like intestine soiled by their own feces, his stripping down is getting serious, and Bagger tries to think what might make this nincompoop stop, and remembers Veck had a daughter, what was her name, ah yes, "Naomi, Veck! What about Naomi? Keep your shit together and get home to Naomi, you hear me?,"

and when the puttees are tossed into a witchy hedge, most of Veck's stench goes with it, which leaves only the subtle but insidious smell of burnt sugar, but Bagger can't focus on it because Veck's unbuckling his belt and dropping his trousers, and like that, Bagger's out of options, he needs to tackle this lunatic before he does something stupider, so Bagger lets the woman slump to the ground and surges at Veck,

and a few inches is all he gets, he's jerked like a leashed dog, what the fucking fuck, and when he throws aside his overcoat, he finds his left wrist handcuffed to the Fahrpanzer, what in the fucking world,

and Veck reaches into the only garment he's still got on, pee-stained army-issue drawers, and draws from it a little silver handcuff key, which he holds so that Bagger gets a good look at it before placing it on top of a rock six long feet away,

and Bagger explodes, "Veck! What are you doing? Veck, you can't leave me here!" and Veck goes back to ignoring him, removing his drawers, cock and balls in winter shrivel, and Bagger pleads, "Jerry will find me! They'll torture me, Veck! They'll tear me to pieces!,"

and Veck kneels, not to help Bagger but to strap the P3 onto his naked shoulders, the flamethrower has been waiting in the frosted weeds, Veck tightens the waist support hard enough for it to bite into his pubic shrub, and Bagger twists around as much as the handcuff lets him, screwing his neck so hard vertebrae crunches, and though he can't see much, it looks like the Germans are gone, the only men left are dead ones,

and that's not good enough, there's foxes in these woods, there's wild boar, there's bears, there's the cold, Bagger rattles the handcuff, the hollow Fahrpanzer chuckling, and since there's no Squareheads about, Bagger flat-out screams, "You listen to me, you bare-ass ignoramus! You leave me here and I'll find Naomi, all right? And you know what I'll tell her? I'll tell her her daddy was a fucking coward! That he died trying to defect to the fucking Heinie! What do you think of that, Veck?,"

and this halts the crackpot, and Bagger pants with the bestial satisfaction of a threat well dealt, but it lasts only as long as it takes Veck to lift the P3 lance, the igniter pointed at Bagger's easily engulfable face, and though Bagger's instinct is to wilt, the only option he's got left is intimidation, so he gives Veck a lupine snarl,

and Veck's red eyes only look tired, they roll upward to watch a biplane trundle across the slate sky, and to Bagger's dread, there's no fear in Veck's voice, no anxiety, only a soft, desolate, homesick sorrow,

and he says, "Sorry, Bagger. For what I gotta do. It's nothing personal. But it's like I said. If the angel's granting wishes, there's only one wish I got left. You read the letter. There's no place here for a man like me. Back home neither. They think shell shock is hysteria. Like I'm a hysterical female. You know how they treat hysteria? Electric shock. They'll cook my brain, Bagger. Burn the hysteria right out of me. And it's not just me. Look around. There's no place left for *any* man, not anymore. It's all gotta end, Bagger. It's all gotta end right now, and she can make that happen,"

---

and it's apocalyptic but also an opportunity, so Bagger says, "You're dreaming, Veck! We were wrong! She's not some magic fucking fairy! She's just a woman! No, she's worse! Can't walk, can't speak! She's more fucked in the head than you! She can't do anything to save us! To save anybody!,"

and Veck gives him a look of pity, poor little ignorant white boy, and raises a palm blistered from flamethrower petrol, and then, slow as a wink, Veck curls it into a fist,

and as he does, the biplane above, as if caught in that fist, explodes,

and Veck doesn't even look at the ball of fire, he merely gives Bagger what could, very charitably, be called a grin, and asks, "You don't think so?,"

XXX

and while Bagger's recoiled in shock, Veck leans down and wraps his arms around the woman, he's taking her, same as Popkin took her, and Bagger grabs for the woman, but with only one free arm, he can only grip the blue cape until it starts to rip, and he doesn't want her unclothed again, so, shit, he lets her go,

and Veck stands tall, not as naked with the P3 on his back and the woman held over his front, yet somehow seeming less whole, as if all the removed corners from Selective Service forms, *If person is of African descent, tear this corner,* have been torn from Veck personally and he's as mortally wounded as Arno, and this scares Bagger the most, Veck's got nothing to fucking lose,

and the instant Veck steps from the tree line he stops, raises his nose and sniffs, which makes Bagger sniff, too, that sweet, scorched odor still there, and Veck reaches into his haversack to remove a tinfoil tube, looks like shaving cream, the guy's lost his mind, but when Veck squirts goo into his palm, the alkaline smell tells Bagger it's what the boys call Sag, a paste to protect from chemical burns, Bagger's used it himself, it soaks into your uniform like bacon grease, only Veck's not wearing a uniform, and that's what the stench is, fucking mustard gas, Jerry must have salted the earth with it before moving on, and Bagger locates the nearest dead bodies and sees the frost around them has melted, the kicked-up mud around them is yellow, that explains all the open collars, the men clawed for air as they died, Bagger's seen it before on burial duty, necks ripped open all the way to tracheas,

and Bagger scrabbles for his gas mask, getting it out of the bag with one hand isn't too bad, but strapping the two-lensed monstrosity over his head is something else, the straps snap and slide, and he cries, "Veck, help!," and struggles, "Veck! Come on, man!," and manages to get the mask cockeyed on his face, nowhere near airtight, he can bite down on the mouthpiece but can't get the nose pinchers applied,

and so he'll have to breathe strictly through his mouth, Bagger tries it and smells the charcoal filter activate, but he's not getting enough air, could be a kink in the tube, and he unbites the mouthpiece to cry, "You're leaving me here to die, Veck!,"

and even as Bagger shouts it, he knows that death is the whole point of what's happening, the mask's circular lenses abridge his view while also bringing it into a theatrical focus, and through them he watches Veck pick the woman back up and turn toward the field, and the crazy thing is, though Veck's body is slathered in Sag, he hasn't put on a mask,

and Veck simply walks away, carrying the woman, there's nothing Bagger can do, so he bites back down on the respirator and hits the mud, stretching himself from shackled wrist to extended toe, but the handcuff key remains a foot away, close enough that he'll figure out how to reach it eventually, but not soon enough, not nearly soon enough,

and Bagger's frustrated cry is stifled by plastic, steel, and cloth, and he contorts to see over the Fahrpanzer, Veck is powering toward the dead, buttocks waxy with Sag and compressed beneath the P3's weight, the woman's head dipped over Veck's right arm, her eyes visible from the hood, staring back at Bagger with a blinding beam of light,

and Veck stops, simply stops, two hundred feet away, nothing special about the spot except that it's within a rough pentagram of corpses like cairns awaiting a final ritual, and Veck stumbles in a circle like a child who has lost his mother, kind of like Bagger lost his, except the mother Veck has lost is the planet itself, and Veck blinks against poison gas, and snorts mucus loosened by chemicals, and speaks to the angel, not loudly, but no other noises compete for Bagger's ears, "All right. Do it. Make it go away,"

and nothing happens, except that Veck drops the woman's lower half to rub at eyes that, even from this distance, Bagger can see grow redder, and Veck grunts in discomfort and gives the woman a shake, saying, "This is my wish. Take the whole world and end it,"

and Bagger pants so hard the insides of his lenses fog, gray cataracts that recede with each inhale, a maddening cycle of blindness that causes lapses in the action, exhale, inhale, and now the woman's sitting up on the ground, legs curled to the side, hood dropped to her shoulders, the light of her curiosity brightening Veck's face,

and Veck's shouting, "Why are you just sitting there? Put an end to it! All of it! Both sides! All sides! We showed you how! We spent four years showing you! Look around! We burned it! Raped it! Killed it! Do that! Do what we did! Do it to everyone, everywhere! Wipe us out! I'm begging you!,"

and Veck hacks, his naked body inverted like a rope bridge in typhoon winds, and he drools pink before choking throttles him again and he spits a kind of ebony ejaculate, making Bagger wonder if all soldiers produce such wicked semen now, capable only of propagating an offspring of stone-hearted destroyers,

and what's left of Bagger's rationality tells him the gunk is Veck's dissolving lungs, and soon the ichor is too thick to stop, it cascades from Veck's chin as blood oozes from his sockets, which makes his eyes stand out like he's wearing red kohl, as big and fervent as two missiles flying Bagger's way,

and Bagger recalls that mustard gas hibernates for a few hours before it kills you, this must be chlorine, which melts your lungs into acid, but chlorine's easy to identify, it turns your brass buttons green, all you need to do to nullify chlorine is hold a wet rag to your face, wet with anything, even urine, and Bagger looks at his groin and wonders if pissing himself might be smart, but then again, chlorine's also highly visible, a slinking cloud of earwax green, so maybe Jerry used a cocktail of whatever chemical dregs they had left,

and a third possibility is that this isn't gas at all, how's that for an awful prospect, this invisible germ liquifying Veck could be the work of the woman, a wrathful reaction to being told what to do,

and Bagger has a malignant memory of his father's final Christmas Eve sermon, four months before the Lusitania, the angel Gabriel announcing Christ's birth to shepherds, but in the Bishop's hands, it was no hark-the-herald-angels-sing, the old man troweled into Luke 2:9, "And, lo, an angel of the Lord appeared to them, and the glory of the Lord shone around them, and they were *terrified!*," how he boomed that last word, children startled from Santa Claus reveries as the Bishop tallied all the times angels slaughtered entire populations, a reputation that would make any shepherd wonder what kind of manger monster had just been born,

and Veck looks like his old self now, terrified, there's no way a melting man can look any other way, and though he's got to be blind now, his hands know their way, one reaches for the P3's block valve while the other aims the lance at the angel, the ignitor prodding her solar plexus,

and Bagger gasps like Arno used to gasp, there are still things in the world terrible enough to shock, and Bagger spits his mouthpiece and screams, "*VECK, YOU FUCKING MANIAC!*," but behind a gas mask he might as well be singing dixie, and Veck starts screaming, too, through a mouth of gummy flesh, "*I'M WARNING YOU! DO IT!*," and Bagger screams, "*VECK! STOP!*," but Veck slaps the woman with the nozzle, which splits her flawless cheek,

and the slash forms an apple-red line through which crystalline light pours as pure as ice, not that Veck can see it, he rams the ignitor against the woman's face, more wounds, and from those wounds, more light from within, as Veck screams, "*DO IT! DO IT!*" and Bagger screams, "*VECK, YOU DON'T KNOW WHAT SHE'LL DO!*,"

and then, for their sins, the angel does it,

and *angel* is how Bagger will think of the woman from now on, for good, forever, he wishes he could grovel before her for having doubted, for when the angel opens her mouth at the last strike of the nozzle, Bagger realizes she's never opened her mouth before, her cryptic smiles have always been tight-lipped, and inside are no white teeth, no pink palate, only the light that has bled through her all along, only this time in concentrate, light beyond light, a uterine passage into another realm,

and it has the effect of a detonated bomb, if Veck wasn't blind this light would take care of that, and Bagger believes it's only thanks to his gas mask lenses that he's able to follow what happens,

and what Bagger first thinks is a *rising mass*, an earthquake up-heaval that convulses tides of mud into the air, he quickly realizes is a *mass rising*, some two hundred German and American corpses dredged upward from hornet-yellow sludge like carcasses on slaughterhouse meat hooks, then operated like a company of mari-onettes,

and the limbs articulate, each cold, dead joint in creaky swivel, obliterated legs arranged in action poses, ravaged arms returned to how they were when they died, most of them gripping invis-ible guns, some in pitcher poses of hurling grenades, several with arms held high to beg their enemy not to shoot, others beckoning encouragement to keep fighting, a ghastly re-creation of men in the final seconds of their wasted lives,

and Bagger's lenses stop fogging because he's no longer breath-ing, it's one thing to chuck corpses into a hole, spray quicklime, shovel in soil, and cultivate a cornfield, another thing to revisit that field and find it peopled by sentient stalks, the angel casts away the world's funereal obfuscations, the tastefully wrapped shrouds, the carefully covered wagons, the sealed grave pits that minimize the enormity of lives lost,

and the risen corpses undulate in the wind, uniforms loose over body parts blown away, emptied sheaths of skin fluttering like the planted flags of pointless patriotism, swaths of purple muscle speckled with snow, exposed bones swaying in ways similar to how the men moved when they were industrious little death machines, it's almost funny how much it meant to them to kill, the ones whose faces have been ripped off grin at Bagger in silent laughter, chattering teeth,

and at the center of this revenant army stands Ben Veck, who knows what's going on by the clucks of broken bones and the slaps of bloody skin, he staggers around until a boot snags and he stumbles, left shoulder planting into one of the dangling bodies, a fellow American, it's like swatting an outfit draped from a hanger, the corpse jiggles and its olive drabs billow, and an arm that was nearly severed finally disconnects, yet still floats midair,

and Veck must feel what Bagger feels, the scope of violence now as naked as him, the angel insisting that Veck's wish has already been granted, the end he pleads for is already here, the Great War a wheel set in motion that's far too heavy to halt,

and Veck appears to comprehend this so rapidly that he becomes the shrieker, caught on uncuttable barbed wire, *"I'M SORRY! NAOMI, I'M SO SORRY!"* he shrieks while bumbling into this dangling doughboy, that suspended Jerry, until he falls, and Bagger doesn't know if Veck's own naked knee does it on purpose or not, but Bagger hears the sucking ping of impact, sharp as musket shot, followed by a whoosh, it's the P3's propellant tank, punctured of its pressurized gas,

and Veck explodes,

and the shock wave shreds his meat off his bones,

and in the red spritz, his tendoned finger bones wrench the valve,

and flame spews into the spouting gas,

and silver fire gouts, a throaty roar, a funeral pyre fifty feet high,

and wind punches Bagger in the chest, and he blacks out,

and he thinks he sees the dead curl back down, a litter of sleepy pups,

XXXI

and in the beginning God created the heaven and the earth, and the earth was without form, and void, and darkness was upon the face of the deep, and the Spirit of God moved upon the face of the waters, and God said, Let there be light, and there was light, and God saw the light, that it was good, and God divided the light from the darkness, and God called the light Day, and the darkness he called Night, and the evening and morning were the first day,

and Bagger's lost somewhere in that cycle, same as he's lost somewhere on the Western Front, same as he got lost in Genesis 5 each time he attempted to read the Bible to impress his father, that pileup of humanity that now reads like a necrology of fallen soldiers, General Adam, Lieutenant General Seth, Colonel Enos, Major Cainan, Captain Mahalaleel, Corporal Jared, and Privates Enoch, Methuselah, Lamech, and Noah,

and it's an order of battle that eventually begets Private Cyril Bagger, how about that, after all the bravado mustered to cover his loneliness, he's most definitely not alone, he's a bud at one tip of history's most expansive root, and if he could turn around, he might be able to follow the root back to its original tree, lording over its original garden, and when he opens his eyes he has to blink away snow that has gathered atop the feather bed of his lashes, a motion that melts some of it, which create puddles he allows to absorb into his eyes, feels nice and cool in the toxic afterburn, and it's only as his sight unblurs that he becomes aware of the monster in front of him,

and Bagger spends a few petrified seconds telling himself this isn't the first time he's mistakenly spotted a monster, there was the time a man's full suit of skin swung from a tree like a winged aberration, the time he saw three heads next to one another in the mud and thought it was Satan's centipede, you see a lot of shit out here requiring a beat of calm decryption,

and so it's a bad sign when the monster doesn't resolve into something explainable, good lord, the thing's hideous, two jet-black eyeballs the size of tea plates protruding from malformed lumps of wrinkled brown flesh, the face narrowing into an aardvark trunk, the end of which is layered in rings of tiny needle teeth,

and when Bagger tries to squirm away he realizes he's flat on his back on the cold Argonne floor, and worse, still cuffed to the Fahrpanzer, which means this thing is floating *above* him, fucking *floating*, its body aligned to Bagger's own right down to the olive drabs, though the drabs aren't quite standard-issue four-pocketed wool, these drabs look more like fur and grow right out of the skin,

and when Bagger turns his head to the right to hide from the shark-like stare, the monster does the same turn, and when Bagger holds up a hand to beg for mercy, the monster raises its hand, too, which looks human enough until Bagger notices the absence of fingernails, the extra joint in the thumb, the total lack of fingerprints, and Bagger whines, it feels like this thing is studying him, like the codger who concluded Bagger's Army physical by cupping his balls and telling him to cough, and as if requiring closer review, the monster floats closer, and Bagger whimpers, what if he touches this leathery mutant and loses his mind,

and when, in fact, the long snout nudges Bagger, he gasps the lungful of air he'll need to scream for eternity before realizing he doesn't feel the thing's skin, he's separated from it by his gas mask,

and that's when Bagger catches his own reflection in the monster's glassy black eyes, and insight leaks in like chemical gas, this monster, flesh and blood, floating and fearsome, is merely mimicking what Bagger looks like, right here, right now, it has shaped its physical form in an attempt to put him at ease, it thinks this is what Bagger looks like now, big-eyed and snouted,

and Bagger pleads, "No, this isn't me, it's a mask," and with his free hand grapples with the resin-infused cloth and spits the mouthpiece and wrangles the suffocating piece of crap off and can finally see clearly again, unimpeded by lenses, which makes the monster's deformities all the more immediate, the slithery blinks of its adenoid eyeballs, the twitching hose of its muzzle,

and the monster cocks its head in apparent interest at Bagger's latest physical change, and there's a pause during which Bagger believes the circular orifice of its trunk distorts into a smile, before the monster brings a malformed hand to its face, pinches its own baggy cheek, and copies Bagger again by tearing its own face off, and Bagger screams, probably, he's no longer aware of his noises, the monster's face comes off and jiggles in the monster's hands like raw chicken breast, and then it's gone, reabsorbed into the monster's hand, which bloats in apparent digestion of the extra flesh,

and, yes, Bagger's definitely screaming now, but it doesn't last, for the monster's olive fur reshapes and recolors into the red dress and blue cape, and its face returns to the one he's come to know, that round, pale, peaceful, feminine face, the half-lidded eyes widened slightly as if to shush him, it's all right, Cyril, everything is all right,

and her lips show no trace of the hideous trunk as they purse, and she speaks, she finally fucking speaks,

and what she says is, *Do not be afraid,*

XXXII

and the words have preternatural force, they are the same words Bagger knows from old sermons, words that angels, over and over, say to those who cower in fear, Bagger recalls his father describing to his appalled congregation how actual biblical texts describe angels, not as gloriously winged cherubs but as gyrating wheels studded in eyeballs, living chariots with multiple faces and hooves, for angels, he intoned, can appear however they wish,

and Bagger obeys, and is not afraid,

and being unafraid, all clues snap together, and Bagger whispers, "He saw you as Naomi. Veck thought you were his little girl,"

and the angel smiles and says, *Sometimes*, and Bagger concedes that she's right, Veck was more certain the woman was an angel than any of them, and yet sometimes, *sometimes*, mistook her for his daughter, a dual vision that shouldn't be possible, though Bagger should know by now anything is possible out here where only duality can save your sanity, you love and hate, you wail and laugh, you kill and rescue, you live and die, and he says, "And Popkin thought you were Effie," and the angel says, *Sometimes,*

and he says, "And Goodspeed," and he has to think harder about Goodspeed, it was a hundred years ago, not yesterday, that the sniveling grave robber was lopped in half over a trench, but Goodspeed had said something odd only moments prior, "Theda," Bagger recalls, "he called you Theda," and the angel says, *Sometimes,*

and Bagger knows Vincent the Vulture didn't want a daughter back or a girlfriend to paw, he wanted money, he wanted to barnstorm the angel before a paying public, and no one could rake in more cash than a star, and right now the biggest star in the world is an actress Bagger has whistled at on movie posters, a woman named Theda Bara,

and this leaves only Arno, and there's no mystery to Arno, never was, from the moment the angel reached the trench, Arno was snuggling into her like the mother he always wanted, he never had to say the actual word, and neither does Bagger, the angel nods and says, *Sometimes,*

and even the rat-eating old man in the village died running for the angel, crying the name of a lost loved one he saw in the angel's face, death, death, death, the angel has facilitated nothing but, and the rancid unfairness of it boils at the back of Bagger's throat, and he says, "You've played me. You've played us. We're all suckers for believing you,"

and she says, *You see what you need to see,*

and Bagger demands, "Who are you really?" and the angel asks, *Who do you think I am?*, a long enough string of words for Bagger to notice her lip movements don't sync with her voice, which tells him the angel's speech is like her physical appearance, to be interpreted differently by different people, one more facade intended to put Bagger at ease, and he can't help but let go of his anger, for when has anyone out here done anything to put anyone at ease,

and the angel's question lingers, then grates like sand, he still can't place her face, her red dress, her blue cape, it's driving him mad, he punches the frozen ground,

and the angel smiles and says, *You do not need to remember,* and Bagger fusses and mewls, "But I want to. I want to remember anything that's not all this shit," a plea the angel ignores, saying, *You are the only one to ask nothing of me,* and Bagger squinches in confusion, the statement has the whiff of a compliment, even though all he's ever done is save his own ass,

and so he shakes his head, sullen, and replies, "I could wish all sorts of things from you," and the angel asks, *Oh? What would you ask for?* in a tone so blithe, so unperturbed by the empyrean devastation that Bagger's stare sharpens into an entrenching tool and digs past the angel's poise, he's got to think of the angel as a mark and find a way into her head,

and he says, "Veck had a wish. Look what happened to him. And Popkin and Goodspeed. Arno too. And they're dead. They all made wishes and they're dead. You think I'm stupid? I make a wish and you'll murder me too,"

and the angel's smile changes ever so slightly, the look of a sister whose much younger sibling has, for the first time, called her out on her bullshit, a mix of surprise and pride, and she replies, *I am not the hand that kills. I am the sword in the hand,* and Bagger understands because his father said this a hundred times, angels are neither bad nor good, what they are, *all* they are, is obedient to their master,

and, shit, that's a good way to describe a soldier, too, Private Cyril Bagger is a sword in Major General Reis's hand, if a dull and cracked one, and now the angel's floating repose over Bagger makes more sense, they are two soldiers from different armies close enough for hand-to-hand combat, but only, it seems, if Bagger takes the first swing,

and, you know what, fuck it, maybe Veck and Popkin and Arno and Goodspeed all wished for the wrong shit, shit that made the angel's boss tell her to strike them down, and it could be the exhaustion, could be the grief or rage, but Bagger has the unstoppable urge to call this heavenly bluff, this invitation to make a final request from inside a guillotine's lunette, what does it matter anyway, he's handcuffed in a poison landscape trying to catch up to a division that might be wiped out,

and so Bagger thinks of all the things he could wish for, a white-clothed restaurant table plunked down here in the forest, a tuxedoed waiter making dishes appear like magic tricks, a course of Russian caviar and canapé of anchovy followed by roast duckling with a side of lobster salad, wait, no, let's get serious, Mary-Louise would taste even better, how about the angel whip up a hand-carved, four-poster, Regency-era bed upon which his favorite Vosges prostituée waits in the repose of a pink-ribboned satin corset,

and the smarter play, though, is to wish his way out of the war, fuck his fantasy farmhouse, materialize back in the blistering Augusts and subzero Februarys of good old Iowa with all the ascotted gamblers and sunburnt rubes he can handle, and maybe the angel, because he's been so good, will throw in a double-breasted black tailcoat, white bow tie, and gloves, so he can be the classiest snake slithering up the Mississippi,

and Bagger wonders how much mustard gas lingers in the breeze, how else to explain the speed at which these succulent desires dry to salt on his tongue, leaving a single wish in the shadows, a little thing, really, a thing that will be of no practical help to Bagger,

and yet he coughs it out, cheeks hot with embarrassment, how has the Hawkeye Hustler, the Sioux City Sharpie, the Council Bluffs Crossroader, the Dean of Dubuque come to this lowly state of mawkish big brotherhood, but come to it he has,

and he says, "I wish for the kid. Lewis Arno. I want him back,"

and if one were to calibrate every smile the angel has given, it would be done in tenths of inches, so subtle are her tranquil adjustments, and this smile ticks a single tenth longer as she says, *You are full of surprises, aren't you?*, and Bagger blushes hotter and turns away, cold cheek to cottony snow and tacky frost,

and the angel says, *This is a significant wish to grant. I will do it, but only if you agree to a wager. You like wagers, don't you?*,

and though Bagger's guts prickle with the rashlike outbreak of hope that the angel can really bring the kid back, he slits his eyes in suspicion, because the angel's finally got something wrong, he *doesn't* like wagers, gambling is for fools unless you're the one fixing the gamble, and right now, the angel's the one holding the marked cards, and yet the pot is too tantalizing to resist, so he nods, cautiously, and replies, "Yes,"

and she says, *I will give you his life. In return, you must promise never to take another's life for as long as you live. If you fail in this promise, a catastrophe beyond imagination will consume your entire world,*

and he stares at her, and blinks, and races his mind around like a trench rat hungry for dropped crumbs but wary of homemade snares, for in theory, Bagger's got nothing to fear, he's not killed anyone since he killed his mother being born, he's not the one who cut Goodspeed in half, or stabbed Arno, or made that prison wall fall on Popkin, or consumed Veck in flame,

and though worries remain, Bagger swats them aside, they are gnats weighed against the marvelous dream of the kid, alive and as irritating as ever, so he squeezes his eyes shut and says all in a rush, "I promise, I promise, I promise, I promise," a torrent he dams with a gasp before doubling up in anticipation of the same violent climax that met the others, a second baptism, this one into the Church of Shrapnel, of Bayonet, of Rubble, of Fire,

and he's tickled by a twinkle of laughter,

and a gentle kiss pressed to his blighted lips,

XXXIII

and what brings Bagger back is the venom sting of his left wrist, the return of blood to handcuff-pinched flesh, and his eyelids open to find Lewis Arno sitting on the Fahrpanzer, a little pale but otherwise still the kid, twirling the handcuff around a finger and whistling "Over There," his helmet a steel yarmulke at the back of his skull, and when he notices Bagger awake, he doesn't halt the twirling or whistling, only smiles, an armistice sun through war's black wool, and says, "Hi,"

and Bagger figures it was all a dream until he sits up, discs cracking, massaging his wrist, and sees the angel sitting against Arno's legs and giving Bagger the coy look of someone with whom you share a secret, and though Bagger knows the secret is his pacifist vow, not their clandestine kiss, he licks his lips anyway, suspecting angels taste like cotton candy, but all he detects is the salty grape of blood,

and Arno, twirling, says, "I've been thinking," and Bagger croaks, their old joke, "Uh-oh," and Arno continues, "You said Korak and Tarzan end up fighting to the death. But that doesn't make sense! Tarzan's an ape man. But he's not an *ape*. What Tarzan would do is stretch out his neck, you know? He'd rather die than hurt his son.

If Tarzan dies, Korak becomes king, and what would make Tarzan happier than that? I think you read it wrong. Or did you make it up? Bagger, did you make it up?,"

and as scorched as Bagger's throat is, and as cymbaled are the plates of his skull, and as cold blue are the aches of his wrist, Bagger feels his organs go buoyant in the helium of joy, this goddamn kid, who's too clever to swallow Bagger's made-up climax to *The Son of Tarzan*, he's going to pester Bagger with questions enough to kill him, and Bagger laughs at the figure of speech, he can't wait to be killed like this each and every day,

and Bagger shrugs and says, "Yeah. But my ending's the only one you get. We lost the book," to which Arno frowns, catches the cuffs in his hand, and digs into his haversack, pulling out, of course, *The Son of Tarzan*, the pages' edges as red as dead leaves, saying, "I brought it. It was just sitting there under the howitzer,"

and Bagger's still staring at the book in blank shock when Arno grins slyly and pulls an improbable second book from the sack, they might be the only two books left on the whole Western Front, where all cognoscenti pursuits have been usurped by jungle ones, and when Bagger sees this book is red as well, he thinks, here it is, the record of our time, authored by the angel, the ultimate Book of Blood,

and it's the Bible, the red leather Bible, the Bishop's Bible, Arno must have noticed it way back in the trench and spent a few death-defying seconds digging it out,

and Bagger nods his thanks like it's no big deal, but has to look away fast, eyes underwater from a rush of tears he palms aside while fabricating a yawn, and when he's got control of himself, he asks, "How'd you find me?," and the kid replies, "You guys left a million footprints," and Bagger thinks of all the mud, all the snow, all the blood, and gives the kid a guilty smile, and notices the blood-snarled bandage under the kid's shirt collar, Veck's handiwork,

and though his heart hammers, Bagger says in an offhand tone, "Nasty cut you got there," and Arno flips the handcuff key like a quarter and laughs, "Yeah, somebody stabbed me! Can you believe it? Wait'll they hear back home," and Bagger's protoplasm bubbles, he's a surgeon gingerly asking questions of a cadaver who just sat up from the slab, if only the Bishop could have seen this, he might never have lost his faith and boarded that boat,

and Bagger probes, "What was it like?" and Arno flips the key and asks, "What was what like?" and Bagger warns himself, careful now, and clarifies, "Before you woke up. You see anything? Hear anything?," and Arno catches the key and gives Bagger a grin and asks, "You mean did I have a dream? When I was asleep?," and Bagger, baffled on how else to proceed, nods,

and Arno chimpanzees the cogitation of a philosopher, stroking an invisible beard, then lights up, and says, "You know what? I *did* have a dream! It was weird," and Bagger dares not speak, only managing another encouraging nod,

and Arno says, "Let's see. I was walking through the trenches. I was trying to find somebody. Anybody. But it was a big maze. I walked for days. And eventually I knew I wasn't getting out. I had to make the trenches my home. So I became the thing that lives in the trenches. And once in a while other people ended up there, too, but by then, I didn't want them there. So I," and here, the kid lowers his voice, "so I killed them, Bagger. I killed them like Korak killed the Kovudoo. With my bare hands. I think I might have ate them? Yeah. I definitely ate them. And the weird part is, I started to like it. The trenches weren't mine to begin with, but I started to think I owned them. So I dug till my trenches spread all over the world. And more people kept falling in. Which meant more people for me to eat,"

and then Arno goes solemn and whispers, "I ate you, too, Bagger. You fell into the trench, and I ate you. Sorry,"

and to Bagger it's less dream than prophecy, one day the kid will kill him, as sure as one day Korak will succeed Tarzan, a fate Bagger can only feel resigned to, so he nods grimly and asks, "How did it end?,"

and the kid pooches his lower lip, eyes faraway, and says, "I think there was a rain cloud? Or a storm? It was dark. Like the inside of a tornado. And I tried to hide. I dug myself into the mud. I kept throwing rats at it! I thought maybe if I gave it enough rats it would leave me be! But it didn't want rats. It sucked me right out of the mud. Then I was up inside it. It was scary. It was loud, like when we're getting shelled. There was red lightning all over. And I felt somebody touch me,"

and Bagger, desperate for just one goddamn happy ending, asks, "The angel?," but the kid looks troubled and says, "Felt like leather. Not leather like your Bible. Like a trench boot. Except alive. It had claws. Cold claws. And a long, cold, leather arm. It flew me out the top of the tornado," and the kid shivers, and blinks, and then he smiles, startled but happy, a kid exiting a carnival ride, and concludes, "Then I woke up and I was alone. And I'd been stabbed!,"

and Arno laughs, a short jolt, the whole story so absurd, and Bagger is breathless at the derring-do, the kid so flippant in the face of death that Bagger laughs, too, there's no other reaction left, and Arno laughs at the sight of the bedraggled Bagger laughing, and that's it, they are howling, rolling in snow and mud, and if someone were to pass by, they would keep their distance, believing the Butcher Birds to be expiring in agony, or dangerously unhinged, or both,

and after a time, Bagger's jubilations relax enough for his happy tears to freeze into pearls, a mentholated counterpart to a rush of air that's too warm to be anything but hope, for if Lewis Arno can be healed, anyone might be healed, the kid, after all, is a messenger, and Bishop Bagger always said that's what angels were above all else, messengers climbing up and down Jacob's ladder between heaven and earth,

and if the job being offered to Bagger is to serve as a bodyguard to messengers, two of them now, he accepts, what a gift that the most cataclysmic event in history has handed him a reason to live, not to simply survive but to *live*,

and so Bagger tells Arno about the promise he made to the angel, it's only fair after the kid shared his dream, and the kid nods along like a pint-sized professor, like it all makes good sense, and when the kid asks, "The other guys are dead?," Bagger nods, the era of mollycoddling kaput, and Arno looks thoughtful but not surprised, and glances at the angel as one might a beloved dog that doesn't remember eating the neighbor's cat, and Bagger stands, wobbly but confident nothing can stop him, and gazes around, a forest iced in celestial white, a battlefield of sloughed flesh, a centaur of ash that used to be Ben Veck, a sky of cinereal clouds somersaulting like fat children, urging Bagger along, the wind at his back, the 43rd surely close now, twenty-thousand men ready to receive the good news of the angel, whether they realize it or not,

and the good news is that the angel can heal, heal the world like it healed the kid's mortal wound, like it delivered every other reasonable thing the soldiers wanted, Popkin's Lucky Strikes, Arno's evaporated puncture wound, the recovery of Veck's squashed kitten, seems reasonable to Bagger she could melt every firearm in Europe with a gesture of her hand, at the very least make the millions of murdered stand up, as they did around Veck, to show everyone alive the true cost of willy-nilly slaughter, it could be the first shot of a new war, a war of shame, one way or the other ending the suffering, he's just got to get the angel to Reis, and get Reis to understand and employ her properly,

and Bagger, dizzy with purpose, finally purpose, picks up the angel, lightweight as ever, turns his back to Arno, and says, "Hop on," and the kid whoops, stuffs the cuffs and keys and *Tarzan* and Bible into his haversack and scampers close, and Bagger squeezes the kid's shoulder, an act of affection he uses to ruffle his thumb through Arno's bandage and get a peek at the should-be deadly wound, and it's there, ugly for sure, but its black crevasse is jacketed with fresh skin, blood sealed away, a flesh wound, nothing more,

and Arno leaps onto Bagger's back, squat-kicking his legs through the loops of Bagger's elbows, and he asks, "Where we going?," and Bagger says, "You tell me," and Arno hums deliberation before slashing his hand east and announcing, "That way!" and Bagger, having fun, he nearly forgot what fun is, replies, "What's that way, cap'n?" and Arno declares, "Dracula!" and Bagger chuckles, *Dracula* is a book the kid's wanted to read since hearing that the Germans defeated the Romanians in the Carpathian Mountains, right at Count Drac's doorstep,

and Bagger nods crisply, a paradigmatic soldier at last, and reports, "Yes, sir!," and the kid gives him a kick in the back to get him going, and Bagger marches out of the forest and through the ossuary of sculptured dead, until the kid kicks him in the right kidney to direct him right, the left kidney to direct him left, and Bagger laughs, the kid always enjoyed how Renault commanders, inside their buttoned-up tanks, signaled directions to their drivers via kicks,

and now Bagger's the tank and he couldn't be prouder, he imagines both of the kid's boots ending in blades, the same model Bagger once attached to gamecocks, Lewis Arno the gaff, he'll spur Bagger to fight as hard as he needs to fight, for as long as that fight needs fought, until all who try to stop him are a discombobulation of feathers,

Mercy Seat

XXXIV

and All-High Warlord Kaiser Willy's never looked better, Bagger thinks in a rush of American zeal, the Prussian's Rottweiler head represented by a cankered jack-o'-lantern, his distinctive pronghorn mustache inked above pumpkin teeth gummed inward like Popkin's trench mouth, the candle flickering through triangle eye holes like mortar fire reflected in Goodspeed's pince-nez, the gourd stem topped with a decent likeness of Kaiser Wilhelm's Garde Du Corps helmet, the ornamental eagle replaced by dead crow, otherwise Willy is naked, right down to a stubby cigar butt for a cock,

and Bagger flicks the dick hard enough for it to spiral off into the fallen night, which makes Arno cackle and the angel raise an eyebrow,

and just beyond, heralded by the fetor of soiled bandages and trench foot, and the sound of a doughboy playing bagpipes like a Scot, is the 43rd's support legion of wagons and trucks and wheeled artillery and horses, lord, the hundreds of horses, kicking shit from their hooves, feeding from grazing masks, and emanating a barnyard stench that raises the temperature ten degrees as Bagger and Arno weave through a torch-lit perplexity of mess tents, water caissons, and latrine benches, which Bagger can tell are being built all wrong,

and what does it matter, though, he's home, back with good old Company P, and as Bagger enters the trench behind Arno carrying the angel in her concealing cape, it becomes clear the pumpkin-head bogey was constructed not by playful privates hopped up on patriotism, but frostbitten woebegoners who might sculpture their own effigies with similar deformities,

and this suggests to Bagger the Butcher Birds have yet to receive a new commander, but something's sure the hell happening, the soldiers ought to be passed out, yet they fidget like men about to go over the top, except no one's preparing to do any such thing,

and Bagger would question them if they didn't stab him with glares of accusation or turn away in disgust, which deflates Bagger, his all-night march has been sustained by the prospect of forging camaraderie with his fellow man, but he tells himself to be patient, these grunts don't know the body he carries will change everything for them, their country, their world,

and in fact, they likely believe he's carrying the shrieker's corpse, and furthermore, that the survivors of Reis's clean-up crew were, of course, its two biggest cowards, the ones who must have looked on as the other three died, which isn't correct or fair, but again, Bagger soothes himself, the doughboys will understand soon,

and finally a boy barely older than Arno waves his arms from above and gestures for the body Bagger carries, he'll take care of it, harvest the ID tag and get it buried, a kindness that makes Bagger regret how grumpily he's dug his graves, so he nods his thanks even as he refuses the offer and follows Arno, and because no one hates Arno, soldiers listen to the kid's repeated plea for directions and keep pointing him down the trench,

and at last they arrive at a reinforced dugout radiating the yellow, orange, and reds of competing lanterns, a sure sign of officers doing officer things, ditto the four armed sentries guarding the downward stairs, the first two of whom are hardscrabble Butcher Birds, a hard contrast to the two guards so snappily outfitted they could only hail from Army HQ,

and Bagger holds Arno back with an elbow, leans into the nearest soldier, and asks, "Who's in there?" and the soldier, knowing he's observed by HQ guards, doesn't move an inch, but bulges his eyes, to which Bagger asks, "Bullard?," and the man bulges his eyes bigger, enough to hush Bagger to a whisper before he asks, "*Pershing?*,"

and the soldier flexes his jaw, holy fuck, the man himself is here inside this junky burrow, General John J. Pershing, commander of the U.S. First Army, architect of the Meuse-Argonne Offensive, so preposterous an event Bagger's instinct is to elongate his spine to salute, no matter all the times he's fantasized about burying Pershing with the quicklimed dead,

and Bagger attunes his ears to the bunker's boss tones and swears he hears Pershing's voice, a bit mumbly, a bit sibilant, but unlike all the times Bagger has heard it on radios, also enraged, a series of attack-dog barks that the dugout's walls mitigate into the soft smacks of wet clay,

and most everyone has cleared the area, unwilling to be excoriated when Reis emerges, if indeed the major general has the balls to emerge ever again, but Bagger stands tall, and breathes deep, he's got to finish this, the stakes are too impossibly high,

and soon the bunker acrimony shifts to the sounds of paper slapped into folders and hats slapped onto heads, and then the lava light is blotted out by uniformed men streaming up the stairs like flamethrower fire, and the guards part ways and Bagger stands at attention, he doesn't know the last time he saw so many gray-haired men, and their nucleus is the grandfatherly Pershing with his shovel jaw and ticket-stub mustache, muttering while his staff nervously checks the sky as if privy to intel the Butcher Birds are not,

and Bagger knows he should stop Pershing, cry out his name, even grab hold of his stripes regardless of the rifle stock he'd take to the face, because here's the one man in the world who needs to know what he and Arno found in Bois de Fays, and how her earthbound fall is a warning to stop firing guns into realms they can't understand,

and yet Bagger says nothing, dumbstruck as the pious,

and then Pershing's gone, nothing but a cold wind, a hallucination of power, Bagger will have to go up the proper chain of command, it's the only way this is going to work, so he kneels to form a private space in which he can open his Bible and take a restorative sniff before handing it to Arno for safekeeping once again,

and Bagger stands before the armed duo and says, "Private Cyril Bagger, Company P, I need to see the major general, it's a matter of life and death," and the guards, groggy from Pershing's holy jolt, share a look to make sure they are both still characters in this nightmare, and black tributaries of soil accentuate their wrinkling eyes as they debate telepathically, then pivot aside like drunkards,

and Bagger pins Arno with a look and says, "Go sleep. I'll find you when I'm done," to which the kid's face pinches as he objects, "That's not fair, I want to stay with her," and Bagger can't deal with this now, there's a window of opportunity and he needs to hurry through it, so he raises his voice like he never has to the kid,

and booms, "Goddammit, Private Arno! Go get some shut-eye and sleep off that subordinance! You hear me, little puke? Why are you still standing here? Get your ass going!,"

and the betrayed look that settles over Arno's face breaks Bagger's heart, but he can't drag a fourteen-year-old kid into Reis's lair, if this goes wrong, Bagger alone must take the blame, so he sharpens a chisel glare to scrape the kid off his boot,

and Bagger turns away, Arno nothing to him now, that's what he tells himself, what he has to tell himself, and he shifts the angel into his left elbow and with his right hand wipes his face, eager to make himself presentable, only for his palm to feel just how many layers of muck have caramelized his skin, it's no use, so he exhales, nerves bouncing, and heads down the steps toward the gas-proof curtain, ocean-cold down here but bright, too, aflame with all the interplanetary possibility of an alien sun,

XXXV

and every time Bagger has laid eyes on Major General Lyon Reis, the man has been standing as if posing for a portrait, no matter the strategical blunder unfurling through his field glasses, an affect Bagger suspects the man has employed all his life to ameliorate the effect of his underdeveloped right arm, so it's ominous to find Reis sitting, all alone in the dusky eigengrau, no staff of sycophants before which to perform his tin-soldier bit, staring into a hissing lantern,

and it's with apparent great effort that Reis rotates his head a few inches to his right to aim his half-lidded eyes on the unbeckoned soldier standing at the base of the stairs, a body in his arms, and Reis delivers a blink of slow odium before staring back into the low flame, saying, in the rasp of the browbeaten, "Private Gravedigger,"

and though Bagger can't salute while holding the angel, he snaps his heels and woofs with a fanatic's brio, "Sir!," in hopes Reis will notice his revitalized soldierhood and welcome him into the fold, but Reis only says, "Too little, too late,"

and Bagger shakes his head, dried mud flaking from his neck, and objects, "Sir, that's why I'm here, it's not too late, not too late for anything, sir, I have what you need," to which Reis gives a rueful puff of laughter that makes the lantern flame duck, and in doing so discovers his left hand and examines the gleaming leather,

and he says, "In your intellectual free time, Private Gravedigger, while digging potties or sepulchering men, do you wonder what will come of us when this war ends?," a question that bewilders Bagger, since Camp Winn he has thought of little else but his triumphant return to rookery, until only hours ago when an angel brought a dead kid back to life,

and yet Bagger senses the question isn't for him, and, sure enough, Reis peels off his glove, feather-dusts it along his ivory coat, and says, "Some of us do think about it. Some of us have devoted our lives to our country. Lived and bled and died for it, only to live again so we could die again. Such was the marinade in which men like myself were cooked, the promise that our devotion would reap its reward. But it's falderal, Gravedigger. Even those of us gifted with vision cannot carry the day. There is no appreciation for the feigned retreats and ambush attacks of Hannibal, the cunning delays of Fabius, the guileful maneuvers of Turenne. Today's generalship is that of a child with toy soldiers, hurling them into the face of a playmate. I endeavored toward a superior design. I should have known better,"

and Bagger doesn't know what to say, so takes a step closer to assert himself, and Reis cuts a look at him, the swiftest motion the major general's made yet, and now he sees Bagger, really sees him, and makes the corners of his eyes sharp enough to chip away at the gravedigger,

and he says, "And who do they supply me with to execute their blunt stratagems? Men like you. Men afflicted with the European

Disease. Are you familiar with the term, Private Gravedigger?,"
and Bagger is pained, if he could only show Reis what he carries,
so quickly he admits, "No, sir, but,"

and Reis runs over him, "Then permit me a professor's privilege.
The European Disease is more insidious than the Spanish flu. 'Tis
a curious scourge, one that has raced across the continent, soldier
to soldier, debilitating millions with a peculiar feebleness of leg,
the inability to fix bayonets, the disinclination to attack. Sufferers
of this condition show an unwillingness to do anything but sit in
place and plead for more artillery. And these are the men with
whom I am supposed to orchestrate frontal attacks?,"

and Reis gazes at the table before him, upon which lays a cartog-
rapher's map, and as much as Bagger disdains the major general,
he finds the stack of wooden-block battalions poignant, whatever
grand plan Reis had hoped to demonstrate to Pershing, the army
commander had ignored, and though Bagger ought to be delighted,
he needs this overweening asshole, and Reis, though he doesn't
know it, needs Bagger, too,

and Reis picks up one of the blocks and says, "See this? This is
you. You and the other leeches I left in Bois de Fays," and he gives
the block a jeweler's inspection before flinging it to a cobwebbed
shelf, where it gongs against a teakettle, a noise that makes Bagger,
trained on ricocheted bullets, squat low, to which Reis chuckles,

and he says, "I did not expect to see you again, Private Gravedigger.
You come like a wraith. It stirs in me a melancholy notion. That I
expired out there in battle. And somehow went awry, for instead of
opaline gates I have been routed to Lucifer's caverns, and instead
of St. Peter, it is you entrusted with my welcome. I can think of

no other explanation for your appearance. This, by the by, is the sort of insight of which the general they are sending here will be incapable,"

and there it is, confirmation that Reis is being replaced, it only hasn't happened yet, and Bagger feels another press of urgency, he may never get an audience with a new division leader, and so Bagger takes a step that brings him to the map's edge, and that's how he feels, on the edge of the world, but it's an insouciance that makes Reis pull away in affront, Bagger knows this look, he's about to be banished back to the empire of dung, he's got to talk fast,

and so he blurts, "The screaming man wasn't a man,"

and Reis's clenched jaw dislodges in repugnance, and Bagger panics, "It was a . . . let me show you . . . ," to which Reis's brow crashes down, "Do not uncover a dead soldier in my presence!" but Bagger's already pawing through the cape to find the hood, and Reis uses his good arm to push himself to his feet, hollering, "Neurological hospital is too good for you! I'll pin you with a blue ticket, Gravedigger! You will die a pariah!,"

and Bagger's fingertips slip through fabric and graze the softest cheek, a scant touch that nevertheless fills him with the equilibrium of hope, and he takes the hood edge and draws it back, whereupon the dugout's tabernacle of lanterns bows in deference to a brighter master, and Reis's rage melts to butter inside the scintillant splendor,

XXXVI

and there's no way for a menial boot like Bagger to know the insides of a command dugout, these cellars of flickering mystery from which ferment the schemes to bend thousands of men forward or back, but in the angel's light Bagger sees all, a fifteen-by-ten stupefaction of gimcrack luxury, walls of sandbag and hay bale and clay brick, a tracery of defunct electric lights, a field telephone box, a dip pen and inkwell and blotter, a stack of newspapers, shelves of books and manuals, an actual fucking bed on wire fucking springs, and a table beneath red-checked restaurant cloth holding the offerings General Pershing spurned, steaming bread, weeping cheese, and wine bottles, two of which hold candles, the rest holding the drinkable stuff,

and a hand-carved cuckoo clock tailed with weighted chains, probably nabbed from a German hutch, hangs where a taxidermied elk would flaunt its antlers in a hunting lodge, the pendulum going *thuck* with every arc, the secret heart, perhaps, that shuttles blood to its soldier capillaries, and for several seconds *thuck* is the only sound as Reis traces the angel's halo with eyes starbursting in white light,

and Reis whispers, "What is she?" and Bagger, adrift in pride, says in a voice that cracks like a new father's, "An angel, sir,"

and Reis studies, and frowns, and blinks, and asks, "Where did
you find her?" and Bagger replies, "In the field, sir. Caught up
in barbed wire. She fell from the . . . ," and he coughs, a throat of
sand, desperate for that wine bottle, but he's said enough, Reis's
eyes roll to the ceiling that's less than a foot over his head, and to
the heavens beyond,

and Reis's good hand touches his heart, a gesture so unplanned
Bagger finds himself stirred, though, on second glance, he sees
Reis's fingertips play along the medals pinned to his breast and loi-
ter at the infamous space left for the Medal of Honor, and Bagger
feels a tickle of unease, rather like Uncle Sam the shamefly,

and Reis whispers, "Minerva," and Bagger hasn't the faintest idea
who Minerva is, but it can't matter much, he didn't know Effie
Weffie or Naomi Veck or Arno's old lady either, so Bagger chooses
encouragement in hopes it greases the wheels, and nods, and says,
"Minerva, that's right, sir,"

and Reis stands taller, his hand pressed harder over his medal-
fortified heart, and his eyes flick over Bagger's shoulder, checking
to confirm the gas curtain blocks any and all prying eyes, before
returning to the angel, only the angel, Bagger all but forgotten,
though the major general manages half a breathless question,
"Does she . . . What can she . . . ?"

and Bagger nods eagerly, this is what he wants, and gestures his
head at the map table, and Reis's reaction is to snatch up his golden
walking stick and hasten backward to allow Bagger the space to set
her down, something Bagger can't believe, the commander of the

U.S. 43rd, scuttling aside as if he, Lyon Reis, is the ignoble private to Cyril Bagger's lofty superior,

and Bagger gentles the angel upon the map, all the wooden warriors of Europe smothered beneath her, and he takes a tailor's beat to adjust her dress, cape, and hood, comb back her fine copper hair as if in preparation for a photograph,

and he pushes up her sleeves to demonstrate the extent of her skin's radiance, which, doubled and tripled now, zeroes out the bunker's pervading decay, corroded trench tools and soot-blasted gadgets reforged into instruments of deliverance as silvered as papal scepters,

and Bagger says, "She saved us, sir. Me and another private. Lifted us out of the path of a minnie, sir," and he's not sure Reis is listening, the major general circles the angel who follows his movement with an unreadable expression, so Bagger continues, more emphatically, "And Private Veck, sir. You remember. The Negro with the P3. He was going to hurt her and she made, and I know it sounds crazy, sir, but she made the dead stand up, and they stopped him,"

and Reis looms over her, a hand floating near her resplendent face, while his hidden hand, tucked into its coat-sleeve pouch, twitches in longing for the same, "Her helmet," he sighs, an odd couple of words, "is as golden as it ever was,"

and because Reis seems so moved, Bagger feels that way, too, and raises his voice another notch, "And then there's Private Arno, sir. The kid. Well, the kid was killed, sir. Killed dead. But the angel brought him back," though Reis doesn't seem to care, so Bagger inserts the name Reis used before, "Minerva, sir. Minerva brought the kid back to life,"

and this gets through to Reis, he looks at Bagger with pupils pinpricked by coursing rapids of light, he seems lost, but at the same time found, a drowning man taking hold of a sudden buoy, a miracle Bagger's father never got to enjoy, and Reis swallows hard, he needs wine, too, and croaks, "Resurrection. Yes. We could all use a resurrection,"

and Reis breaks away as hard as a snapped rubber band, the heel of his walking stick snapping against floorboards, and when he wheels back around, he looks more like the Lyon Reis that Bagger knows, sharp and shrewd, and in a familiar tone he asks, "She is capable of the impossible, is that so?,"

and Bagger distrusts the question but can only respond with a nod, and Reis draws an inhale through his nostrils for what must be fifteen seconds, face pink, ears purple, left hand curling into a fist, and he says with trembling resolve, "Then the impossible is what I shall request,"

and before Bagger can warn off this request, explain what happened when Veck made an equivalent demand, Reis hurls his coat to the ground, revealing the polished and holstered Colt .45 implicit to officers, as well as the sleeve tailored to snug his withered arm, a jolt to Bagger, it resembles a flaccid cock in prophylactic rubber, and then, accelerating the shocks, Reis grips the left shoulder of his blouse and rips it downward, a moist tear, and there's his concave chest, his baby-fat tummy, and one more tug and Reis's right arm flops free, nothing like the ham-hock stumps amputees tote back home, this arm resembles a thick noodle, milk white from lack of sun, glossy as wet clay, dimpled at a neonatal elbow and ending in a flipper with one-inch vestigial fingers, far less terrible than the mutations imagined by Butcher Bird busybodies, but far more terrible, too, for Bagger need only glance at it to know it's the parasite that has fed off Lyon Reis his entire life,

and the revealed arm reveals Reis, ego stripped as bare as his torso, every button and fold and cuff and trinket rendered irrelevant, he's the spindly, off-center, poorly assembled human male General Pershing knew him to be, and his hungry left hand claws at the air, wanting, needing,

and Reis orders, or urges, or pleads, or sobs, "Give me my arm. Give me the arm God took from me. How hard I've worked for those who only see me as incomplete. If my career must end here, give me the arm with which I might forge a new one. That might make a woman look upon me with something other than dread. If you really are Minerva, bring to me that which I deserve,"

and shit, fuck, the major general's weeping, nothing could make Bagger squirmier, back when the 2nd Battalion was repelled at Cuisy by mustard gas, Bagger couldn't even look at the soldiers who cried carbolic tears, and even forced himself to laugh at how they jumped into his latrine ditch to splash sewage into their burning eyes,

and that's Reis now, chest hitching like a well bucket on a rope, skin ruddy except the right arm, the accursed right arm, still custard white, still flexing happily like a dreaming puppy, and when nothing happens, Reis's face takes a magenta plunge and his lips curl into his mouth, over his teeth, inchworming toward self-ingestion, and Bagger thinks Reis might tear the arm off himself, a club with which to thrash the angel,

and so Bagger looks at the angel and whispers, "Please," and hears Reis gag through spitty slobberings of tears, and Bagger hisses, "Please, do what he says," and Reis's coughs sawblade through his humiliation, while the angel's eyes go from Reis to Bagger, she's the map now, and her shifting geography asks Bagger if this is really what he wants, and he nods, this time it's her own skin the angel needs to save,

and the angel closes her eyes,

and every lantern in the dugout curtsies for half a second, and the angel's white light pulses, silent, incandescent, and too much for human eyes, Bagger peels away, covering his face, and from across the table comes the gamy reek of slaughter or birth, and a wet sound, almost flatulent, like venison mashed through a grinder, noises quickly overtaken by Reis's shriek, he's the shrieker at last,

and in the maelstrom of wincing and yawning flame, Bagger sees a thing he wishes he could scrub from his eyeballs, Reis's doughy little arm flayed open as if by scalpels, the eggy epidermis, the yellow pudding of fat, the chocolate red of toneless muscle, the skin undulating like a bedsheet over cockroaches,

and then the muscles unthread as if guided by invisible fishhooks, the underdeveloped radius and ulna unsheathed like two bamboo stalks, at which point the unstrapped muscles ripple like ribbons while the tiny hand swells until it explodes, an orderly explosion, each scroll of skin, cartilage, and tissue arrayed like tools in a toolbox,

and Bagger gags, how in heaven could any miracle be so repellent,

and with the arm unraveled, sectioned, anatomized, and exsanguinated, a biologic basket-weaving begins, knots of tissue slugging down from Reis's shoulder like snake-swallowed mice, a journey that, per Reis's moan, is unspeakably painful, before the bone, larger now and stinking of sweet marrow, is enveloped by nets of nerve, knits of muscle, needlepoints of skin, all of which start pink and finespun but thicken and darken until the skin fuses smooth like melted rubber and arm hairs blade upward, a garden at breakneck growth,

and the angel, simple as that, opens her eyes,

XXXVII

and once again the lanterns are as steady as potted flowers, the angel's light a sunny canopy in the underground box, and Bagger's canine panting is overcome only by Reis's, the major general viscous with sweat, face a slick mask of bug-eyed incredulity as he slowly, slowly takes the right arm held away from his body like a torch and brings it nearer, his look of terror lightening, smoothing, going slack,

and, for the first time in his life, Lyon Reis makes a fist with his right hand, and wrist bones gristle, knuckles pop, veins extrude, tendons articulate, and Reis is breathless as he opens the fist and stares into the empty palm as if it holds the universe, and it just might,

and Reis's head snaps up hard enough to fling sweat, and he stares at the angel with a garbled expression that might break into anything, shock or disgust or rapture, and after a pregnant second, his face delivers the most unsettling possibility of all,

and it's a grin, a sinuous, gleeful grin that taints Reis's eyes with a jubilant jaundice, this man Bagger believed was incapable of anything but embittered scoffs, a bubbly giggle that percolates into a toddler peal, a spill of broken glass, so sharp Bagger flinches away, and Reis giggles, "You," glancing at Bagger before returning his admiration to his refurbished hand, and it's the hand he talks to now, "You have brought me this incredible gift,"

and as rare as it was for Bagger to be in a frontal trench when an officer rang the gas klaxon, he still viscerally feels the routine, the reflex fumbling for his mask, the worry that gas will sperm its way into his crevices, and that's what Bagger hears now, *clang clang clang*, he brought the angel here for a reason, to help the army if not the world, but there's no hint of any of that in the word Reis emphasized most, the word *me*,

and something, maybe Bagger's heart, tells him to abort, snatch up the angel and race up the stairs, find a trench ladder, run away, he was a goddamn idiot to bring a being like this to man like this, but Bagger deliberates the extra second it takes Reis to approach the table, thread his newly muscled arm beneath the angel's neck and lift her into the crook of his capable elbow,

and Reis tries to suppress his gaiety, being a combat visionary requires sobriety, after all, and he says, "From the start of this war, men have spoken of wonder weapons. Planes phased with interrupter gear to fire through propellors. U-boats that hunt like sea serpents. Tanks that spit bullets like dragons spit fire. No one saw chlorine gas coming before the Germans opened those cylinders at Ypres. As no one, Private Gravedigger, will see the coming of this, the most wondrous weapon of all. My Minerva,"

and Bagger's gut cramps, he's made a blunder all right, the worst blunder of his life, if not the worst blunder of the war, and he stutters, "She's, no, sir, she's a healer, I told you what she can, listen, sir, she could *end* it, she could end the entire,"

and it's pathetic how Reis talks right over him, he became Private Gravedigger again the moment he handed over this miracle in flesh, and the major general talks to himself now, himself or a full house of imagined admirers, "General Pershing just described to me how the Great War crawls toward its end. A matter of weeks, sayeth our vaunted leader, if not days. The Germans are pushed to the Heights of the Meuse. The Hindenburg Line will shatter and they will be chased all the way to Luxembourg. The world about to phoenix from the ashes will belong to the Allies, and America will soar highest of all,"

and Reis bends to the angel, a Valentino pose, though Bagger wonders if the real target of his adoration is his naked right arm, and he says, "And yet Pershing wishes to replace me. Wishes the ruination of my career. For what purpose? Humiliation. Duly, duly, General Pershing, I am humiliated. Only how great, I ask, can a war be that lasts but four years? Look to the Peloponnesian War. The Punic Wars. The six hundred years of the Crusades! Those were wars. Wars given space for proper prosecution. Never again will I be offered a war. This is my only chance. To show them how they underestimated Lyon Reis. Oh, I shall show them. I will let them pin their medal upon me before I make them kneel,"

and it's baffling how Bagger's mind ties it all together, but it does, he need only picture the medal Reis desires, the five-pointed star around a woman in golden profile, hair flowing from beneath her helmet, a likeness Bagger recognizes thanks to a bit of schoolhouse trivia, and it's Minerva, goddess of war, who is imprinted on the Medal of Honor, the only woman Reis has ever lusted after, finally that gap over his heart can be filled, and maybe his actual heart as well, filled with black blood, the commingled grout of good and evil,

and Bagger wonders if this consummation would have been better left to Goodspeed, the angel as freakshow capitalism, or Popkin, the angel as a body upon which men could demonstrate domination, or Veck, the angel employed to scorch the earth of injustice, an apocalyptic turn, but preferable to the rule of one nation, indivisible, with liberty and justice for all, so long as *all* is Major General Reis,

and Reis laughs, full-throated, the laugh of a groom swirling his bride in post-nuptial waltz, which is exactly what happens next, he lifts the angel, glorying in his right arm's effortless might, and away he whirls, his Colt .45 flapping in its holster, the angel's blue cape rising like a petticoat at a barn dance, Reis's leather-gloved paw swallowing the angel's fine-boned fingers as they spin across the dugout,

and Bagger would not have believed one arm more or less could result in such a change, but the evidence is in a three-step sway as steady as the cuckoo's pendulum, Bagger's a fine enough waltzer, it helps pass the time on riverboats, but Reis is poetry, a dashing master of the chassé, hover corte, hairpin, oversway, and developpé, and what's more, dancing for two, manhandling the angel into each position and kicking her feet to where they ought to be,

and Reis talks as he dances, "End the war? No, no. Prolong it. Lengthen it. Draw it out as one does a waltz, until the only cartridges we have left are scrounged from the dead, the only food our own boiled belts, until the Reichstag has our armies inside its closing fist and all hope is lost," which Reis illustrates by bending his torso in the feminine lily, a position of yielded conquest,

and it's only to pivot on the next one-count, reversing positions, the angel dipped low, halo scraping dirt, "Only then do I reveal my hand," Reis crows, "the wonder weapon I alone wield, and with which I win the war and save the world," and he kisses her, hard, as the position might suggest, and the angel doesn't resist, forcing Bagger to wonder if she might accept this plot, even consent to it, and his viscera festers in jealousy, all the times he rescued this ungrateful bitch,

and yet if Bagger could speak, if Reis would allow it, if the angel would accept it, he would plead, *Don't do anything he says, he's talking about sabotaging the war, turning a victory that's weeks away into years more of gruesome attrition, the deaths of millions, all so he can be the hero rewarded with his country's highest honor, though even that might not be high enough, emperor of the world will be the only role he accepts with a wonder weapon such as you loaded at his side,*

and Reis disconnects the kiss, the angel's face marred with the profanity of a sleazy smudge, and swings her around, only this time he miscalculates, either his right arm has some learning to do or the angel is upset by the kiss and no longer playing along, either way, she's slung too far and the inexperienced Reis overcompensates, and they end up colliding, the tasteful distance between them collapsed, hip bones crashing,

and Reis hisses and pulls away, and the angel drops to the floor like a haversack, and Reis holds his right hand before him, it has suffered its first big-boy wound, a nick on the palm, a check mark of blood wrought by an angelic fingernail, perhaps, though who knows, maybe it was something beyond an earthbound man's perception,

and Reis pants from the dancing and chuckles at the cut before bringing it to his lips and sucking it clean, harder and wetter than the kiss, and he gives the angel a jailer's leer, "So the lady has claws, does she? Tut-tut. I was hoping we could be friendly. It is of no consequence. The Adversary will learn to be friendly," and the way he says the word, *Adversary*, feels truer than anything said about the angel thus far,

and that's because she's lovely, and unassuming, and perfect, and yet, and yet, and yet, just look at the blood in her wake,

and Reis checks Bagger for the first time in minutes, making Bagger realize that he hissed, too, at the dancers' collision, and Reis frowns, displeased to find an observer to the bloodshed of man and virgin, the wrong one deflowered, and directs his eyes at the stairs and says, "I am obliged, Private Gravedigger. Your contribution to the Allied effort will be remembered. That will be all,"

and now Bagger knows what Arno felt when dismissed at the dugout entrance, *You hear me, little puke?*, the sensation of being cloven from a family you helped create, but what else can Bagger do, he's the one who brought the angel here, he can hardly attack Reis, a division commander with two strapping arms, and besides, Bagger's thirsty, starving, and needs to sleep for a million years, which is exactly how long it might take for Reis's new world order to come and go, and so Bagger salutes, and wonders how he ended up weaker leaving the dugout than when he entered, Cyril Bagger used to be a man, or so he believes, but now he's something else, and he stretches his neck to try and see the angel one last time, but she, in her cape-and-dress puddle, faces the other way, having given up on him, same as everyone else,

XXXVIII

and Bagger sleeps in straw munched by horses that will soon be dead, breathing the odor of moldy oats and uric acid, his helmet hugged like a stuffed toy, stubble cottoned with crumbs of crusty bread and gut sloshing with non-muddy water, all tortured thoughts erased, he makes sure of it, that nudge of horse muzzle is the turning hips of Marie-Louise,

and he awakes to thumps and slaps, echoes of sex, which he dreamed of all night, Marie-Louise disrobing, and disrobing, endless layers shucked until she was nothing at all, but after he swipes straw from his face, he locates the source of the sounds, soldiers in dawn's gray putty using rifle butts to bash frozen extremities back to life, as if angry at the apostate feet that led them here, the treasonous arms that carry the weapons that make them targets,

and there's a rhythm to the self-battery that inspires admiration in the sleepy Bagger, it's not quite right to compare the soldiers to flagellating monks, those idiot vandals of their own bodies, these soldiers are more like farmers, rising in cold fog, same old, same old, the creak of their bones answering the bickering of birds and the umbrage of unmilked cows, while silver hoarfrost uplifts the gutted terrain into something you could paint and hang over the hearth,

and though both France and Iowa are filled with farms, Bagger accepts they represent a life he'll never know, scoundrels like him belong alone, it's part of the deal, but for this agrarian, frost-muffled instant he can pretend, what's the harm, that these are his farmhands, his horses, his equipment, his land, his morning, his planet, his eternity, all distilled to a drop of honey sunlight he might yet catch with the tip of his tongue,

and it's this same sun blading men's eyes that prevents them from seeing the telltale streaks in the sky, so when a wall of clay bounds upward from a trench three hundred yards away, it seems to happen spontaneously, the earth upchucking an epochal breakfast, though the tiny bodies of soldiers flung wiggling into the air mark this as Hun handiwork,

and it means Jerry has both caught up and caught the 43rd un-awares,

and the crackling booms of curtain fire hit seconds later, like a boot camp prank of palms slapped over Bagger's ears, and he rocks up-ward, gasping, horses overhead neighing and rearing, and Bagger rolls away, hooves can crush skulls, and when he's face up, the whole regiment has appeared out of nowhere, five thousand men scrambling like ants from a booted anthill,

and soldiers strap on bandoliers as they leap into reserve trenches, men toss other men Springfields and Enfields and Garands, knights in olive drab storm through craters with Vickers guns strapped to their backs, a team of artillerists wheel out an eighteen-pounder, engineers emplace bridges over trench tops, and staff sprint across them to string cable to telephones already being shouted into by officers, cooks drop breakfast tins in favor of rum rations, medics raise aid posts and dash off with stretchers, never enough,

and Bagger, to his breathless shock, is among them, finally among them, racing to a front carapaced by mud and straw, the horizon lit by wrath's votive fires, ground sliding like calving glaciers, ghostly afterimages stamped onto his retinas from staccato blasts, all of which resolve into the shape of the angel, she's probably still in that dugout, and as bad as it is that Reis has her, letting the Krauts get her would be worse, so Bagger's got to do what he can to protect her, and that means fight, finally fight,

and someone, from somewhere, throws him a rifle, cold matte black in his hands, the weight nearly sinks him, gotta be twenty pounds, so heavy it's got its own handle, Bagger glances down as he runs, holy shit, it's a BAR, a Browning automatic, the sons of bitches finally arrived, the thing's practically a myth, shoots a Springfield's .30-caliber round but from a twenty-round box mag, it's a mobile machine gun and he, Private Bagger, inveterate coward, has got one,

and he bellows, top of his lungs, can't hear it over the barraging drums of a new round of Jerry's shells but sure the fuck feels it, larynx shredding in the force of his war cry, holy shit, Cyril Bagger's got a war cry, same as the other boys, it expels from his guts with the same skyward explosion as the missiled earth, he's bloodthirsty, he'll do anything he needs to protect she who needs protecting,

and a piece of him, a tiny, Arno-sized splinter, knows there's something awry with all this, something awry with *him* as he fuses into the bloodlust funnel, the precise act he's always avoided, individuality swapped for the exhilarating namelessness of being a ball bearing inside a mechanism, he's succumbed, but lord, don't it feel good, ain't it the easiest way to bash past regret and shame, feels so much better to lose himself to a mass, to dilute into a flood of fury,

and Bagger vaults the reserve trenches, grunts with helmets askew and whistle-blowing officers flashing beneath him, though his eyes are on the front, a hundred yards off now, great quilts of smoke unfurling across No Man's Land to divulge screaming Squareheads charging the 2nd Battalion, they haven't seen a charge like this in weeks, it's as if Jerry's already heeding Reis's plan of providing a few more years of Yank slaughter,

and the support trench yawns open and Bagger jumps into the rabble, no telling the company, Bagger doesn't care and neither do they, the gravedigger has traded his shovel for a BAR and that's good enough, a whoop goes up and Bagger's ragged heart sings, it's not too late for him after all, boys are slapping him on the back, shoving him up the line, and he can't think of anything grander, now *this*, this is how to die,

and he's into the frontline trenches, men leaping onto dirt parapets to lay out defensive fire, and there's an officer gesturing Bagger up a ladder, a prime spot, and he follows orders, just watch him follow orders, doesn't feel so bad to be a cog in a machine, to accept you're a hinge and your only job is to do that, to hinge,

and he lodges himself on the top step, elbows driven into red clay, the soundscape yawping wide, a thunder of Roman conquest, boots in beating ritual, muzzles cracking, shells pealing, bayonets clashing, the first wave of Germans close enough to fence, and more than that, to stab, Bagger hears the raw-meat squish, the Revelations of the Bishop's fiercest sermons, the scourge of frogs and lice and flies, of water into blood, of pestilence, of boils, of hail, of unbreathable darkness,

and *whomp*, the trench to Bagger's right is throttled into a tidal wave of black dirt, Jerry hurling grenades, *whomp*, the trench to his left convulses like a gagging throat, men left without jaws, without scalps, without faces,

and it's all the more reason for Bagger to fire and kill, he plants the BAR's bipod into the mud, kill, the gun feels like a strong new arm, how Reis must feel, you get yourself a new arm, you goddamn use it, kill, he grips the gas tube, kill, whole body longing, kill, for the pulverizing thrust of the initial spray of lead, kill, the jellification of his biceps, kill, the tintinnabulation of his bones, kill, he tries to line up the foresight amid concussions buffeting his eyeballs, kill, and curls his right index finger, no, not even his, it's Uncle Sam's, the finger belongs to the shamefly, and he loops it over the trigger, kill,

and but one hair of a second before he squeezes, he's yanked down, as if by a shark, and his very first shot of the war goes wild, rounds spitting into the wolfen mat of smoke, fog, grease, and blood, and then he's on his back in six inches of water, staring up into the darting cardinals of traded fire, mind in cyclone, either he fell or got shot,

and a soldier's head eclipses the destroyed dawn, a face of filth claw-marked by the tears of smoke-stung eyes, Bagger instinctively hates this doughboy, the war machine unto which Bagger gave himself to must be built of anonymous men, and this face isn't anonymous at all, it shouts, "Bagger! You can't! You promised her!,"

and of course it's Lewis Arno, the kid the unluckiest of pennies, always turning up even after Bagger hurled that penny off the highest available cliff, and Bagger has the urge to smash the BAR into the kid's nose, he'll show the brat, he's here to kill, kill, kill, but the kid's more balanced than Bagger and finds the automatic rifle first and throws it away,

and Bagger screams, "Fuck!" and the goddamn kid slaps him, a rifle crack of its own, and Bagger gasps, and the kid grabs his drabs and slams him into the water, mud sliming over both their faces, and screams, "You promised her you wouldn't kill!," and Bagger disinters his arms from grave muck to strangle the boy's puny neck,

and the kid's slapping, pounding arms wind around Bagger's shoulders, extracting him from mire, embracing him, punching little fists of fury into Bagger's back like the tank directions he kicked into Bagger's kidneys, instructions on what to do, where to go, and though Arno's orders defy those of Uncle Sam, they have the timbre of truth, and Bagger's arms of strangulation hug the kid right back,

and he sputters into Arno's ear, "I'm sorry, I'm sorry," not even sure which transgression he's apologizing for, there's been so many in such a short, ugly time, and though he knows what this clinch looks like to any doughboy who spies them behind the hailstorm of detonated dirt, two chickenshits holding each other in the last chickenshit seconds of their chickenshit lives, he doesn't care, he's worked with chickens before and they happen to be Earth's bravest beasts,

and Arno shouts, "We gotta save her!," and Bagger holds tight, men exploding all over, and screams, "She's not your mom, kid!," and the kid yelps, like he's been stuck, and screams, "We still gotta save her! You've got to save her, Bagger!," and Bagger sobs, "Why?," and the kid hollers, baritone now, suddenly a man, "Because she's *yours* more than *ours*," and Bagger pulls back and stares at the kid, who nods and says, "Or you've always been *hers*,"

and the feeling isn't confusion, or even surprise, it's astonishment, for he knows the words as truth the second he hears them, they answer the question he never had the wherewithal to ask, it was never Bagger who found the angel, it was the angel who found Bagger,

and the astonishments mount, that first mortar blast back in Bois de Fays, the one that should have killed him, maybe it *did* kill him, maybe he dwelt in the razor world of death long enough for the angel to notice him before the inadvertent resuscitation of a corpse thrown atop him brought him back to life, and from that moment, he and the angel have been in unbroken contact, everything Bagger has wanted, the angel has tried to deliver, and what he's wanted has been violence, just think back to Rochambeau, the symbols he used to win,

and how Goodspeed fell to scissors, and was scissored by shrapnel,

and Popkin fell to rock, and was buried in the rock of a falling wall,

and Veck fell to paper, and perished after finding Reis's paper note, and Bagger, why, he was the one to kill all three, he was the major general shaking his walking stick, each Rochambeau victory translated by the loyal angel as a direct order to kill each loser, kill them in a specific way, and though Veck died believing he could bend the angel to his will, that was a fool's mistake, *I am the sword in the hand*, she said, and it has been Bagger's hand the whole time,

XXXIX

and with Uncle Sam roaring, no way in hell can Bagger maze the path back to Reis's bunker, but again the kid proves he's a born runner, he weaves around and between the legs of fighting men, and nuzzles deep into clay when shells rock the earth, and jumps straight through fires crepitating with scorching oil, and climbs half-buried corpses whose limbs extend like branches,

and Bagger focuses on Arno's dervish body through blood, sweat, smoke, and soot, he can't risk taking his eyes off the kid because Bagger defeated him in Rochambeau, too, same as the others, only he can't remember what symbol he threw to beat Arno, and if he can't picture the symbol, he can't predict what kind of death is barreling toward the kid at locomotive speed,

and he collides with Arno, maybe that's how the kid dies, a blow to the back of the head, but being thrown to his knees doesn't stop Arno from pointing, and Bagger will be damned, there's the stairwell to Reis's dugout not ten feet away, behind a scrim of dirt thickening from embeddeding bullets,

and Bagger grabs the kid by the scruff and shouts, "Stay here!," which makes the kid glower like he could kill Bagger for pulling this shit again, there's no keeping the kid back a second time, nor is there time to argue it, so Bagger bolts ahead and nearly somersaults down the stairwell, the stairs took a direct hit and are a pile of matchsticks, but enough solid wood clings to the left side for Bagger to prance down, metal cleats pinging rusty nails,

and the gas curtain's on fire, so Bagger tears it down and stomps it into the dirt, then scans the dugout, blinking in the dark, it's chaos, all four walls tilted inward, the map table knelt with a broken leg, the map itself crumpled and doused in ink, the wee wooden blocks scattered just like the companies they represent,

and Bagger kicks aside rolling wine bottles and ducks beneath the drooping wooden ceiling that drains muddy water like Popkin's drool, but the place is vacant, "No," he says, there's no stopping Arno's death if he can't find the angel and demand she stop it, "No!," and he hurls aside Reis's chair, "No!," and spikes the cuckoo clock, somehow still going *thuck*, boot-heeling it to splinters, "No! No! No! No!,"

and Arno's lost it, too, he's wrestling a wooden trunk like it's a bear, and Bagger crabs over to join in, eager for something to punish, only to realize Arno's trying to wrench the lock off, knuckles bloodied from the effort, and the kid's insight gusts through him, the trunk's plenty big enough for a woman, and Bagger presses his ear to a dowel and blocks out the war to listen,

and there's the verseless chorus, *Save me,*

and this time, the words invoke Bishop Bagger, who once preached how angels pulled double duty as God's protectors, flanking God in a space called the Mercy Seat, a site of unfathomable terror, where only the truest hearts dared plead for mercy, a higher-stakes gamble than anything proffered aboard a riverboat, but what bothered Bagger as a child was the notion hidden inside the story, the notion that God *needed* protecting, which, by extension, posited that God could be hurt, even killed,

and hold on, now, if Bagger's been drafted to protect God's protector, simple logic holds that he, then, is the most powerful of all, maybe all humans have the valence to overthrow their creator and establish a better world, all they have to do is join together to topple God's ramparts, which might mean war is God's defensive tactic, slabs of meat earth's factions can tussle over while the Mercy Seat goes unchallenged,

and so Bagger elbows the kid aside and kicks the lock from the bottom, drives his heel into it from the top, up, down, up, down, while the dugout walls teeter and the girders overhead shit soil, and the lock yields whine by whine, black steel unplugging from pale wood, and then tubes of brilliant light shoot through new holes, and Arno eeks and undoes the hasps, and Bagger fumbles for the slats and hurls off the lid,

and let there be light, and let there be blue cape, and let there be red dress, and let there be halo, and also that sulky comma between the angel's eyebrows, as if it took Bagger longer to rescue her than she would have preferred, and Bagger apologizes, "Ma'am," and begins to unpack her, tougher than it looks, it's barbaric how Reis smushed her inside,

and then she's in his arms, where she belongs, she fits so well, and Bagger tucks her face into his chest, tenting her precious light, yet feels no canine jealousy when Arno encircles her by the waist, tears slipping, lips tapping a pattern that looks like *Mommy, Mommy*, and despite the prospect of another shell burying them alive, Bagger allows himself a few seconds to dream, one family lost, one family found, perfect for this broken shard of time,

and pain shatters across Bagger's face,

and he's on his back with no memory of getting there, vision hot and knotted like his face is cinched in barbed wire, and he feels foolish until agony shrills from his cheekbone like a scream, he brings both hands, empty of anything angelic, to his face, and finds slippery blood and a soft, weeping tear in his cheek, his pinkie tip slides inside it, could be a bullet hole, could be he's been shot in the fucking face,

and he rolls to all fours and a liter of liquid shifts in his mouth, and, aghast, he opens wide and a gallon of blood dumps to the floor, along with three teeth, cracking hard and rolling funny like his weighted dice, except these bones roll from the toss of a player even sneakier,

and hawking and spitting, Bagger looks up at a looming Lyon Reis, devolved into the negative of a French mime, his face blacked with soot but red eyes still stabbing, stabbing, and he's got the walking stick, the gold plating gone marmalade with Bagger's blood, in the grip of his right hand, his new right hand, and Bagger, unable to speak through blood soup, holds up a hand to ask the major general to wait,

and Reis does not wait, he strikes again with the wonder weapon of his right arm, all the gears of his body finally working in factory synchrony, and the stick cutlasses through air too fast for Bagger to track, he only hears the whistle and feels the wind quiver his eyelids, one second Bagger's outstretched hand is whole and a blink later, his index, middle, and ring finger are snapped flat against the back of his hand, three metacarpals poked through the skin, all smaller bones demolished,

and somewhere Arno's snarling like a little mutt, but Bagger's lost inside white wallops of pain and doesn't see when Reis swings the golden stick a third time, only hears the same whistle again and feels the same breeze, and on instinct retracts his demolished hand into his chest, one more hit will rip the fingers clean off,

and so he takes the blow in the eye and that's it, the lamp goes out, sure as a shattered bulb, his left eye gone, the pain a strange electricity in the fat of his brain, though worse is the crisp, alien feel of air inside an open socket and the syrupy crawl of vitreous humor down his face, some of it dribbling into the hole Reis knocked through his cheek, all of which tells Bagger that this is how he dies, the eggshell obliteration of every single piece of his body,

and Bagger waits, but the final strike doesn't come, so he spends time choking, the imbroglio of his sinuses full of blood, he gags and strangles and retches, and tries to catch it, like Father Muensterman once palmed his puke, but the vile potage ends up in his finger wounds, now he's dying of his own poison, if he hasn't been poison all along, a lying, cheating, stealing, walking bottle of arsenic,

and his ears pick up the sounds of a struggle, he wants to know what kind, but must first relearn how to see, his field of view is halved, all depth flattened into a sketch by an artist obsessed with the color brown, and there, brushed into the background, two familiar figures frolic, and the first is Arno, spider-monkeyed around the angel, trying to keep hold of her through his full weight, and the second is Reis, who has the angel by her wrist and is pulling her with madness and might, he's liable to detach the angel's arm from its socket, while his other arm, the new one, bludgeons the kid with the walking stick, the red leeches of welts erupting across Arno's skin, his hair raspberry with blood, blood fluming from a forehead gash, blood spouting from an ear, the kid's about to be killed, no third chances for Lazarus,

and yet the heroic brat doesn't let up, he levers a boot heel into a floorboard crevice and leans the opposite direction, a tug-of-rope for the fate of the world,

and all the while, Reis squeals, *"Minerva is mine!,"*

and Bagger plants his good hand into his own jellied blood, curls a leg under him, and sways, or else it's the dugout swaying, about to collapse, and he pistons his thighs, by some miracle his legs still working, and he's up, somehow up, forehead batting the boards that dangle from the ceiling, salty spit eddying in the chasm of his three lost teeth, each gasp crackling like a straw at the bottom of a drink,

and Bagger's bones sling back into their sockets like he's made of pool cues and billiard balls, his left foot lands and the world slants leftward, same routine on his right, like he's on the observation deck of the Lusitania, trying to reach his father in time to save him, and if there wasn't a war lusting overhead, Reis would hear the hiss of Bagger's sliding feet and the splat of his sleeting blood, but as it is, he closes the distance unnoticed, and there on the floor, right behind the tug-of-ropers, lies the Model 1911 Colt .45 that Reis wears on his belt, incredibly it has fallen free, perhaps bungled while trying to point it at Arno, a black steel beauty, the slide already pulled back, the recoil spring tight, aching to empty its seven-cartridge mag,

and Bagger doesn't believe the gun's really there, must be a trick of one-eyed vision, until he drops to a knee and picks it up, ice cold, scapula smooth, redolent of mulled wine, and anchor heavy, it's a struggle to lift with a sprained right wrist, but also a palpable joy, the textured butt in perfect union with his calloused palm, the half-moon trigger another match for the crease in his index finger, and the Colt's steel freeze creeps up his hand's bones, wrist bones, and onward, a whole new arm to rival Reis's,

and quickly the steel undergirds Bagger's whole body, he's no man anymore and he's sure as hell not made of dough, he's a .45-caliber tool built for a single purpose,

and he rises without pain because he's solid metal, and finds Reis has nearly taken full possession of the angel, Arno's a mallard color, warted in bruises, bathed in blood, yet still clinging to the angel's legs, prepared to die before giving her up,

and Bagger wonders if he'll be able to line the V of the .45's sight with only one eye, but at this range aim shouldn't matter, he extends his arm and points the Colt at the back of Reis's skull, not two feet away, and Bagger feels a grin, October air burning through the hole in his cheek, into the abscess of his missing teeth, he's eager, it turns out, for the symphony of broken bone and splattered brains, and echoes of his promise pelt him like attacking gulls, *You must promise*, oh fuck, *never to take another's life*, fuck fuck, *for as long as you live*, the angel said. *If you fail in this promise*, fuck this, *a catastrophe beyond imagination*, not fucking now, *will consume your entire world*, and Bagger's grin wilts into a toddler's frown, it's not fair, the vow must be voided, a few strikes more and Arno will be killed,

and with his single-eyed vision screwing into black vignette, Bagger bellows in a voice mangled into unintelligibility, but of course the angel understands all, *"HELP ME! PLEASE! I DON'T KNOW WHAT TO DO!,"* a cry not too different, after all, from *Save me,*

and the reply comes from the Argonne and beyond, the world and its peaceable creatures, not quite extinct, the lion's roar, the wolf's bay, the robin's call, the puma's growl, the frog's croak, the dolphin's click, the bee's buzz, the elephant's trumpet, the grasshopper's rasp, the snake's rattle, the monkey's chatter, the antelope's grunt, the alligator's hiss, the bat's squeak, the cicada's chirp, the deer's bleat, the donkey's bray, the hawk's screech, the elk's bugle, the goose's honk, the horse's nicker, the lemur's whoop, the leopard's snarl, the mosquito's whine, the owl's hoot, the pig's snort, the pigeon's coo, the raven's caw, the seal's bark, the songbird's warble, the turkey's gobble, the boar's grumble, the zebra's yip, the whale's song, and the chicken's buck, oh, the emphasis of the chicken, prodded by the sharpest of gaffs,

and together, you could call it a shriek,

XL

and stop,

and what stops is the whole shebang, war's babel severed sharply enough to produce a pop as dry as a desert thunderclap, leaving Bagger gasping in the hush, all movement stopped, too, everything fixed in upheaval, one arm-length board fallen from the ceiling just hanging there midair, clods of dirt, too, suspended like fruit from an earthen tree, even smoke hovers like giant cobwebs intricate in turmoil and mystification,

and Reis, too, has stopped, body petrified, the last strike of his walking stick undelivered, and cautiously, suspiciously, Bagger lowers the Colt and tiptoes around Reis, it's like the man's trapped in amber, regal face fatted into rolls of arterial sausage, red eyes protuberant and glassy, the ribbons of spit between his jaws turned into translucent stalagmites and his coughed beads of spit strung up like floating pearls,

and Bagger's eye catches something else and he looks straight up and finds the entire dugout roof in mid-downfall, a vortex of lumber and clay and soil and roots that, ten feet up, peeks into the outer world, Bagger spies a fringe of barbed wire up there, the sideways wheel of a wagon, a puffy artillery streak like a keloid scar, and a red aircraft faraway and perfectly still,

and Bagger shivers with the awe of cheated death, the men down here oblivious to the cave-in about to bury them,

and he shuffles away from the overhead hole, better safe than sorry, and turns to Lewis Arno, in hopes the kid will blink back at him in shared wonder, but Arno's as deadlocked as Reis, teeth bared in frozen agony, each cut and bruise on his head, neck, shoulders, and arms more hideous as a still life, the flaps of skin, the exposed collarbone, the kid was being ripped apart,

and only then does Bagger notice the angel is gone,

and he whirls, he's lost her again, but no, she's behind him, standing on her own two feet and watching him, everything coy, amused, or dreamy about her turned as sharp as an entrenching tool, her arms dangled like readied weapons, chin lowered, chest forward, lioness ribs expanding, legs in the stance of a dauntless boxer,

and the silence stretches thin, her disappointment, his anxious panting, the pressure building, until abruptly the angel moves, striding at him, so much poise and vigor that Bagger recoils, he can't help it, he's a low beast and she's the huntress, look at the rolling strut of her hips under the red dress, the flick of the blue cape off her swinging elbows, she looks like she could end this war by simply glaring into the faces of the kaiser, Ludendorff, Hindenburg, the whole Reichstag lot, until they begged for clemency,

and this reveals to Bagger the upsetting truth, that every quality the angel has so far displayed, the meekness and mildness, the lameness and languor, has been an act, and she stops in front of him, and he withers, he can't hold her gaze, even though he's held her, carried her, slept beside her, all he can do now is look at her feet, remarkably clean for this landscape of offal and ooze,

and Bagger covers his face with his hands, one floppy of finger, the other clinging to the pistol, and doubles over enough to feel the remnants of his left eye drip out, which tells him all of this is real,

and he whimpers, "I didn't know," and her skeptical grunt turns Bagger back into the whippersnapper scolded before the congregation for horseplaying in a pew, and his face, ablaze in injury, burns blacker in disgrace, he's bowing now, begging, "I mean, I knew, I knew you were, I knew you had, I knew you could," but he's unable to finish a thought, thoughts don't matter in this oblivion of pure sensation,

and when Bagger dares peek again, the angel has him trapped in the same glare, but she's also holding out her right hand, palm up, and he doesn't know what else to do, so he places his left hand there, the three busted fingers dangling in three different directions, and it does, in fact, hurt when she folds her hand over his, it's all goddamn real,

and then they are rising, that's real, too, Bagger looks down and the floorboards, jumbled with detritus and laked with blood, grow smaller and smaller, so he looks up and finds that he and the angel are moving through the hole in the roof, into the cold loam channel blasted out by some explosive, the stony subsoil, the greasy clay, the weeping mud, it's strangely gratifying to understand the trenches at the level of the rats that own them, and then Bagger is born unto a battleground turned epic diorama, a square mile of toy soldiers staged in poses more disturbing than can be purchased at the store, bayonets through chests, bodies dragging satchels of their own guts, tiny faces etched in horror, as well as giant bags of smoke as motionless as mountain buttes, mortars hanging like coconuts, rounds of machine-gun bullets gathered midair like strands of fish eggs,

and right below Bagger, the boys of the 2nd Battalion are arranged like mannequins, look, there's Sergeant DiStefano, an ersatz stretcher bearer tilting at the field hospital, neck cords like rope, there's Captain Greisz, dragging an absconder trenchward at such velocity that neither of his boots touch dirt, there's Major Chester, battalion honcho, mouth ovaled against a telephone, photo-flashed in the act of taking a bullet to the heart, the ejected blood like the petals of a red flower that only grows in doomed flesh,

and Bagger wants to snap off one of his broken fingers and plug Chester's hole, but he and the angel keep rising through constellations of detonated dirt clods, high enough to see the enemy trench to the north, the supply trains and big guns to the south, the wales and fissures carved through a France not only dead but disfigured by autopsy, all morticians halted in unnatural armistice,

and then gasping shock, a massive bloodbeast beside him in the sky, wingspan so vast that Bagger ducks, but the angel tightens her grip, so Bagger clings back and realizes it's the triplane he saw from three thousand feet down, black Iron Cross painted on the cherry-red chassis, the golden propeller halted and yet the thing doesn't fall, nor does the pilot, clad in leather cap and goggles, bearing down on his gun, bullets from which are so solidly situated in air that birds could perch on them, and still they rise, getting colder now, the Colt an icicle in his hand, Bagger afraid the angel doesn't know he needs air to breathe but equally afraid to tell her, with that expression of hers, with her hair and cape whipping, not to mention that they are fucking *flying*, all signs that she's done with his bullshit and is liable to drop his ass if he says a word,

and they rise until, another hundred feet up, the angel reclines and their path goes obtuse, and like that, Bagger spots the largest object he's encountered in his life, seems impossible to have missed it before, but Bagger cuts himself slack, his father had a portrait of Christ in his study and once asked little Cyril if he could see Christ's temptation, and he studied the portrait and said no, so the Bishop repositioned him to the side so he could see the red worked into the thickness of paint, visible only from an angle, Bagger's only true moment of religious marvel,

and it's like that, suddenly Bagger can see a great fold in the air, a pocket stitched into the sky, one that grows in size as they approach, big as a mountain, big as the Alps, big as France, and this close, Bagger can discern only a soft, fleshy edge, and his heart accelerates, and his cock stiffens, the fold is labial, it's soft and warm, and he gives in to it, back in Marie-Louise's bed but shrunken to weevil size, and in they go,

and, sure enough, he's been here before,

XLI

and it's been so long since he's seen his father's church that he feels what he always feels when revisiting a childhood haunt, that combination of offense that the place had the temerity to keep existing without him, and awareness that the place has hoarded part of him and only by returning can he reunite with that lost fragment,

and crossing the mewling floorboards, his senses are flushed with memory, the sickly sweetness of the narthex and its vases of dying flowers, the lambent mystery of the frosted-glass door stenciled with CRYING ROOM, the red-carpeted nave Bagger processioned up and down hundreds of times as an acolyte, his candlelighter unsteady, the guttering wick, all those faces anticipating his failure,

and the caramel varnish of the pews hasn't changed, nor have the merlot pull-apart men of the stained glass windows, nor have the ancient light fixtures hanging from above, each holding a quartet of bulbs that are the spitting image of shrapnel shells, the clues to his ultimate demise hinted at way back then,

and then he's up the altar steps and scuffing his iron-heeled boots across the gray blotches of wax on the carpet, dropped there each time he mishandled the candlelighter and glanced up to find crucified Christ looking disillusioned, and the Bishop, just below the cross, looking sad, and making Bagger, the son, sad too,

and now Bagger wonders if the sadness had less to do with Sunday fuckups and more to do with his lockstep march toward a redundant future, he was baptized here, he'd be married here, he'd be mourned here, but not for too long, another acolyte was already donning the surplice,

and lying on the altar is the very red leather Bible that Bagger carried with him to France, so Bagger, still the acolyte, pulls back the front cover, and the broken spine flops the book open to the section of images that, as a boy, Bagger preferred to the flavorless text, one image in particular,

and it's a painting by Raphael called *Solly Madonna*, depicting the Virgin Mary with Baby Jesus on her lap, his arms too stubby, thighs like drumsticks, belly distended, weird little naked penis, and the head of a balding old man, a depiction young Bagger found unsettling, and so he always focused on Mary, the placid, patient, half-closed eyes, rosebud lips, center-parted copper hair, skin so white it looked as if lit from within,

and the blue cape,

and the red dress,

and all at once Bagger can't breathe, for he *does* know her, he's *always* known her, she's been present in a way his original mother never was, she's been with him always, always, always, the tender half his father lost the instant Bagger was born, and Bagger feels his wearied knees give and folds himself over the altar so as not to fall, and it's here, inches from the Bible, that Bagger notices small dark circles on Solly Madonna, something pushing from behind the image, and Bagger drags a hand up to turn one page, two pages, ten, a hundred, until he finds three black holes drilled through the book's back cover, which means Jerry had, in fact, shot Bagger while he fled across No Man's Land with the angel,

and that means Bagger would have died but for the Bible that stayed the bullets, which is to say, the father who stayed the bullets, as the Bishop had forced the Bible into his unappreciative son's hands the last time they saw each other, Solly Madonna the sacrificial lamb as surely as Bagger's mother, their lives relinquished all so Bagger, a petty swindler, could keep on swindling, he wasn't worth it then and isn't worth it now,

and Bagger puts his hands over his face and feels the most surprising thing, tears from his right eye, and though it's the only eye he's got left, it's capable of everything a son needs, it all makes sense now, his lack of faith never mattered, there might not be a God or a Jesus or a Mary, but there *was* a Bishop Bagger, and all this time, it's him that Bagger has been saving, from the cold, lonely frights of his wavering belief, from the straying of his flock, from the cold, salty waters that pulled him under with a barbed-wire grip,

and a sob breaks from Bagger's chest, and other sobs come pell-mell after it, a jailbreak, he's wailing now, tears raining like bullets and softening the charred holes in the red leather,

and the angel's voice comes from behind and above, "Each of the others wanted something particular from the person they imagined me to be," and sounding every bit as human as Bagger, she asks, "But what do you want?,"

and Bagger doesn't have to think, "All I wanted was to protect you," he gasps through sobs, "like he protected me,"

and when he's emptied of tears, he turns toward the narthex and sees the angel standing there, and is unsurprised to find that she is six stories tall, halo like Saturn's rings, dress the red curtain of a theater, knees at balcony level, and he's also unsurprised that she holds a massive medieval sword, the tip stabbed into a pew, the polished blade, the hilt of obsidian, the pommel bright as the moon, if not an actual moon,

and, of course, the church isn't large, never was, yet the angel hasn't crashed through the roof, the roof is gone, the church walls simply go up and up, and though it's hard for Bagger to say for sure in the night-sky dark, the plaster, brick, and wood appear to twist and twine into a towering jungle canopy, the stained glass redispersed into the glimmering beaks, claws, and scales of unspecified jungle life-forms,

and Bagger has to squint, the angel's face is hard to see way up there, for once she exudes no light,

and Bagger asks, "Was that you? At Mons?" and the angel replies, "Mons is a fairy tale. None of you understand time. What does it matter which nations win which wars? Future wars will reverse all gains. God is on no one's side,"

and it's foolish to do anything but fall to his knees and beg for grace, but maybe it's being back in the church, maybe it's the mystery of the jungle beyond, but Bagger asks, "How can you say that? There's right and there's wrong," and to this, the angel raises an eyebrow the size of a howitzer and replies, "You ask me that? You, who has never cared for anyone?,"

and the ghost congregation chuckles, and Bagger, angry now, demands, "How many times did I save you? Three? Four? I risked my life. Over and over I risked it!," and the angel retorts with a temper this time, "You wanted to save who you saw. The same as the others. None of it was for the good of anyone but yourselves,"

and though Bagger wants to make the angel tell him about Arno's impending death, as foretold by Rochambeau, and how to avoid it, indignation pulses inside his empty socket, "My father used to talk about the Destroying Angel," he says, and he stomps the kneeler bar of the closest pew, snapping it off, "He said the Destroying Angel could kill thousands with the flick of the sword," his father loved that word, *flick*, he'd pair it with a flick of his finger to illustrate the ease of mass murder, and Bagger javelins the kneeler bar at a window,

and the stained glass shatters into kaleidoscopes, and vines flop through the breach, vines that seem to thread through his veins, did Bagger weave the jungle, or did the jungle weave Bagger, and he looks up at the angel and demands, "So why don't you do what Veck asked? Stop messing around and wipe us out?,"

and the sword, all fifty feet of it, turns in the angel's fist, a minute gesture that nonetheless grinds a pew to splinters, a pew Bagger's father used to varnish on his bloody knees, which must mean Bagger's getting to her, good, maybe she will end this endless nightmare, but instead the angel asks, with aggravating patience, "How did your father say the end would come?," and the old man might as well be back at his pulpit, the answer springs automatic from of Bagger, "A divine plague,"

and the angel responds with nothing, her eyes two boulders dangling over Bagger's grape head, and Bagger recalls his father inserting silences like this to make his guilty audience squirm, but being aware of the tactic doesn't make Bagger less susceptible to it, and after a few seconds, his own squirming begins,

and the reason is the flu, the one army leaders insist is contained to neutral Spain, though the letters doughboys get from home paint a darker picture, one of churches, ballrooms, barracks, and gymnasiums full of sufferers writhing on cots beside nurses whose white masks cover the only helpful tool they have, their pretty, sympathetic faces, and of undertakers sneezing sawdust from so many coffins being built, and of cemeterians pink-handed from covering corpses with ice, where's the quicklime when you need it,

and the ice freezes Bagger, too, there's no known origin of the plague, the plague on track to kill more people than any silly war,

and here's a thought to scare off sleep, imagine this, a squadron of angels soaring over Bois de Fays in an attack formation called Revelations, what if this angel was midwifing the missile to end all missiles when she was shot down, and that by saving the angel, Bagger has only ensured the resumption of her mission, the end of humankind, and if that's true, it begs a question, the only question left, probably the only question that ought to be asked of a visitor like her,

and so Bagger asks it, "Why?,"

and the angel's cunning grin is so paradoxical to her former modesty that Bagger's blood goes gelid, the old church a polar tundra beneath the sultry swamp, and as he cradles his goose-bumped arms, the angel vanishes, but for only a blink, then she's back and says, "I have returned," and to his confusion she laughs as you laugh at a dog that doesn't recognize its master in a new hat, and says, "I told you that you have no understanding of time. I have been gone for sixty thousand years,"

and Bagger only stares, unable to grapple with a declaration so mad, and the angel says, "It has been approved. I am allowed to show you why. But I warn you, once we begin, we must see it through. There will be no going back. No chances to look away. What you will witness will haunt you until your final moments. You will regret wanting to know. And yet, when I ask you if you truly want to be shown, you will say, 'Show me.' No human has ever been able to leave a box unopened. So I ask it, Would you like to be shown?,"

and Bagger believes there is nothing in life, possibly in death as well, that he loathes so much as doing what's expected of him, and his every particle galvanizes to reply a resounding no, do not open the box, do not pluck the fruit, do not look back at Sodom, until he accepts that he shares his ancestors' blood and recrudesces with their ills, which leaves nothing but to look up into the jungle, defeated and doomed, but at least aware of it, which has to count for something,

and he says, just as the angel predicted, "Show me,"

XLII

and the floorboards fold down on hinges and screws and swivels
that don't exist, braiding into a whirlpool of lumber, a black cavity
that falls like a bomb all the way to earth, driving into the trench
and then further, into the body of mud, the heart of clay, the dead
soldiers buried by landships and gun wagons and millions of boots
in melee, bedfellows to ritualistically buried ancient humans, and
forgotten dinosaurs, and the single-cell organisms that started it
all, each stratum more innocent than the one above it, and yet
shooting downward from each buried body are stems twining together to form a root as thick as an arm, a leg, a torso, a body, a
house, a town, a country, until the root is not a part of the planet's
mantle but the planet itself and Bagger, cupped inside the angel's
free hand, is inside that root, utterly dark, until he notices a mist,
swirling like Argonne fog but crimson, lit by a fire at Earth's core,
and Bagger's afraid now, but nothing can stop them, they pass
through a cloud that stinks of scorched kerosene and tastes like
motor oil, stinging Bagger's empty socket, and there it is, the center
of the world, not rock or magma or primordial ether but an engine,
sixty thousand wheels, gears, blades, pulleys, pistons, and pumps
in calamitous clatter, hot air shrieking from chimney whistles, soot
coughing from behind the blistered teeth of metal grills, an intricate labyrinth of puffing, chugging, gasping, hacking machinery

arranged around a flywheel cauldron into which the master root feeds, all of Earth's murdered smelted into tar, scorching and bubbling but fanned by wheezing bellows of sheet metal before being sucked down the mazy throats of corroded pipes, each elbow so tenuously bolted it bleeds black lifeblood muck, a continuous draining action that powers a great windmill of threadbare cams and rotors reptiled with generations of spindrifted blood, and rolling from the firebrick of a throbbing, banging oven are tray after tray, chainmailed together, of human tar cooled to an ebony gelatin, knobby with bone, cartilage, and gristle, and with a factory honk and a puff of xanthous smoke, dozens of rusty guillotine blades drop in unison with the ungodly cymbal of overturned silverware drawers, dicing the inky jelly into thousands of patties of rubbery pulp, which luge down a slide of ludicrous design, careening all about the infernal machine, the steel support rods planted into undergirding oil pans whining with each bend until the slide abruptly ends and the jiggling black cakes shoot into a chickenwire bin studded by crooked nozzles that shoot flatus of anhydrous powder, coating the gelatin in off-white spoor, and when the accumulated weight trips a trigger, the bin screams downward on frayed elevator cables that sway like black gallows until it locks in place atop railroad spikes and dumps its contents into a tin tank floored with a jerky, clacking conveyer belt that bounces the material along, a transport that reminds Bagger of the entry conduit of Iowa slaughterhouses right down the bars that spread apart livestock legs, only here the bars route the black gel into an aluminum matrix drilled with holes, and Bagger watches as the patties are shoved into a hotbox of tunnels that iris smaller and smaller, rounding the blobby goo into smooth black cylinders that drop, like rabbit poop, out the tank's other side and into an oxidized gutbucket that spins on sheaved sockets like a centrifuge, if not the original centrifuge, aged and wobbly and thumping, its underside papuled from the blue flames that sibilate from a cauterized vent, and the black cylinders harden until it sounds as if the bucket is filled with teeth, and it's this dryness, Bagger thinks, that sets off the bray of a timer, which triggers the bucket to upend with a jack-in-the-box twang, hurling its contents into the most frightening piece of machinery Bagger's ever seen, a long, gray, greasy grid of stone grinding wheels, hundreds upon hundreds, snagging which-ever end of each cylinder lands first and, with a piercing shrill, shaving that end to a point, the fountains of yellow sparks forming a feverish marquee, and just as Bagger feels his eardrums bleed from the decibelic insult, a huge gray monolith, chipped and pitted from billions of strikes and twitching with diaphragmed tubing, swivels via pneumatic post, magnets the pointed cylinders onto it, then rotates vertically, setting off a series of moldy overhead spig-ots that squirt white cooling liquid amid a dragon's huff of steam, and though Bagger recoils from the scalding cloud, his one eye observes the cylinders, one by one, wash from the magnetized slab and rain down into brass clockwork, each cylinder slotting into the chambers of what looks like a rotary dial, each tick of the dial like the rolling action of a revolver, a detail that makes Bagger so cold his perspiration steams in the diabolical heat, the dead, all the dead ever slain in war's killing fields, have been forged into *bullets*, flesh and blood recycled into ammo, for once you see enough human bodies broken into pieces, insensate arms and legs and heads, it's simple to rethink them as fodder, Genesis incorrect after all, life doesn't beget life, it's death that begets death, so foundational a principle it has become civilization's engine, an inferno of grief that, nut by screw by rivet, is refashioned into outrage and hysteria and vengeance and moral polarity, a cycle perfected by the so-called War to End All Wars, which, Bagger understands with hor-ror, is really the War to Begin All Wars, countries carved into furious parcels and technology matured to a stage of perpetual regeneration, an entire industrial complex, the hatreds of one age inherited by the next, the next, the next, broadcasted, promulgated, and liked via glass screens yet to be invented but inside which we see our barbarity reflected, and Bagger knows what's coming and doesn't want to see, yet feels the angel's arm swoop him sideways so he must behold the gun, the Brobdingnagian gun, the titanic, breathtaking, wondrous, bewildering, obscene, detestable, venomous, ferocious, world-destroying gun, the size of a redwood, leveled upon cast-iron wheels that could trample entire countries, no BAR, no P3, no Hotchkiss, no Bergmann-Schmeisser, no Stokes, no Jack Johnson, no Big Bertha, no A7V, no Beutepanzer wagon, no Renault, no Mark IV, no Fokker, no Sopwith Camel, no Albatros, nothing could equal this deranged patchwork cannon of brass, steel, wood, and leather, a buzzing, clanking, coughing device that inhales through throbbing plastic hoses and exhales through valves jointed like a suit of armor, the smoothbore barrel whirring with fans on serrated axels, dog springs plunging to lock iron pyrite jaws, hammers like Thor's mjölnir and ramrods like Athena's spear stoking a muzzle so big it is filled with uncountable other muzzles in constant Gatling rotation, while a hotwired ticker-tape machine tap-tap-taps a blood-spatter language on carbon paper that loops like innards over the weapon's inlaid bone and gilded steel, all of it engraved with the scrivenings of the homicidal, the church-bell gleam of the gun disrupted only by the black snow of wafting gunpowder, yet despite all of this there's no rigamarole before it fires, it simply fires, the glib effortlessness of its operation the most horrid thing of all, no one has to suffer the gun burning their palms or watch bones splinter or brains spew, no one must feel guilt, it's the future of warfare, even a soldier as feckless as Bagger recognizes that, and he watches the projectile shoot through space, passing a series of other engines still being built from the earliest and most cursed of innovations, saltpeter, charcoal, sulfur, and internal combustion, engines that will be ready for the next war, the next, the next, a metal blimp being constructed inside a mushroom-cloud haze, stylish personal assault rifles with bottomless magazines produced at a scale necessary to satisfy global demand, pilotless planes capable of murdering hundreds of people hundreds of miles from their emotionally disengaged operators, and artificial men instilled with artificial brains, no telling what kind of hell they prefer, and from the rafters of this dark place drop wooden marionettes, hanged proxies of the future dead, and a shocking few of them look like doughboys, or Huns, or Frogs, or Russkies, they hail from places Bagger only knows for how the dead announce themselves with off-stage shrieks, Iraqi, Turkish, Kurdish, Chinese, Ethiopian, Spanish, Japanese, Greek, Italian, Vietnamese, Pakistani, Indian, Colombian, Burmese, Korean, Algerian, Sudanese, Angolan, Filipino, Indonesian, Laotian, Cuban, Iranian, Sri Lankan, Somali, Rwandan, Bosnian, Burundi, Mexican, Nigerian, Syrian, Yemeni, Ukrainian, Israeli, Palestinian, tens of million shredded, poisoned, tortured, deformed, mutilated, incinerated, melted, and just plain blown away, and Bagger prays to God, to the opposite of God, to anyone or anything, for it to end, but sorry, sucker, it's not even close, the next puppets that drop tremble like Ben Veck and stick gun barrels or bottles of rotgut down their throats, and they beat up smaller puppets, a chain of traumatic violence that spirals onward, a cast of millions that Bagger sees, as the stage lights shift, are lodged inside pitched ravines, the trenches of the Great War evolved into the entrenchments of ideology, of hatreds and superiorities and vanities and comforts and riches, most of all riches, whole races subjugated for the convenience of entitled others, a cruelty worse than any Bagger has seen in this war, because it's all for nothing, the game is fixed, the same way he fixed every game he played with others, and Bagger feels a vertiginous tug as the angel stands, or flies, higher and higher, until the rotten core of the world, as well as the world itself, shrinks to a ball, and only at this scale can Bagger see that Earth is a naked giant balled up in agony, shot in the stomach, the drops of her blood coagulating into ill-fated galaxies, she won't live forever, and Bagger wonders, screaming now, if the giant's corpse will end up buried, too, and fed into a bigger engine that forges bullets capable of sundering the fabric of existence until everything in heaven, too, is a No Man's Land, a telling phrase, a Land With No Men, or at least what men have represented till now, the slavering instinct to conquer, a momentum unstoppable unless some hero jams the hardest detritus he can find into the machine he helped create, break the cogs and overheat the engine, and accept being burned alive in the resulting explosion, thereby inspiring everyone else toward heroism, too, the same self-sacrifice of Mr. and Mrs. Bagger, which might graduate into blanket nonviolence, an impossible dream, yet what else could be the point of being shown this, by chorusing *Save me*, the angel tried to get Bagger to save anything other than himself, to make it a habit, and do so without throwing more gas into the furnace, *You must promise never to take another's life for as long as you live*, at last Bagger feels the angel's soft palm fold over his body, closing him off from the terror of another trip through space and time, until he is delicately deposited onto a floor, the smell of which tells him he's in the trench dugout again, the trounced walls whispering the deal the angel offered and he accepted, *If you fail in this promise, a catastrophe beyond imagination will consume your entire world*, though now he gets the joke, it wasn't a vow but a condition that already exists, the angel only did exactly what Bagger asked of it, with rock, with paper, with scissors, what they all asked, with Theda, with Effie, with Naomi, with Ma Arno, the angel's as much a machine as the underworld engine, though she might still give humanity a reprieve if Bagger turns his back on all of it, refuses to be a cog, refuses to be a bullet, if he just walks away as Bagger's father walked away, no matter how badly it goddamn fucking son-of-a-bitching hurts,

XLIII

and when the world's engine restarts, it does so gradually, a crotchety thingamajig, and in that elongated first second, Bagger opens the last eye he'll ever own and sees the reserve trench overhead sag into the bombarded dugout, where he currently stands, right arm outstretched, the .45 aimed at the back of its owner's head, Reis ignorant of being the target, his torso in full torque about to deliver the blow that will kill Lewis Arno, who, visibly concussed, plumskinned with macerations, blood condensing through his skin, still clings to the angel with his last paroxysms of muscle,

and the angel looks right at Bagger in calm curiosity over which option he will choose, one, break his vow, shoot the megalomaniac, save the kid, and damn the world, or two, let the kid die, climb from the dugout, defect from the front, get collared, and spend the rest of his life under the penumbra of the worst of dishonorable discharges,

and the characters begin moving again, the walking stick revved to quarter-speed, half-speed, blood from Arno's mouth drooping like wax, then molasses, then milk, and for a flash, Bagger entertains a third option, putting however many bullets are left into the angel, how about *that*, except Bagger's certain bullets won't pierce her skin, just as Jerry's bullets failed to pierce Solly Madonna, and there's also the fact that shooting the angel won't prevent Arno's death, Reis will finish him off regardless,

and then there's no time left to think, and, in fact, he can't think, his brain's erased, all he's got left is heart,

and so Bagger does what he's always done with cards, dice, dominos, a poker chip hidden under one of three bottle caps, but rarely, if ever, done fairly, he gambles, an honest gamble, no thumb on the roulette wheel, everything placed on red, and though the world may be damned as a result, what's the world even worth without the one person Bagger wants in it,

and so to hell with it, he shoots,

and the hair at the back of Reis's head flutes outward playfully, like a Marie-Louise blowing on Bagger to wake him up, only Reis won't ever wake up, there's an emphysemic crack like a man expiring from a flu, perhaps a Spanish one, and globs of tissue spray at a wide angle over the dugout corner, a storm of blood as bright as any artillery barrage, rinds of skull tumbling like cups of pulped brain, while tabs of skin, pink on one side, red on the other, flap through the air like wet doves, including a strip of skin containing Reis's Van Dyke, which glues to Arno's back,

and the walking stick falls from Reis's brand-new hand, then Reis, too, falls like a sheet, as if his ejected skull took the rest of his skeleton with it, and this leaves Bagger with a clear view of the angel, Arno in sole possession now, and she blinks up at Bagger, surprised, perhaps even impressed, it takes a certain size of balls to condemn one's own species, and still Bagger registers the sandy shift of the ceiling collapse, and he dives forward to tackle the angel and the kid, dropping the pistol to enclose them in his arms and shove them against the wall, a collision Bagger's pretty sure rips one of his own broken fingers clean off, but what's one fewer finger at the beginning of the end,

and the roof falls for a while, Bagger feels mud and clay gathering over his outstretched legs, the Butcher Bird's burier buried, there's justice to that, and hell, he tries to enjoy it, holding Arno close, the first time he's ever really done it and probably the last time, too, making up for the brotherhood they didn't get to grow up with, all the scraped knees and bloody noses, it's going to be okay, kid, even though it's not going to be okay, not even close,

and when Bagger hears war screaming louder than before, he knows the earth above them has finished falling, and how about that, they didn't get buried after all, he shakes soil off his back, the dugout behind him now a dirt hill topped with that most routine of Great War accessories, the dead horse,

and he shovels the three of them out, not easy with one hand, but then two other hands join in, the kid's hands, Arno's still kicking, and Bagger gets so occupied extracting the kid that he doesn't notice that, once again, the angel has vanished, until he sees Arno, muddy and dazed, gaping dopily at the stairs,

and the angel stands at the dugout entrance, the gas curtain crumpled where Bagger stomped it, and she's as spotless as she was in Raphael's painting, though unlike Mary, she looks as resigned to catastrophe as any zero-hour commander, and she beckons with a hand, to which Arno responds by struggling to his feet, and

Bagger's appalled, he tries to grab the kid, but his grabbing hand is mangled,

and the kid slips away, punch-drunk from wounds he can't fathom, and the angel offers him her hand and, to Bagger's horror, Arno takes it, of course he does, in his eyes she's his mother, and the angel begins picking her way up the blasted stairs, and Bagger knows she's leading the kid to his demise, one of rock or paper or scissors, whether it comes right now or later with the demise of the world, it's like the angel told Bagger, he's got no appreciation of time,

and what he does appreciate, however, is the nearsightedness of his choice, the kid's saved, sure, but future conflicts will seize Arno, and Arno's children, and Arno's children's children, whole family trees of corpses to be fed into the woodchipper that outputs only fury, Bagger was a buffoon to break his promise, and he looks away, unable to watch Arno head into a world unfit for any child,

and that's when Bagger's eye falls upon Reis's pistol, packed under clay and wood, and he leans over, works it free, nearly laughing now, desperately inspired,

and he holds the muzzle two inches from his temple,

and shouts, "Hey! Listen to me!," and Arno turns, and the angel as well, and a bursting delight effervesces through Bagger's blood, maybe he can throw a loaded die one last time, he thinks of Gavrilo Princip, the nutty Serb who started the war by shooting Archduke Ferdinand, and only because the Archduke's driver took a wrong turn, a minor goof that flipped the switch on a war machine that seemed impossible back in 1914, when every nation's king was married to another king's cousin, and how Princip tried to shoot himself seconds later but failed, only Bagger will not fail,

and he shouts to the angel, "You said I couldn't take *another* human's life! You didn't say I couldn't take my own! I'll give it to you! Let me give you my life! To balance the scales! To make up for Reis! To make up for everything! For everybody!," and the angel cocks her head like an animal puzzling over human industry,

and she asks, "You would do this?," and Bagger nods, spattering flecks of bloody sweat and gasping laughter through the hole in his cheek, certain that his father laughed at the end, too, it's all so perfect, this damaged dugout is Bagger's Lusitania, a ship with which he will happily go down, just listen to the men dying overhead, what's one man more, and his forefinger twitches against the cold steel trigger,

and the angel's eyes fog as she says, "You do not get to change the deal," and Bagger waves his free hand, flopping two obliterated fingers, and laughs, "I always change the deal! Changing deals is what I do! You said our promise was a wager! I know better than anyone you can always increase a wager! Always up the ante!,"

and though the angel looks unconvinced, it's Arno, the dumb kid, who shoves the moment over the cliff, his perplexed features sharpen as he recalls Bagger's promise and clocks this violation, and the kid yelps, "Bagger, don't!" and rips his hand from the angel's, bolting back across the dugout landslide,

and, honestly, it's an uplifting thing to see at the end, brother protecting brother, but older brothers are wiser than their rascally youngers, so Bagger smiles, lips splitting, gums bloody, he hopes the kid can tell he means it, he fucking loves the little bastard, and realizing there's no better thought to exit on, Bagger pulls the trigger, the report cracks, and he hopes the bullet has kick enough to exit the other side of his skull and drive to the center of the world, lodge into a critical cog, and break the engine, for the sentence has gone on for too long, it's past time for a period to end it,

XLIV

and he's heard of point-blank shots going awry, suicide bullets that ricochet off a condyle of bone, or frolic with physics by shearing around the skull, or destroy a part of the brain that turns you into a vegetable but doesn't let you be topped off, gone west, bumped, clicked it, pushing daisies, a new landowner, napooed, just plain dead, and Bagger thinks this is what happened, for he feels no pain at all, he's neither sailing through the sky nor back in the celestial church, he remains grounded in the destroyed dugout, the photoplay finished and spinning on its reel,

and it's through purls of gunsmoke that his eye finds Arno standing over him with his hands over his ears, probably screaming but Bagger's not sure, the gunshot gonged his eardrums, all he hears are subaquatic rumbles, what Lusitania passengers must have heard as they all went down, but there's the peppery charcoal of a spent cartridge and the warmth of the Colt, confirmation the gun fired, yet still there's no pain,

and the angel strolls past Arno, right up to Bagger, who follows her only with his eyes, afraid if he moves an inch, he'll feel the nose or jaw he just shot off, but when the angel stands before him, she shows no alarm, only the half-affectionate exasperation Bagger has seen on her before, *What am I going to do with you?,*

and she reaches for his face with index and thumb shaped to pinch, and Bagger grimaces, she's going to snap off a twig of splintered bone or pick a blob of brain from his cheek, but she frowns in a silent request that he stop being a baby, so he clenches his teeth and carefully, carefully rotates his head toward the smoking gun,

and the bullet floats there, a hair's breadth from his eyeball,

and there's a heart skip, of course, rarely does a man get to see his death so close, the lead tip, the copper jacket, the whole bullet warped by the Colt's propulsion, just suspended there, an aneurysm in caesura, though Bagger shouldn't be surprised, it's the second time the angelic boxing ref has halted the bloodshed,

and this time, it's only the bullet she's stopped, war itself shakes and squeals the same as ever, the angel has rescued Bagger, Bagger specifically, in what he assumes is reciprocation for the times he rescued her, until he sees the exquisite care with which she plucks the bullet from the air and cradles it in her palm, as if it's the bullet, not him, that is precious, she beholds it like Solly Madonna beheld baby Jesus, eyes beatific, lips pursed,

and she peeks at Bagger, and though he's never sired a child, not to his knowledge anyhow, he knows what he's feeling is what any father feels when the mother, holding her baby for the first time, locks eyes with him over the child's head, that boil of pride and fear, but also melancholy, it's a farewell of sorts when a father meets the child who, as of this moment, will begin to replace him,

and the angel's beauty intensifies, no, exacerbates, it's nearly painful, she's moonbows, arctic auroras, desert roses, her satisfaction
brighter than any interior glow, and Bagger's moved when she takes
a moment to palm his cheek, his skin of rash and scab against her
skin of silk, and gives him a small, sweet, earnest smile, and says,
"Always full of surprises,"

and Bagger can't tell if she's referring to him or humans in general,
it seems vital to know even though he never will, for her right hand
slips off his cheek and joins her left hand in cradling the bullet,
and too late does Bagger realize her jeweled gaze had a warmth,
a warmth now gone forever, somehow he knows he'll never feel it
again,

and the angel turns, eyes to the bullet, and walks silently on tidy
bare feet around the hill of landslipped ceiling, past the bewildered
Arno, and up the ash-swirled stairs, her toes finding all the dregs
of board available to climb,

and Bagger's filled with loss, but also the manic need to understand
the loss, his only chance to properly grieve, so he stands, every muscle spasming from the contraction his body made when he pulled
the suicide trigger, and staggers forward, and though his ears remain
too stunned to hear what Arno's saying, he gathers the kid under his
arm and drags him along as fast as their tumbling feet can go,

and it takes too long to scale the shattered jaw of the dugout steps,
exploding shells cleave mud, break apart handholds, cause ava-
lanches of soil, but eventually he and Arno make it, and enter into
the flames of earthbound hell, the gasp and sick and song and
fury, the miasma of pooled blood, the torridity of molten metal,
and peer through the fiery black of scramble and surrender, and

there, dead ahead, striding fearlessly across duckboards laid over trenches, goes the lightning bug of the angel, straight into battle,

and they run after her, no strategy to their charge, the kind of full-bore rush that built the war, brick by cadaver brick, racing over trench tops filled with gray tides of human meat, bayonet blades spearing skyward, spumes of hot blood frothing Bagger's exposed skin, and with a giant leap they hurdle the frontline trench and spin their oaf bodies away from barbed-wired bulwarks, and end up in mud, and dead men, and the sludgy solutions of both,

and there she is, fifty yards ahead, parading into No Man's Land like no man ever has, hood down, face of sunlight held high, an easy target for thousands of bullets crisscrossing through smoke, some missing the angel by inches, yet she proceeds unperturbed,

and there's no way, absolutely no way, that Bagger and Arno enter this hornet's nest and aren't pulled like pork, and so, by silent accord, they enter anyway, no weapons to speak of but the ferocity of their cries, Bagger's the fermata of the final hymn echoing through his father's church, Arno's the high-pitched yap of apelings as they sling themselves through jungle eaves, élan, boys, élan,

and gunfire passes so close it's like piano string plucked against Bagger's ears, parting the dry-mud tangles of his hair, tugging at his drabs like the small hands of a hundred buried children, but he torpedoes on, pausing only to hoist Arno by his collar when the kid trips over a helmet, a pair of shoulders, horse ribs like a bear trap, nitwit pratfalls against the psychedelic pageant of a world in total rupture, neon arches of lobbed minnies, the red rain of strafing planes, white fountains of flamethrower fire, iron sparking off cycling tank treads, all florid in night's inkwell, and at last, chests crushing, bodies oiled in sweat and dusted with the ash of a thousand near misses, they arrive at the dead center of No Man's Land, equidistant between American and German earthworks, amid the ejecta of a body-strewn crater, the angel kneeled at the lowest point six feet away,

and Bagger slides down the wall, kicking aside the top half of a corpse, Arno sliding beside him to kick aside the bottom half, and they are painted black when they reach the angel, who is, as ever, immaculate,

and on all fours, coughing and gagging, Bagger and Arno watch as the angel, using the pert motions of a flowerbed gardener, finishes digging a fist-sized hole in the yellow clay and inserts the bullet, the one that ought to be embedded in Bagger's brain, after which she buries it at a leisurely pace, unmindful of the ear-bleed booms and the overhead fronds of exploded earth,

and bullet as seed is a nonsense idea, yet it fills Bagger with unexpected hope, if the infernal engine could turn dead people into ammo, perhaps ammo could turn into something alive if imbued with enough longing, handled with enough care,

and with his head leaned against Arno's, watching the angel pat the clay nice and flat, Bagger allows his fatigued mind to dislodge from the realities of mud and oil and fire, and try to overcome what the angel said was his weakest trait, his failure to allow for the mystifications of time, ever too fixed in the present to imagine how things might yet bloom,

and he sees, before his stinging, dirt-filled eye, night turn to day, then day turn to night, then both at once, time moving too rapidly to differentiate, and he watches this stretch of the Argonne repair itself, craters filled, detritus cleared, grass daring to regrow, braver each season, each year, until suddenly the gray is green, and the exquisite antenna of saplings sprout branches and bud,

and decades pass, a generational blur of sun and rain and snow, and the forest becomes a forest again, weeds, creepers, and lichens clabber over hills and valleys the precise contours of Marie-Louise lying on her side, faster and faster, home base for the expeditions of boars, deer, rabbits, foxes, and wildcats, how they scamper, reproduce, live, die, and reabsorb into the chestnut and pine that unfold like bears from hibernation, stretching arms, interlocking with neighbors to form a compound body, not as large as the giant balled up to create Earth, but with enough fingers to salve the giant's wound in abundances of aloe, echinacea, and turmeric,

and no tree is more splendid than the one that grows from the bullet seed, a magnificent beast with a trunk of bison girth, bark like elephant skin, bowed under the weight of moss-furred branches varicose with twig squiggles no machine could ever predict, not even in this distant future, with leaf coverage so total sunlight has to bleed through chlorophyll, which turns the air green and the shade as cold as the Celtic Sea,

and Bagger sees a group of people approach in numbers uncertain, though it's clearly a family, outfitted in brighter clothing than Bagger's ever imagined, walking in shoes of colored leather and taking photographs with tiny cameras, and at their forefront is an old man in a Panama hat being pushed in a wheelchair through mowed grass until the bullet tree's roots thwart the wheels, at which point a middle-aged fellow supplies the man with a double-handled, four-footed cane of lightweight metal, and the feisty old bastard waves off the younger man's attempts to help and proceeds toward the tree alone, the family holding back in deference, stab after stab of the cane over twisted terrain, Bagger can't help but smile, he likes this stubborn codger, and when the old man reaches the trunk, he tosses his cane, and drops to a kneel, and Bagger feels the pain in his own knees,

and the old man reaches out with a hand that looks like part of the tree, knobby and gnarled, and lays it against the bark as if checking if the thing still breathes, and then, reassured, takes off his hat in a gesture of respect, revealing his eye patch,

and the old man is him, Old Man Bagger, and Private Bagger's heart breaks, he's so old, so old, scant hair wisped to either side of his head, but Bagger's heart soars, too, look at how long he lived, his old skin wrinkled from so much time in the sun, look at the family that loves him enough to haul their asses all the way to France, look how the man's sagged flesh maps all the places he's been,

and the suspension cables of Old Man Bagger's flabby neck sway as he begins to murmur, and to hear, Private Bagger has to lean into the vision so far that he feels the sticky peach of summer sun and feels the caress of living leaves, and hears Old Man Bagger whisper to the tree, "You were right about everything,"

and Private Bagger shivers, it's the worst possible thing he could know of the future, that the angel kept her promise, that the engine of death kept cranking, that wars kept warring, that blood kept spilling, that all the lives lost in this forest were worth jack shit, but then Old Man Bagger cracks a smile that strikes breathtaking new intersections of wrinkles,

————

and he whispers, "But I regret nothing,"

and Private Bagger's frail heart pounds back with force, and his bloodstream makes music, and he laughs, just once, but it's the best laugh of his life, joyful surprise, and with it comes a tickle in his throat, inside his mouth, within the new gap in his teeth, and then the shamefly, good old Uncle Sam, comes buzzing out through the hole in his cheek and flies away, finally, finally away,

and Bagger's tears are hot enough to steam the filth from his face, and this part of him, he believes, will always stay clean, and he turns to Arno, wondering if there's any chance the kid was the middle-aged man pushing the wheelchair, anything is possible, but the kid's staring straight ahead, having seen none of Bagger's vision,

and there's a brisk, snapping, wet-dog noise, and Bagger looks forward, the sunny vision gone, the husked gray world returned, the bullet tree only a buried bullet, and finds the angel has moved several paces away, and she's shaking, not at all like her, a graceless, bestial buck,

and the blue cape kilts outward as if punched from within, and the red dress bulges as if containing tumors at rapid growth, and Bagger reaches for Arno and feels Arno's fingers interlace with his own,

and the angel's garments sunder, dress and cape torn into segments that fly like soft shrapnel before braiding ugly in the mud, the angel as naked as she was in Popkin's ambulance, except this time she's changing, her Old Glory hues polluted into the smutch of a profaned flag, smooth skin ridging into alligator scutes, lean limbs thickening with ropes of outlandish muscle,

and with a wet crunch, her spinal cord rips apart into twin columns of bone, two spines, both of which push out at the distended sable skin,

and the skin splits, and two knuckled sickles of bone emerge and unfold, unfold again, unfold again, spiked bat wings as long as the crater is wide, fingers of black bone, membranes of red leather, Bagger's seen that color before, and the giant wings flap once, experimentally, and then again, this time with enough might to lift the angel off the ground and into the air, dirt and ash corkscrewing into Bagger's eye,

and then she's aloft, elevating over the crater, rising over the battlefield, wingspan elongating until it dwarfs every aircraft yet invented, each leather flap powerful enough to change the trajectory of shells, to blow back volleys of gunfire, to tumbleweed soldiers and medics, the living and the dead, until she's high enough that the moon, peeking through grit, gleams off two obsidian horns that have grown from the angel's head where the halo used to be,

and Bagger hears Father Muensterman's curse, *You'll find the devil out there, Private Bagger!*, maybe the old padre was right, though here at the end, here at the beginning, there's no telling what's an angel or a devil or if the two are the same, it's just the Adversary, forever the Adversary, having left a good world to a rotten people who turned it into a butcher box, a box with a lid called the Mercy Seat,

and all Bagger knows is that they need to hang on so they don't get blown away, and Arno, reading his mind, holds his hand harder, any fantasy of the angel-as-mother ripped from the kid like a scream, while someone else holds Bagger's mangled left hand, which hurts, but not in an unkind way, and Bagger recognizes the grip from boyhood, calloused from too many turned pages, arthritic from scribing too many sermons, rather like a leather Bible, rough but familiar, as useless as it is perfect,

and Bagger grips both hands back and the being above ascends, and vanishes into the sky, and Bagger waits to see if he has enough life kicking inside to climb out of this crater, get back to the front, back to the world, to live and persevere, to love and suffer, to become that old man who will one day come back to measure the page turns of an ever-turning world, and he inhales and waits for either the story to end or for the story to start over, and waits, and waits,

and,

and,

and,

and,

and,

and,

and,

and,

and,

and,

and,

and,

and,

and,

and,

and,

and,

and,

and,

and,

and,

and,

and,

and,

and,

and,

and,

and,

and,

and,

and,

and,

and,

and,

and,

and,

and,

and,

and,

and,

and,

and,

and,

and,

and,

and,

and,

and,

and,

and,

and,

and,

and Cyril Bagger considers himself lucky,

ACKNOWLEDGMENTS

Thanks to Richard Abate, Natalie Argentina, Alan Axelrod, Bryan Bliss, Hannah Carande, Adam Hart, Elizabeth Hitti, James Kennedy, Gretchen Koss, Falon Kirby, Amanda Kraus, Mary Jo Kraus, Loan Le, Adam Egypt Mortimer, Heather Norborg, Cynthia Pelayo, W. Scott Poole, Grant Rosenberg, Michael Ryzy, Marcus Sedgwick, Julia Smith, Christian Trimmer, and Meghan Walker.

ABOUT THE AUTHOR

DANIEL KRAUS is a *New York Times* bestselling writer of novels, TV, and film. His latest novel, *Whalefall,* received a front-cover review in the *New York Times Book Review,* won the Alex Award, was a *Los Angeles Times* Book Prize Finalist, and was a Best Book of 2023 from NPR, the *New York Times,* Amazon, the *Chicago Tribune,* and more.

With Guillermo del Toro, he coauthored *The Shape of Water,* based on the same idea the two created for the Oscar-winning film. Also with del Toro, Kraus coauthored *Trollhunters,* which was adapted into the Emmy-winning Netflix series. He also cowrote *The Living Dead* and *Pay the Piper* with legendary filmmaker George A. Romero. Kraus's *The Death and Life of Zebulon Finch* was named one of *Entertainment Weekly*'s Top 10 Books of the Year. Kraus has won the Bram Stoker Award, the Scribe Award, two Odyssey Awards (for both *Rotters* and *Scowler*), and has appeared multiple times as Library Guild selections, YALSA Best Fiction for Young Adults, and more.

Kraus's work has been translated into over twenty languages. He lives with his wife in Chicago. Visit him at danielkraus.com.

ATRIA BOOKS, an imprint of Simon & Schuster, fosters an open environment where ideas flourish, bestselling authors soar to new heights, and tomorrow's finest voices are discovered and nurtured. Since its launch in 2002, Atria has published hundreds of bestsellers and extraordinary books, which would not have been possible without the invaluable support and expertise of its team and publishing partners. Thank you to the Atria Books colleagues who collaborated on *Angel Down*, as well as to the hundreds of professionals in the Simon & Schuster advertising, audio, communications, design, ebook, finance, human resources, legal, marketing, operations, production, sales, supply chain, subsidiary rights, and warehouse departments who help Atria bring great books to light.

EDITORIAL
Loan Le
Natalie Argentina

JACKET DESIGN
Jacket Design by Claire Sullivan
Jacket Photograph © Sylvian Deleu

MARKETING
Zakiya Jamal
Morgan Pager

MANAGING EDITORIAL
Paige Lytle
Shelby Pumphrey
Lacee Burr
Sofia Echeverry

PRODUCTION
Laura Jarrett
Vanessa Silverio
Stacey Sakal
Esther Paradelo

PUBLICITY
Falon Kirby

PUBLISHING OFFICE
Suzanne Donahue
Abby Velasco

SUBSIDIARY RIGHTS
Nicole Bond
Sara Bowne
Rebecca Justiniano

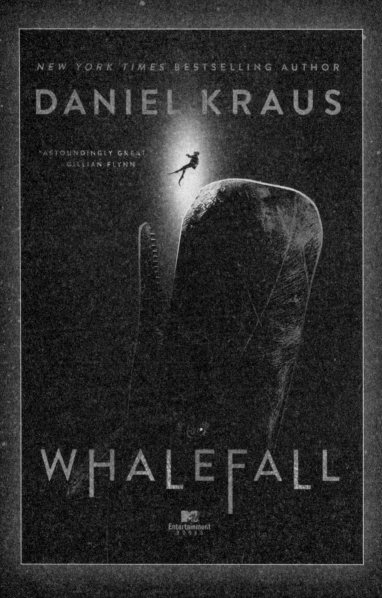